A CAPTIVA WEDDING

CAPTIVA ISLAND SERIES

BOOK TWO

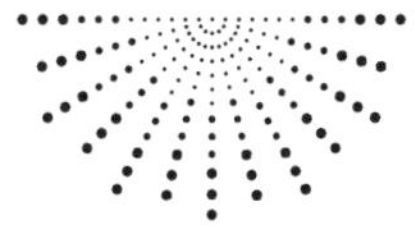

ANNIE CABOT

CABOT PUBLISHING GROUP

ISBN ebook, 978-1-7377321-2-9

ISBN paperback, 978-1-7377321-3-6

Cover Design by Marianne Nowicki, Premade Ebook Cover Shop

For the latest information on new book releases and special giveaways, click here to be added to my list.

Created with Vellum

PROLOGUE

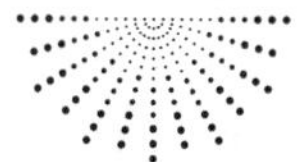

Maggie let the sand sift through her fingers, and watched the sun come up. The coolness of the early morning sand covered her bare feet, as she wrapped her sweater close to her body. The fragrant smell of the ylang ylang tree on the edge of her property made this spot a particularly favored place to recover from a night of tossing and turning.

The same haunting dream rattled her nerves, yet again. Daniel stood at the foot of her bed complaining that she didn't get the spot off his shirt. He asked her several times to clean it, but somehow, she didn't have the skills to bring it back to its pure white color. Almost comical, Maggie thought him silly for being so particular, but her mood shortly after changed to a more somber tone.

They were in the bedroom getting ready to attend an important gala. Daniel made a point of instructing Maggie on who she should make a special effort to talk to, and who to avoid. His voice rising, he emphasized the importance of the evening. Daniel needed this promotion, and everything depended on Maggie saying the right things.

Maggie's hand grasped her throat. She couldn't breathe and

tried to tell Daniel that she couldn't go to the party because she had lost her voice, but he didn't hear her. She tried to speak, but the words wouldn't come, so she reached for him instead. Her hands passed through his body, and she fell forward. She tried to stop her fall, but descended through the floor, hearing Daniel's voice as she plummeted to the ground.

She woke in a panic state. Her body wet from perspiration, and her heart racing, Maggie continued to gasp for air. She looked around the room, aware that she was safe and no longer in Massachusetts.

Sliding out of bed, she removed her nightgown and changed into jeans and a t-shirt. She didn't want to disturb her guests, so she quietly walked down the stairs to the mud room and slipped on her sandals. She grabbed a sweater and walked out the back door and onto the porch. Running as fast as she could, she breathed in the salt air. The beach lay just beyond the gate and soon she'd be at her safe place—the ocean.

How long she wondered, would she continue to be tormented by such memories? Daniel had been dead for over eighteen months, and she had moved far away from her old life. Nothing from her past could touch her now—she was safe.

More than anyone, the person she wished to talk to about her dreams was Rose Johnson Lane, the previous owner of the Key Lime Garden Inn, and her friend. She hadn't known Rose for very long, but the minute they met, Maggie knew she had found a kindred spirit. Rose had the ability to cut through the chaotic mess of her thinking and get right to the point. Maggie smiled when she thought of her friend, and even laughed out loud at how silly she would look to Rose.

"You just need to get on with it, Maggie. You can't go wrong if you follow your heart. What is it you want dear girl? When you find it, run, don't walk toward it."

Maggie felt that she had done that very thing. She'd moved to Captiva Island and refurbished the inn. She had opened her heart to Paolo Moretti, who shared the ownership of the property with her. Her best friend, Chelsea Marsden, lived nearby, her daughter, Sarah, worked with her at the inn, and Maggie had the support and love of her family and friends. Grateful for her blessings, she wanted nothing more than to live a peaceful life on the island.

But Daniel wouldn't let her be. He'd destroyed her ability to trust, and although she could forgive him for that, she couldn't forgive the pain he caused their children.

Her daughter, Lauren, and son, Michael, had families of their own, and were raising their children with unconditional love and security. Her son, Christopher, was serving his last year in the Marines. He had been in both Afghanistan and Iraq and had, mostly, been spared the trauma of Daniel's indiscretions.

It was her daughters, Sarah and Beth, who struggled the most from their father's cheating and subsequent death. Maggie did everything she could to protect them from a future of mistrust in marriage and motherhood, but her daughters had minds of their own. Whatever decisions they made, Maggie would support and be a guiding beacon if they needed her.

What she needed most, was to be done with these constant frightening dreams. She couldn't understand why they continued to haunt her when everything in her world was going exactly as she wanted, but she wasn't blind. Maggie understood that the body had a way of getting your attention when you refused to look deeper.

Now, sitting on the beach listening to the sound of the waves, she made a promise to herself to pay attention to the cracks in her life. Never again would she be a victim to her numbness. If there was pain, there was a reason, and no matter its intensity, she'd discover why it held her prisoner.

CHAPTER ONE

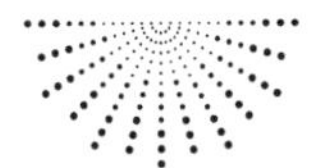

Sarah Wheeler navigated around the lumber stacked beside the carriage house. The smell of shaved wood filled her nostrils, and the dust stuck to her navy-blue skirt. She watched as two construction workers packed up their tools and got in their trucks to leave for the day.

Sarah came to Captiva Island to help her mother open the Key Lime Garden Inn only a few months ago. The establishment's popularity in such a short amount of time surprised everyone. The inn was so successful both Sarah and her mother, Maggie, needed to find other accommodations to free up all six bedrooms for guests.

Paolo, the inn's co-owner, and her mother's partner came up with a solution. They would renovate the carriage house to provide the necessary room while keeping the women close enough to take care of guests no matter the hour.

Construction was well under way. Maggie talked non-stop about her plans for the new apartment. However, the arrangement wouldn't work for Sarah. She needed to speak up before the project continued much further.

Except for two guests having tea in the garden, the inn was

quiet. Paolo saw Sarah from the vegetable garden. He stopped working, wiped his hands on a towel, and met her in the driveway.

"Hey Sarah, be careful where you walk around here. Those expensive heels of yours are bound to get scuffed. How is work going? Ciara says you're doing a great job."

"Hi, Paolo. It's been busy for sure, but I love it. Have you seen my mother? I need to talk to her about something."

"She should be back any minute. She went over to Chelsea's to pick up a painting for the front room."

Sensing Sarah had something important on her mind, Paolo asked, "Is there something I can help you with?"

She considered the question. Paolo's opinion on Maggie's reaction might help.

"I know my mother was planning on us living together in the carriage house, but I don't think that's going to work. I decided to see what I might be able to rent and found a condo not too far from the bridge on Summerlin. It's perfect for me to get to work and to Captiva. I just don't know how Mom will feel about it."

"Your mother wouldn't want you to be unhappy. It can be difficult to travel back and forth. My sister complains about it all the time. Don't worry. I'm sure your mother will support whatever you want to do."

"I'm feeling a little guilty."

"About what?"

"I came to Captiva to help her with the inn. Then I go off and get a job and rent a condo off island. So much for me helping around here."

"Don't be silly. We never could have managed the computer program you set up. You've done so much on top of your work at the Outreach Center. Besides, your mother isn't alone. She has a staff to help run this place now."

At that instant Paolo spotted Maggie walking up the driveway carrying a large, framed painting, and ran to help her.

Sarah loved to see Maggie so happy. She smiled, watching her mother with Paolo; anyone with eyes could see that they adored each other.

"Thank you, Paolo," Maggie said. "This thing weighs a ton."

Paolo lifted the painting and motioned toward Sarah.

"Let me get this inside and hang it up. I think Sarah wants a few minutes with you."

As Paolo walked away, Maggie turned to her daughter. "Is everything all right, honey?"

Screwing up her courage, Sarah said, "Mom, I know how much you want the two of us to live in the carriage house but driving back and forth to work is too much for me. I really need to live off-island."

Maggie smiled and nodded. "That makes sense. I wondered how long it would take you to come to that conclusion. I know how difficult traffic on the island can be. Why don't we see what's available and go look at some apartments?"

"We don't have to. I already did and I found a place. I signed a one-year lease this afternoon. I thought about buying something, but I'm not ready to make that kind of commitment."

The speed of the decision took Maggie aback, but she supported Sarah's choice. "Oh, wow. That's great. So, you'll be moving right away?"

Sarah looked down at the broken shells in the driveway. She moved them around with her foot.

"Mom, I feel awful about this. You know I'll be over here all the time when I'm not working. Whatever you need, all you have to do is call me."

Maggie put her arms around Sarah and tried to comfort her.

"Don't worry about me. I have plenty of help. It's not your job to look after me. I love that you want to, but you need to think about what works best for you. Just come to visit. You don't always have to help with the inn. I can't wait to see your place. We'll help you move into the apartment if you need us."

"Thanks, Mom. You're going to love it. It's modern and has a super open-concept look. I've got a pool, too. It's a house in a gated community and was listed as a condo. It's probably bigger than I need, but the price was right."

"It sounds amazing. I'm glad you're going to have your own place. You need some privacy. After all, you don't want to bring a date back here."

Sarah knew that was her mother's way of opening a conversation about her dating life. A life that was starting to pick up, even though she kept that information to herself.

"We're not going to discuss that, Mom, no matter how many times you try."

"Oh, come on. I've been good. I haven't been that nosey. You know I've been waiting for you to tell me what's going on between you and Trevor. Give me something. Please?"

Sarah laughed. "All right, all right, don't beg. What do you want to know?"

"You seem happy. Can I assume that's because of Trevor?"

"I'm happy about a lot of things, and yes, Trevor is one of them."

"How about we go inside, and I'll make us some tea? You can tell me about him."

Sarah nodded and let her mother guide her into the house.

"Mom, I swear there isn't a conversation that happens in this family without a cup of tea."

"Don't complain. A lot of wisdom has been shared over a cup of my tea. Come on, you can spare a few minutes with your mother."

The women climbed the stairs to the porch arm-in-arm. Inside, Maggie started the flame under the kettle. She used her bone China teapot and covered it with a warmer.

When they settled in her mother's favorite room, Sarah admired the new artwork. "Chelsea certainly is talented. I'm glad she agreed to show her work at the gallery."

"Chelsea's been painting steadily and has several pieces ready for the gallery showing. I'm her biggest fan. She generously donated this one to the inn. I love it."

Her mother poured their tea and sat back. "So, tell me about Trevor."

"We've been seeing each other for a few months. There's still so much about him I don't know. He comes from a wealthy family. They own lots of commercial and residential real estate all over the country, but especially here in Florida. They have properties overseas as well."

"So, Trevor has money?"

"He could have all the money he wants, but he decided to go a different way. He's worked at Oxfam International and America. He's volunteered at several non-profits focusing on poverty and hunger. He's a real humanitarian."

Sarah tried not to gush and watched her mother closely to gauge her reaction.

Maggie smiled, but Sarah knew her mother wanted more information. All Sarah would give her was what she felt in the moment. She didn't share that the very man she found rude and irritating at first, had captured her heart and invaded her every thought.

"He sounds like a nice guy," Maggie said. "I hope I get to meet him one of these days."

"Mom, that sounds an awful lot like pushing to me. You see? This is why I don't tell you stuff."

"What did I say?"

"You know what I mean. I want to take it slow."

"Fine. I'm just saying when the time is right, bring him around."

"As it happens, he's coming to pick me up in an hour. We're going to Sweet Melissa's for dinner. You'll get a chance to say hello. Right now, I've got to take a shower and get ready."

Sarah got up and kissed her mother's forehead. "Thanks for

the tea, and for being so understanding about the condo. I love you, Mom."

"Love you too, honey."

Sarah doubted this was the last time her mother would question her about Trevor. Determined to keep as much of her thoughts about him to herself she avoided her mother's questions as best she could. What good would it do to tell her mother every detail about Trevor? Sarah had no way of knowing how long the relationship would last. She had the kind of romance track record that typically kicked you out of the game. For now, she would enjoy her time with Trevor, and keep her expectations low.

Trevor Hutchins lay in bed thinking about the last time he spoke with Sarah Wheeler. The way her freckled nose crinkled every time she smiled made him laugh out loud. He teased her about her freckles and insisted she must be years younger than the age on her driver's license. No one could be that cute and be over thirty. Cute or not, Sarah could stand her ground and keep him on his toes. Being formidable and adorable at the same time only made her more intriguing, and he couldn't take his eyes off her.

Keeping his focus on the food pantry distributions and inventory control proved difficult whenever he ran into Sarah. He had mastered the ability to sneak a glimpse of her without her knowing, and when she did catch him, she smiled. She let her guard down long enough to accept his invitation to lunch on the lawn.

After that day, they ate their lunch together whenever they crossed paths. Eventually, he found the courage to ask for a date. They'd gone to dinner several times in the last few months, but they were less frequent since Noah came into his life. Trevor felt bad that he hadn't told Sarah about his son, but he never felt the time was right.

Trevor decided to tell Sarah about Noah at dinner tonight. Their relationship had grown stronger, and he wanted to share everything about his life with her. He'd never felt this close to anyone and wondered if his nomadic life had been the reason. It mattered to him there be no secrets between them.

Noah opened the door and ran to Trevor's bed, jumping on it as hard as his little body could.

"Hey, buddy. Why up so early?"

The little boy's eyes were wide, and his face was full of excitement.

"You promised to play ball with me. Can we go outside now?"

Trevor smiled at Noah and looked at the clock.

"It's only seven o'clock. Do you know what that means?"

Noah shook his head.

"It means I sleep for another hour before I get up."

Noah didn't agree. Seven o'clock meant that the sun was up—a perfect time for ball-throwing.

"No. It's time to go outside."

Trevor tickled Noah and made him giggle.

"I tell you what. How about we have breakfast first? If you want to catch a ball, you'll need your energy. Not to mention, I need my coffee."

Noah reluctantly agreed, and so they made their way to the kitchen.

Since Noah had come to live with Trevor, every day felt like a new adventure. Seeing the world through the eyes of a five-year old boy forced him to slow down and live in the moment. He was happy about his new role as Dad, but it was unchartered territory for him.

Learning that he had fathered a child was a shock. It had been only three weeks since Noah came to live with him. Noah understood that Trevor was his father but had yet to call him Dad. That, plus the constant questions about his mother, made Trevor feel uneasy. He had only the briefest amount of information about her death and wasn't sure he'd be able to ease Noah's confusion and his inevitable worry about losing Trevor.

Ava died of a drug overdose. Her brother, Cameron, reached out to Trevor when she died. She had little communication with her family, but when she was in trouble, a call to Cam almost always followed. When she was pregnant with Noah, Ava called Cameron sporadically. Cam said it was because she felt that he was the only person she could trust. She kept the identity of Noah's father a secret until a few weeks before her death.

In Trevor's eyes, Ava's parents had given up on her because they were tired of trying to get her off drugs. Other than what Ava had told him, Trevor had no other information about her parents. When she found out she was pregnant she had made it clear to her brother that if anything ever happened to her, Cam should get in touch with Trevor. Under no circumstances was her family to have anything to do with Noah's upbringing.

A day didn't go by without Noah asking about his mother. Where exactly was heaven? Would he be able to talk to her from here? Would he ever see her again? Was Trevor going to heaven too? He did the best he could to answer Noah's questions but found it difficult to know the right things to say.

Having a child scared Trevor. He didn't know the first thing about being a father. For now, their day-to-day activities amounted to getting to know one another along with ball-throwing, tickling sessions, hide and seek, and an occasional nap together. Often, when Trevor read a book to Noah, they both fell asleep.

They spent the day playing in the sand and eating grilled hot dogs. Trevor made sure to cover Noah with suntan lotion and kept him in the shaded area whenever they weren't near the ocean. When they approached the edge of the water, Noah would only go as far as the seashells. In the late afternoon, Trevor noticed Noah's mouth twitching. He couldn't tell if it was something serious of if the boy was just tired.

"You ok, buddy?"

Noah didn't answer Trevor.

"How about we go inside? It's getting late and Ciara will be here soon."

Noah pouted, "Do you have to go out?"

"You remember I told you I was meeting my friend, Sarah?"

"You mean, your girlfriend?"

Trevor smiled. "Yes, she's my girlfriend." For now, Trevor didn't want to say more than that.

"Come on. Let's go inside."

As they walked toward the house, Noah began to shake and then fell to the ground.

Trevor dropped on the sand next to his son.

"Noah! Noah!"

Noah's body shook, and his eyes rolled back in his head. Trevor had seen this before. He remembered once in New Zealand, a child, not more than Noah's age, having what turned out to be a seizure.

Ciara arrived and ran to them. "What happened?"

Trevor felt panic but needed to stay in control for his son.

"I don't know, I think he's having a seizure. Call an ambulance!"

Trevor turned the boy on his side and stayed close to him. He tried to remember everything he learned in New Zealand. What to do, and what not to do. He couldn't be certain this was a seizure, but until the paramedics arrived, he couldn't do more than stay close to his son.

Fear tried to overtake his emotions, but he wouldn't let it. He would stay strong for Noah's sake, but he was panic-stricken. A month ago, he had no idea Noah existed. Now, he was terrified he was about to lose the most important person in his life.

CHAPTER TWO

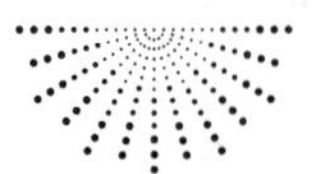

No one could blame Sarah for wanting to keep most of her thoughts about Trevor to herself. She could barely understand her feelings, let alone explain them to anyone else. What she knew with certainty, was that she couldn't go a day without hearing his voice.

Looking through her closet, she tried to find something to wear, selecting a white blouse and a skirt with a tropical design.

Her cell phone rang, and Trevor's name appeared on the screen."

"Hey. I'm getting in the shower now. Is everything all right?"

"Sarah, I'm sorry, but I'm going to have to cancel our dinner tonight. Something's come up and I can't make it."

She didn't want Trevor to hear the disappointment in her voice. Staying upbeat, she tried her best to act like it was no big deal.

"I understand. Don't worry about it. I'm sure we can do it another time."

She was about to hang up when Trevor stopped her.

"Wait."

There was silence for a moment before he spoke.

"I'm sorry. I wanted to be with you tonight, but I'm at the hospital. It's my son. We spent the day playing on the beach when he collapsed. I don't know what's happening. I'm waiting for the doctor, but no one has come out to talk to me. I'm about to lose my mind."

Stunned, Sarah didn't know what to say. Trevor never mentioned that he had a son. She had a million questions, but this wasn't the time. "Do you want me to come to the hospital? I can leave right now."

The connection fell silent, again. She didn't know if he was still on the line. He might not want her there and couldn't find a polite way to say no. Sarah didn't know what to do, so she waited.

When he finally answered, her heart jumped out of her chest.

"Please come."

"I'm on my way."

Stepping into her sandals, Sarah grabbed her purse and ran to her car. Halfway through Sanibel, she realized that she didn't know how to get to the hospital. The traffic was unusually light and there were no bike-riding tourists to slow her down.

Her hands shaking, she pulled into a parking lot and used the GPS to locate the closest hospital's information. Her mind raced with unanswered questions. Trevor had told her a few things about his family life, but never mentioned a son. Why would he keep such an important detail from her?

She had no right to expect Trevor to divulge anything he wasn't ready to share, but she couldn't shake the possibility that his past might somehow come between them. If there was a son, then there was an ex-wife or girlfriend in the picture.

Taking deep breaths, she felt calm by the time she reached the hospital. The emergency room was quiet except for the two nurses talking to each other behind the desk.

"Hello. I'm looking for my friend. He brought his son here tonight."

"What is his name?"

"The last name is Hutchins. I don't know the boy's name, but his father is Trevor, Trevor Hutchins."

The woman looked at her computer screen, and then back at Sarah.

"Are you family?"

"No. I'm a friend."

"I'm sorry. You'll have to wait over there. I'll let Mr. Hutchins know you're here."

The woman got up and walked through the electronic doors. Within seconds, Trevor came out and put his arms around Sarah.

"Thank you for coming. I'm sorry they made you wait out here."

Taking Sarah's hand in his, they walked through the doors. "I just finished talking to Noah's doctor. They're doing more tests, but they think he's had a seizure."

Sarah saw the anguish on Trevor's face and the tears in his eyes. He ran his hands through his long hair.

"I don't know if he's ever had a seizure before. Nothing like this has happened since he came to live with me three weeks ago. I tried to talk to him, but he couldn't speak. God. I feel so helpless. I can't answer any of the doctor's questions. I didn't know what to do. All I could think to do was to call an ambulance."

Sarah's heart broke for Trevor. She didn't want to upset him more, but she couldn't help without better information.

"Where is his mother?"

"She died a month ago from a drug overdose. I didn't even know I had a child until her brother, Cameron, got in touch with me. He was the only person in her family she talked to. I guess she confided in him. He said the family couldn't take Noah. I was shocked, of course, but there was no way I would turn away my child, even though I haven't a clue how to be a father. I assumed between the two of us, we'd figure it out."

"Why wouldn't his mother want you to know about him?"

"I don't know. Her brother couldn't answer that question when I asked him. She put my name on his birth certificate, so at least we have a legal record of my relation to him. Ava and I dated several years ago. I met her in Bolivia. We volunteered for the same organizations and traveled together. It was an on-again, off-again kind of thing. Whenever we ran into each other, we'd start the relationship all over again. It wasn't serious. We liked it that way. Neither of us stayed in touch with our families. As you can imagine, her family had issues with her drug use. We finally broke up because of the drugs. I couldn't deal with it."

"Is it possible that her drug abuse is the reason for the seizure?"

"I asked the doctor about that. He said it was possible. He asked if Noah had suffered any kind of physical abuse because that could be a possible reason. That scares the hell out of me. Noah is five years old. He's probably had seizures before, but I don't know. I don't want to think of Ava doing anything intentional to harm Noah. The doctor said they would know more after the tests."

Trevor shook his head and had tears in his eyes. "You should have seen him, Sarah. He looked so frail, and I thought..."

He couldn't finish but Sarah knew what he was going to say. He feared his son would die. She pulled Trevor close and tried to comfort him.

"Noah will be fine, and you are going to be a wonderful father. This is what they call trial by fire. You've got lots of sleepless nights ahead of you, but you've also got a lot of joy coming your way. You'll see."

He pulled back and looked at Sarah. "I'm so sorry. I should have told you about Noah before this. It was all so new, and I didn't know what to say. When you and I first met, I knew right away I wanted to be with you, but then Noah showed up. I've been trying to find the right way to tell you about him. This wasn't what I planned at all."

Sarah smiled, "Did you have a plan?"

Trevor smiled at her. "Yes, I did. I thought Noah and I would invite you on a picnic. I figured you could make sandwiches and after we had our lunch, we could play catch with Noah. I'd wear my baseball hat and glove and bring a couple of baseballs. You look like you can throw a ball."

That made her laugh. "I do know how to throw a ball, and I'm pretty good at football, too. My family had games in the backyard every year. I have two brothers who showed me a few things about sports. We can still have that picnic as soon as Noah is well. Have you told him about me?"

"He first asked me if I had a wife. When I told him I didn't, and mentioned you were my friend, he asked me if you were my girlfriend. I said, yes."

Sarah could feel her cheeks flush, and she hoped Trevor didn't notice.

"So, I'm your girlfriend?"

Trevor pulled her close. "If you want the position, it's open."

She didn't get the chance to tell him how happy she was because the doctor interrupted.

"Just to be safe, we're going to keep Noah overnight. All indications suggest he's had more seizures in the past. He's able to speak and I talked to him. He's been in hospitals before. It would be helpful if we could get his medical records. I understand you know very little about his medical history."

Trevor nodded. "I have a list of the vaccines he's received, but there was no mention of seizures. His mother had a problem with drugs, but I don't know if she was using when she was pregnant. I didn't know my son existed until a few weeks ago."

The doctor handed Trevor some papers. "Noah may have more episodes in the coming days, and he may outgrow them in time. We can talk about treatments and medications that could help. The nurse will take you to him, and you can walk with her as they bring him up to his room. We'll talk again tomorrow."

"Thank you, Doctor."

Around the corner from the nurses' station, a wheeled bed rolled toward them. A small voice called out, "Daddy."

Trevor ran to Noah. It was the first time his son had called him Daddy. "Hey. How are you doing, buddy?"

Noah lifted a stuffed animal. "They gave me a giraffe."

"Wow, that's great. Does he have a name?"

"No. Not yet. I didn't pick one. It's a girl."

Looking beyond his father, Noah locked eyes with Sarah.

"Hi, Noah. I'm Sarah."

"Are you Daddy's girlfriend?"

"Yes, I am. I'm happy to meet you. That's a cool giraffe you've got there."

"She doesn't have a name. I think her name is Nessa."

"Oh, if it's a girl, I think Nessa is a very good name for her."

Noah nodded and hugged the giraffe as the orderly wheeled him into his room.

Both beds were empty so, at least for now, Noah wouldn't have a roommate. She knew Trevor would stay the night and wondered if she should leave and give the two of them private time together.

While two nurses came to get Noah into bed, Sarah pulled Trevor aside.

"Is there anything that you and Noah need? Have you had anything to eat? I can go downstairs to the cafeteria or pick something up from outside the hospital and bring it to you."

"No, thank you, I'm not hungry. Oh, man. I just realized that you haven't had dinner. I'm so sorry. You must be starving."

"No. I'm fine, but I probably should get back home. Hopefully, there won't be much traffic getting to the island at this hour."

She turned and looked at Noah. "I have to go, Noah. It was very nice meeting you. I hope I get to see you again soon."

"The doctor said maybe I can go home tomorrow. Will you come to my house tomorrow?"

Sarah looked at Trevor. He smiled, and asked, "Will you?"

"I'll come as soon as you get home. Send me a text when you get there."

Trevor hugged Sarah and whispered, "Thank you for being with me."

Sarah nodded. "Of course. Call me if you or Noah need anything at all. I'm glad I got to meet your son. He's a wonderful boy. I'll see you tomorrow…Dad."

At the door, Sarah turned and looked back. In only the blink of an eye, she found herself connected to two men who unexpectedly captured her heart. For now, she'd leave that unfamiliar feeling in the room with Trevor and Noah. Her emotions threatened to overwhelm her otherwise. In the safety of her private thoughts, she'd revisit the feeling. No point in making a big deal out of nothing.

CHAPTER THREE

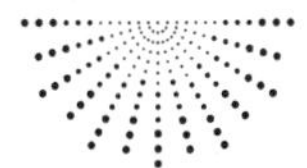

While her guests slept, Maggie worked her magic in the kitchen. She loved to bake breakfast pastries and quiches in the morning before the sun came up. Her chocolate pecan and cranberry orange scones were the most popular, but the blueberry lemon ones were Maggie's favorite. She always made extra for family and friends.

She pulled the chocolate pecan scones out of the oven and put them on a cooling rack.

"Something smells amazing. What's on the menu this morning?"

Maggie turned to the screened back door and smiled at her best friend Chelsea Marsden, who stopped at the inn most mornings for a cup of coffee and a scone.

"Chocolate pecan. Your favorite."

Chelsea came inside and peeked around the door to the dining room.

"Looks like you've got two couples up already. I don't know how anyone could sleep with this smell wafting through the house."

Maggie put her finger to her lips. "Shh, they'll hear you."

Chelsea whispered, "Are all the rooms booked?"

"Only three. If two couples are up, I'm guessing the newlyweds are still in bed."

Maggie grabbed the coffeepot and walked into the dining room. She filled cups and took their orders, which she placed with Riley, the breakfast chef.

"Yup, I was right," she told Chelsea. "The lovebirds are still in bed. So, how are preparations coming on your showing?"

"Everything is done that needs doing. Did you get the invitation?"

"Paolo, Sarah, and I will be there. You must be so excited."

Chelsea selected a scone from the tray and poured a cup of coffee. "To be honest, it feels like a dream. I don't think I'll believe it's happening until the day arrives."

"Your paintings are gorgeous, Chelsea. Everyone is going to love your work. I bet you sell every one of them."

Chelsea pressed her hands together in prayer. "From your lips to God's ears. Did Sarah leave for work already?"

"I don't think so. Her car is still here. She must have the day off. She had a date with Trevor last night. I didn't get to talk to her when she came in. Paolo and I took a long walk on the beach after dinner. When we got back, I stayed up for a while and then I went to bed about nine o'clock."

Chelsea rolled her eyes. "Nine o'clock? You live such a wild and exciting life. How are things going with Paolo? Do I hear wedding bells?"

Maggie got up from the table and poured herself a cup of coffee. "Chelsea, can a day pass without you asking me that? You know how I feel about him. I need time."

"Time? How much time do you need? The man is crazy about you. Not to mention, you're in love with him, too. What else is there to think about?"

It was true, Maggie was in love with Paolo, but she didn't trust her judgment and wanted to take things slow. Her husband's infidelity and subsequent death had left Maggie reeling. Getting married again was not high on her bucket list. Running the inn and adjusting to her new life on Captiva Island was all she could handle.

Thankfully, Paolo gave Maggie the space she needed. They ran the inn together, and when they weren't working, explored the island, met up with other couples, and enjoyed trying new restaurants.

Their friends considered them a couple but there had been no declarations of love or promises about the future. The stability of their relationship was enough for Maggie, and she often wondered why anything needed to change. Her only concern was whether Paolo felt the same way.

"Whatever Paolo and I decide to do, I promise you will be the first to hear about it. Until then, can you do an old friend a favor and let this be? I know you don't mean to, but you are stressing me out."

Chelsea's constant pushing for Maggie to remarry was a reminder that somehow what she and Paolo had wasn't enough for other people. Chelsea had always been a hopeless romantic and saw a trip to the altar as the ultimate brass ring. Whatever her motivation however, Chelsea's comments made Maggie uncomfortable.

"Maybe you should take your own advice. I don't see you in a hurry to walk down the aisle again."

Chelsea laughed at Maggie's words. "Find me Mr. Wonderful, and I'll consider it. As far as you and Paolo go, I'll drop the subject."

Chelsea moved her finger over her lips from left to right, pulling an imaginary zipper. Maggie bent down and hugged her friend, happy this subject was closed, at least for now.

When Maggie updated the kitchen, she installed a second door to shield the view from the dining room. Customers didn't need to see Sarah walking around in her bathrobe. As her daughter came into the kitchen, Maggie realized the wisdom of that decision.

Sarah looked like she was sleepwalking. Watching her daughter grab a coffee mug from the cabinet, Maggie said, "Maybe you should have stayed in bed. You look like you're still sleeping. How was your night?"

Sarah poured coffee, took a sip, pulled her bathrobe close, and yawning, sat at the table. "Eventful."

Maggie and Chelsea looked at each other. Chelsea pressed for more information. "This is why I come over here every morning. Nothing exciting ever happens at my place."

After Sarah shared as much as she could about the events at the hospital, Maggie said, "How sad for Noah. Did he mention his mother at all?"

Sarah shook her head. "No. Nothing about her. He acted like a happy little boy with his stuffed giraffe. The whole episode was an adventure for him. I think he's been in hospitals before. Trevor doesn't know much about his son, including his medical history. It's heartbreaking."

Remembering Sarah's declaration to stay single and childless, Maggie wondered how this new development might change things between Sarah and Trevor. Maggie always hoped Sarah's feelings would change, but now, she worried that Sarah might grow attached to the little boy. Maggie didn't want her daughter to marry Trevor out of sympathy and a sense of obligation to help. But she kept that fear to herself.

"I assume you're not working today?"

"No. I'm waiting to hear from Trevor. The doctor said they might send Noah home today. I promised him I would visit. I should take a toy or something to celebrate his homecoming."

"That would be nice."

Chelsea remembered a toy store in Sanibel. "I forget the name, but it's on Periwinkle, on the right side in that strip mall that has the coffee shop you like."

Sarah grabbed a scone and refilled her cup. "I know the place. I'll stop on my way. You ladies have a lovely day."

Chelsea waited until Sarah was out of earshot. "Seems like things are getting serious between her and Trevor."

Maggie nodded. "I don't know if that's a good thing."

"Why do you say that?"

"What if she gets tied down with all this because she feels bad for Trevor?"

"I don't think that will happen. Sarah is a smart woman. She won't marry someone she doesn't love. Trust her to make the right decision."

Both women knew Maggie would still worry, so Chelsea changed the subject. "How's the carriage house construction coming along?"

"Oh, I didn't tell you? Sarah is moving off-island. She's renting a condo on Summerlin."

Chelsea laughed. "I wondered how long it would be before she got a place of her own."

"I know. It's the right decision for her. There's no way she would have privacy around here. I'm happy for her, but a little sad for me."

Chelsea walked her plate to the sink. "Listen, my friend. At the risk of bringing up the subject of your romantic life again, it won't hurt you and Paolo to have a bit of privacy as well."

Maggie blushed and pulled her apron over her head. "I better get out and tend to the garden."

Chelsea took the cue. "I've got a million things to do before the showing. I'll see you tomorrow night?"

"We'll be there with bells on."

Before Chelsea left, she pinched a few stems of basil off the plant in the window. She brought the leaves to her nose. "Don't you love the smell of basil? I'll use this in my pasta sauce for lunch."

The kitchen windowsill held several herb pots. Oregano,

basil, parsley, and thyme reminded Maggie of her greenhouse back in Massachusetts. She liked to refer to the inn's cuisine as garden-to-table, and the herbs played a large role in that image. Her chefs, Riley and Grace, created mouth-watering gourmet dinners that drew guests to the inn.

The garden continued to be Maggie's oasis and private retreat. Whenever she needed quiet alone time, she sought out the maze leading to her flowers. At least three times a week, Paolo and Maggie walked on the beach right after breakfast. On the other days Maggie put on her straw hat and headed for the fenced-in section of the backyard. Her fresh-cut flowers decorated the inn's rooms, but for clients with allergies, she thoughtfully substituted with books.

Although she didn't have a greenhouse on the island, she couldn't imagine life without flowers and said a prayer of gratitude for the colorful blossoms in her garden. She used the private moments among the plants to talk to her late friend, Rose Johnson Lane, the former owner.

Maggie promised Rose she would restore the inn. Now, people from all over the world visited the property. She knew Rose was watching with pleasure from heaven.

When Maggie's cell phone rang, she took a video call from her daughters Beth and Lauren. "Hey, you two. How are my girls?"

Lauren spoke first. "Everything's fine here. We have news, but first, Beth wants to show you the garden."

"Let me get out of this glare. I need to look at your pretty faces."

Maggie left her basket on the ground and walked up to the porch. "There, that's much better."

Beth took the phone from her sister and walked around her garden, stopping at Maggie's favorite rose bush.

"Mom, can you see the roses?"

"Oh, my goodness! They're beautiful. Bethy, you're doing a great job."

"I talk to your plants all the time, Mom. They want to know where you are."

Maggie laughed. Here she was in Florida, talking to plants, and her daughter was in Massachusetts doing the same thing.

Lauren pulled the phone from Beth. "Brea had the baby last night. It's a boy. His name is Jackson, and he weighs seven pounds, six ounces. He's perfect. Brea and Michael had come to our house for dinner, but we never got to eat. She'd been having contractions, but they weren't that close together. I guess she thought there was time. They drove to the hospital from our house. She was in labor for seven hours. He was born at 2:16 am. Michael wouldn't let anyone call you until this morning."

Tears of joy filled Maggie's eyes. Michael and Brea lost a child the year before. They struggled with their grief, but Maggie felt the trauma of losing a child strengthened their marriage. Maggie couldn't wait to tell Sarah the happy news.

"Oh, girls, this is wonderful. I've got to call Michael when we get off. Sarah isn't here right now, but I'll tell her as soon as she gets back. What else is going on up north? Beth how are things at work now that you're a big-time lawyer?"

"I wouldn't say my job is the big-time, but it's good. There's a lot to learn. I'm in the newbie phase where all the lousy work none of the other attorneys wants lands on my desk."

"Honey, that's what they call, 'paying your dues.' You'll move up the ranks. Lauren, how are things with you, Jeff, and the girls?"

"The transition has been much easier than we expected. Jeff is in heaven being a stay-at-home dad. The girls and I love his gourmet meals. My job is great, and I love going to work every day. Sometimes, I get home early and can be there when the girls get out of school. How about you, Mom? Do you still love running the inn?"

"I'm happier than ever. The business is booming. Of course, I want all my children to visit me, but I know that you're busy. So, when you can, plan to come down. I miss you all."

"We miss you too, Mom," Lauren said.

Beth added, "It's going to be a while before I get any vacation, but as soon as I can, even if it's for a long weekend, I'll be there."

Lauren turned the phone so that Maggie could better see her face. "Mom, we've got to run, but we're glad everything is going so well. Tell Sarah we're sorry we missed her and that we'll call her soon."

"Will do. Love you both."

Maggie returned to the garden feeling the bittersweetness of living the life she wanted but at such a distance from her family. She hoped she would still be there for the important events in the lives of her children and grandchildren.

Later, she would call Michael and Brea to congratulate them and see her new grandson, but no amount of video calls could replace that new baby smell.

CHAPTER FOUR

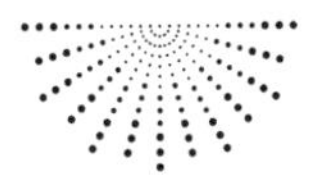

Sarah pulled the rearview mirror down to take a last look at her face. Hours in the sun resulted in several freckles on the bridge of her nose. Pushing the mirror back, she shrugged and accepted her fate. No matter how much sunblock she applied, nothing stopped the tiny dots from appearing. Her skin's sensitivity to lotions and creams made makeup out of the question.

She turned the car off and went into Toyz 'n Stuff. The toys stacked from floor to ceiling made the store a favorite with locals and tourists.

"What do you have that a five-year old boy would love?" she asked the woman behind the register.

"My younger brother likes to make things, so maybe some clay?"

The idea of Trevor and Noah working on a project together made Sarah smile. "That sounds perfect. I'll take it."

The young woman pulled the box from the shelf and handed it to Sarah. "Would you like it gift-wrapped?"

"Thank you, but no, that's not necessary."

Sarah paid the saleswoman and got back in her car.

The drive to Trevor's place was a short one. Without his directions she would never have found his house. The beach shack stood on stilts down a sandy, bumpy road she'd previously taken for a driveway.

Trevor was on the porch when Sarah arrived. "Have any trouble finding the place?"

"No trouble at all."

"I'm so glad you could come today. Noah's been talking about you ever since we left the hospital."

"How is he feeling?"

"He seems like he did before the seizure. You'd never know anything was wrong."

Noah came out of the house and walked toward his father. He was wearing a bathing suit and held the stuffed giraffe Sarah remembered from the day before.

"Hi, Noah. I kept my promise to come visit you."

Noah seemed glad to see her, and asked, "Can you come to the beach with me?"

Trevor held Noah's hand as they walked down the stairs to the driveway. "You did bring your bathing suit, didn't you?"

Pulling aside her collar to reveal the suit's straps, she said, "I'm wearing it. Wait. Noah. Before we go, I have something for you."

Sarah walked back to her car and grabbed the gift. "I thought maybe we could make something today."

Noah took the box and, without instruction, thanked Sarah.

"You are very welcome. How about we play in the sand for a bit?"

Noah seemed pleased with the suggestion and grabbed Sarah's hand, pulling her toward a blanket.

Even though drama and loss marked his short life, Noah showed no signs of unhappiness or stress. Sarah wondered how long it would be before another seizure ravaged his body.

While Noah and Sarah filled their buckets, Trevor busied himself digging a hole.

"I assume you have plans for that hole?"

Trevor smiled. "Nope."

"What do you mean, 'nope'?"

"Just what I said. I have no plans."

"You mean, you are digging a hole, just to dig?"

"Uh-huh. That's exactly what I mean."

Clumps of sand flew from his shovel, and she was glad the wind carried it in the opposite direction.

Trevor explained. "You dig because the sand is there to be dug. Simple enough. People unnecessarily complicate things."

Noah got up and went to his father. "Daddy, can we go see the water now?"

"Absolutely. Sarah, are you ready?"

Sarah pulled off her top and pushed her shorts to the ground. "Let's go."

They didn't run to the ocean but walked together slowly instead. When they got to the edge of the water Noah didn't reach for Sarah, but rather lifted his arms for Trevor to pick him up.

"How about you go in a little and then if you don't like it, I'll pick you up."

Noah squirmed and fussed, seeming on the brink of tears.

Sarah tried to help. "Noah, have you ever been in the ocean before?"

He shook his head and put his finger in his mouth, turning toward his father's body.

Trevor looked at Sarah. "He doesn't seem to like the water. He's always asking to stand near the water, but won't go in. Maybe it's the waves? I've tried several times, but this is as far as we get."

Rather than try talking to the child, Sarah ran into the sea, jumping up and over the waves before they hit the shore. Each time, she screamed like a little kid. She made a point of splashing and laughing as much as possible.

Noah watched with interest. After a few minutes Sarah ran back toward them and pulled on her braid, intentionally spraying water on Trevor.

"I think I'm going to do that again."

Sarah continued playing in the water until Noah let go of Trevor and walked toward Sarah. She reached for Noah. "Would you like to hold onto me? I won't let go. I promise. We'll go in as slow as you like and when you want to stop, we will."

Noah took Sarah's hand. They stayed in that spot for a few minutes. She let him lead and with every step he took, Sarah took another. Noah was learning to trust her. Trevor smiled and watched from the water's edge.

Noah never made it farther than letting the water flow past his knees, but it was a start. As they walked back to the house, this time he held Sarah's hand. It was a small gesture but his tiny hand in hers felt like the best gift. She hoped there would be more days like this one. Not just for Noah and Trevor's sake, but for hers as well.

At the hospital, she hadn't noticed how much Noah looked like his father. Now, she saw that they both had the same blue eyes and light brown hair with golden sun streaks.

When they got back to the blanket, Noah took his gift and went inside. Trevor and Sarah followed him to the kitchen where the boy had already opened the box and started to play with purple clay.

"How about I make us some turkey sandwiches?" Trevor asked.

Noah wanted peanut butter and jelly instead.

Sarah decided to join him. "I like peanut butter and jelly too. Can I have that instead of the turkey, please?"

"Looks like it's peanut butter and jelly coming up."

They enjoyed their sandwiches and watched Noah play. After they ate, Trevor put Noah down for a nap. The boy was asleep before his head hit the pillow.

Sarah changed out of her swimsuit and put her hair up in a messy bun. They went onto the porch, and Trevor took Sarah's hand. "Thank you for helping Noah. He needs more adults that he can trust in his life."

"He's been through a lot. I'm sure things will get better. The two of you need a period of adjustment. It's going to take time. You've spent years traveling the world, never staying in one place for long. Noah's not the only one whose world has been turned upside-down. How difficult is it going to be for you to stay put?"

"I've been thinking about that a lot lately, and now with Noah's health issues, it's more important than ever to create a stable environment for him. I'm afraid I have no choice but to do something I hoped I would never have to do—contact my family."

Sarah knew little about Trevor's family but understood his relationship with them was strained at best.

"Would it be so terrible to connect with them again? It might be good for Noah to have family. Maybe for you as well."

The tension in Trevor's jaw made Sarah immediately regret the suggestion.

"If not for Noah, I wouldn't even consider it, but for his sake, I have to put my feelings aside and think about what's best for him."

Trevor saw his property with new eyes. "Look at this place. It might be fine for a guy who looks like he's perpetually on spring break, but it's unsuitable to raise a child here. Noah deserves better."

Sarah rubbed Trevor's back. "Don't be so hard on yourself. You can always change where you live. You've done a lot of good in the world. Caring for people you don't even know. You have an empathetic heart. I don't think Noah could have asked for a better father."

Trevor took Sarah's face in his hands. "We're both lucky to have you in our lives."

He gave her the softest kiss and pulled her close as they watched the tide come in.

They were interrupted when her cell phone buzzed and although she didn't want to pull away from Trevor's embrace, she worried it might be her mother. When she saw that it was her brother, Michael, she answered the call immediately.

"Hey, big brother. Is everything all right?"

"Better than all right. Brea had the baby. We have a son. His name is Jackson and he's perfect."

Tears welled in her eyes at the news. "Oh, Michael, that's wonderful. I'm going to cry. How is Brea?"

"Mom and son are both doing great. She was in labor for seven hours, much less than the girls. We had gone over to Lauren's for dinner, but her water broke, and we had to get her to the hospital right away. We never did get to eat anything."

Sarah laughed. "I know how much you love your food. That must have been tough. Did you ever get to eat?"

"I wasn't even hungry to be honest. All I could think about was Brea and the baby. Now that you mention it, I think I need to get something to eat. I'm starving. I just wanted to call you before Mom shared the good news. I had Lauren and Beth call her, but you know Mom. I expect a call from her any minute. Everything good where you are?"

There was so much that Sarah wanted to talk to her brother about, but now was not the time.

"Everything is fine. I'll call you in a few days. Lots to talk about. It's all good though."

"Sounds good. Give Mom a kiss from me. Love you bunches."

"Love you too."

Sarah wiped the tears from her eyes. "My brother and his wife have a son. My new nephew's name is Jackson, and I can't wait to meet him."

Trevor hugged Sarah. "Congratulations. There is nothing in

the world as wonderful as a new baby. I'm happy for you and your family."

Sarah rested her head on Trevor's shoulder and imagined what being pregnant would feel like. She had heard women say that they've never imagined a love so strong. For the first time in her life, she envied those women.

CHAPTER FIVE

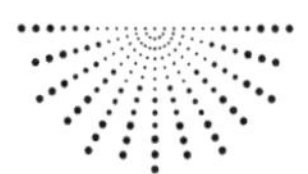

Trevor parked in the circular driveway directly in front of his parents' house. Wanting a quick escape if the meeting with his father went badly, he made sure the car was facing toward the gate. He got out of the car and looked around. The mansion looked exactly as it had so many years ago. He could still hear his father's voice yelling at him as he walked down this shell-covered driveway. "And don't expect a penny from me. You're on your own from here on out."

Money never mattered to Trevor the way it did to his father. There were times when he struggled to make ends meet, but he refused to compromise his life and values. Working to care for those who could not care for themselves mattered more to him than anything his father could provide. He felt proud of his accomplishments but understood the cost. He had a son now, and his pride would have to take a step back. He had nothing but love to offer the boy. But love alone wouldn't buy medicine or put food on the table.

Palm trees adorned the front of the house with topiaries on either side of the arched front door. The house screamed money and opulence. For his father, maintaining the status quo conveyed a certain superiority within their perceived social class. The thought disgusted Trevor, but today he couldn't indulge the luxury of contempt.

He remembered seeing his parents on the cover of Architectural Digest standing in the middle of their living room. Floor to ceiling glass windows behind them, an infinity pool with the ocean not far in the distance. Except for playing with his siblings in that pool, he never thought the house was designed with children in mind. A strange reality considering his parents chose to have five children.

There were camps, and boarding schools to attend, and rarely any children-themed entertainment on the property during the summers. Most parties involved cocktails with the rich and famous, something Trevor found intolerable. He thought it more fun to climb out the window of his bedroom, and down the trellis to escape the adults. He'd walk past manicured gardens and courtyards around to the canal and smoke his forbidden cigarettes. He'd sit wishing the years away, counting the months until he was eighteen and legally free to do as he pleased.

His dream to travel dominated his thinking. He kept a map on his bedroom wall with pins stuck to areas of the world where he planned to visit. A small part of him didn't believe he would actually get to these places. No matter the challenge, even if he had to wait until after college, he promised himself he would get there eventually. And he did. Along with his desire to see the world, Trevor developed a deep empathy for those who were less fortunate than he. To combine both things seemed a perfect plan.

His dream finally come true when he began his work with Oxfam, infuriating his father for not joining the family real estate business. He left this house, his family, and the money behind and only returned once, when his mother was ill.

Now standing at the front of the house, he put aside his memories for the sake of his son. He would give Noah everything he could, even if that meant humbling himself before Devon Hutchins.

He scheduled the appointment with his father, a necessity since childhood. No one got in to see the man without an appointment, even his children.

As usual, the butler answered the doorbell.

"Good evening, Mr. Hutchins."

"Hello, Jeffrey. Nice to see you. I assume my father is waiting for me in the study?"

"Yes. I can take you to him."

"No need. I know the way."

Jeffrey bowed in acknowledgement.

Trever walked into the large living room. The white terrazzo floor, a stark contrast to the darker furniture, appeared polished, and barely walked on. A Steinway & Sons grand piano sat in the corner of the room. Flowers adorned several accent tables, one covered with family photos. He ran his finger over the frames.

Trevor walked out of the room and toward his father's study. Italian marble flooring under his shoes, he had to remind himself that he wasn't a child anymore. He found himself thinking about the days when he would slide along this floor in his stocking-feet.

How many times as a little boy did he find himself standing in front of these doors? Memories of his mother's words, "Wait until your father gets home," came flooding back. He would stand at the entrance waiting to be summoned. Behind these doors his punishment lived. Now, a grown man, the doors represented the divide between the old and the new, between prison and freedom. Crossing the threshold into the study was easy. A few steps, only a foot or so, but this time, on Trevor's terms.

He took a deep breath and opened the doors.

Devon Hutchins stood as Trevor entered, emphasizing his height and personal power. Trevor recognized the manipulative nature of the stance. He recoiled from what others admired about the older man, and rather than speak first, waited for his father to acknowledge him.

"Have you seen your mother?"

Trevor shook his head, using silence to gain the illusion of control.

"Make sure you do before you leave. It's been almost four years since we've heard anything from you. I assume you want something from us—from me. Is it money?"

"I don't want money. I'd like to see if we can be a family again."

His father walked to the table and poured himself a scotch. "Would you care for a drink?"

"No. Thank you."

"Since we never stopped being a family, am I to understand you wish to reclaim your place as our son?"

Trevor ran a hand through his hair.

"Do you really believe we've always been a family? When has that ever meant anything to you? You loved money more than us. I've never heard you say that you loved Jacqui, or Carolyn or Wyatt, or Clayton. Not even our mother."

Devon slammed the glass on the table, and stormed toward his son. Trevor stood his ground. He learned as a boy that any sign of weakness gave his father the upper hand.

"Why did you come here? You clearly have no desire to make amends. You talk about being a family. That relationship goes both ways. What do you propose? What exactly do you want from me?"

For a moment, Trevor almost allowed old, learned behaviors to ruin his plan to give Noah a real family. Even if he didn't believe they were good enough for his son.

Coming home was probably a mistake. Maybe he didn't have a mansion or money, but he loved Noah and could give him everything that truly mattered.

Without thinking, Trevor blurted out, "I have a son."

The room went quiet. Then the questions began.

"Is he with his mother? Did you bring him with you? How old is he?"

"His name is Noah. He's five and his mother is dead. He's being cared for by a friend. I want him to be part of a larger family and to know his ancestry. More than anything I want Noah to be loved. Not just by me, but by the members of his family."

For a moment, Trevor thought his father's expression softened.

"Were you married to his mother?"

"No. We loved each other, but no. Does that matter?"

"What about her family? I assume they know about the boy."

"They don't want anything to do with Noah."

"You say that now, but don't be surprised if they change their minds when they realize who you are."

"Who I am?"

"Are you so naïve to think they won't come around looking for some connection to this family? To wiggle their way into our lives and bank accounts. I'm sure they don't care about your son, but that only means they don't yet realize that he's a Hutchins."

Trevor worked to keep his temper in check. "You are unbelievable. You can't see anything, but money, can you?"

"I see plenty, but I'm not so ignorant as to assume any connection to this child would be out of love. Who rejects their own blood?"

"Who indeed, father?" Trevor asked, seizing on the palpable irony of the words.

The two men stood at odds and as defiant as ever.

"I never rejected you, Trevor. Can you say the same?"

"Your love has always been conditional. Wyatt, Carolyn, and I at least had the courage to leave and build lives with meaning, even if you disapproved."

"If your life here was so terrible, why put your son through that same misery?"

"Because he's your grandchild and I foolishly hoped he might bring us all together. I won't put Noah through the hurt and the pain I endured. He'd get more love and affection from a stranger on the street than from you."

With that, Trevor turned and walked out. Devon called to him, but Trevor didn't look back. He almost reached the front door, before Clayton and Jacqui appeared.

Clayton smirked and threw his hands up in the air. "Well, well. If it isn't the prodigal son. Did Daddy not welcome you with open arms? No big party for the favorite son?"

Trevor wheeled around. "Favorite son? Are you out of your mind? What would make you think that man has an ounce of affection for me?"

Jacqui tried to intervene. "Clayton, stop."

She walked over to Trevor and kissed his cheek. "I'm glad to see you, but by the look on your face, I guess you won't be staying."

Trevor hugged her. "I'm sorry, Jacqui. I can't. I don't know how you stay in this house. Don't you want to have a life away from here?"

"What makes you think I don't? There's more than one way to get what you want, Trevor. You don't have to fight all the time."

Trevor looked at his brother. "You're just like him, you know that? You're still Daddy's little boy, aren't you? Ready to do his bidding whenever he calls."

Clayton smiled as if he'd been complimented.

Before Trevor walked out the door, their mother appeared. Even at seventy-two, Eliza Hutchins retained her beauty. With immaculate hair and makeup, dressed in Chanel and adorned with expensive jewelry, she made a striking impression. The cost of her handbag alone could feed hundreds of families.

Eliza went to her son and put her arms around him. “Your father told me you were coming. Are you leaving so soon?”

Clayton didn’t miss a beat. “The prince has to go mother. Things didn’t go so well with the King.”

“I’m sorry, mother.”

Trevor kissed her and walked as quickly as he could to his car, without looking back.

CHAPTER SIX

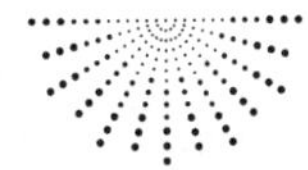

Sarah twirled and bowed at her mother and Paolo. She wore a black dress and heels with her hair up to showcase sparkling drop earrings. "I decided to dress up a bit, although I can't hold a candle to the two of you."

Paolo Moretti looked handsome in his crisp white shirt and summer blue blazer which contrasted beautifully against his tanned skin. With his full beard and mustache peppered with gray and ocean blue eyes he could have stepped out of one of Chelsea's paintings. Her mother looked equally stunning in her pale blue dress.

Paolo complimented his date. "Wow. Maggie. You look amazing. I don't think anyone will be looking at Chelsea's paintings tonight with you in the room."

"You look rather handsome yourself, Mr. Moretti."

Paolo kissed Maggie's cheek and, when Sarah walked into the room, blushed.

Maggie hugged Sarah. "You look beautiful, honey. Is Trevor joining us?"

"No. He's going to see his father tonight. I'd love to be a fly on the wall at that meeting."

"I'm confused. I thought he wanted nothing to do with his family?"

"He doesn't. Not really, anyway. Now that he has Noah, he thinks he owes it to him to have a family, even one as dysfunctional as his. I'm not sure I agree with him, but then again, I don't know the specifics of why they're not close. He has this idea that the way he's been living isn't good enough to raise a child."

"Well, I have to commend him for putting Noah first. I realize Trevor has lived a carefree existence, but things have changed. I'm glad to see he's responsible."

Sarah shrugged. "I guess."

As usual, her mother sensed her concerns. "Don't worry. Everything will be fine. Let's get going. I want to be one of the first at the showing. We need to give Chelsea all the encouragement and support we can."

Paolo drove, and by the time they reached the gallery, the party was underway. A steady stream of people walked into the building and a small line formed outside.

Sarah leaned forward. "I can't believe how many people came. Chelsea must be overjoyed."

Maggie agreed. "My dear friend has tons of confidence about everything except her art. I hope this convinces her that she has real talent."

Paolo led the way, as they edged inside. A waiter circulated with a tray of champagne. Paolo reached for glasses, one for Maggie and Sarah, and took one for himself.

They searched for Chelsea among the guests, and Maggie suggested they check the other room.

Sarah nodded. "We'll follow you."

Chelsea's paintings adorned every wall throughout the gallery. As they moved from one room to the next, a voice in the crowd called Sarah's name. She turned to see her college roommate, Emma Thurston walking toward her.

The women hugged. "Emma! What in the world are you doing here? I thought you were in Germany?"

"Among other places. I needed a break. I'm home for a while. It's been a long time since I've had a vacation. Besides, I need to think some things through, and home seemed like the right place to do that. Hello Mrs. Wheeler. It's been a long time."

"Oh, my goodness, Emma. How nice to see you. Paolo, this is Emma Thurston, Sarah's friend, and roommate from college. Emma, this is my friend, Paolo Moretti."

"Nice to meet you, Mr. Moretti. Sarah, I'm so sorry about your father. I hope you got my flowers. I wish I could have been at the funeral. I was on an assignment and couldn't get away."

"Don't be silly. We all understood you couldn't make it. And yes, we did get your lovely flowers. Thank you."

Maggie interrupted. "Sarah, Paolo, and I are going to see if we can find Chelsea. We'll catch up with you later?"

"Of course, Mom. I'll find you. I want to spend a few minutes with Emma."

Maggie took Paolo's hand. "I hope we'll see more of you, Emma. Have Sarah bring you over to visit us on Captiva."

"I will, Mrs. Wheeler. Nice to see you again."

Sarah and Emma watched as Maggie and Paolo walked away.

"Your Mom looks good, Sarah. It must have been a terrible shock to her, and all of you when your dad died."

Sarah signed. "You have no idea. We'll have to get together one of these days and I'll bring you up to speed on everything. So, tell me what's been going on with you? How long have you been home and why haven't you called me?"

Sarah remembered being jealous of her tall, beautiful friend in college. With her hair styled half-up and half-down, Emma turned heads. Her light, carefree attitude made her popular. Boys who couldn't date her counted themselves lucky to be her friend.

Emma landed a job as a photographer's assistant at the

National Geographic. Now she traveled the world taking photos of the most iconic and history-making figures and events.

"I've been home about two weeks. My parents think I'm here to visit for a few weeks and then will return to Europe. The problem is, I'm not sure I want to return. Naples hasn't changed at all. I was counting on that. Sometimes you just need to be among familiar surroundings. I'm sorry, I'm being so vague. This probably isn't the best time to talk. Why don't we make plans to get together? "

"I'd love that."

Emma handed Sarah her card. "Here's my number. Call me soon."

Sarah looked at the card, and when she looked up found herself alone. She spotted Emma approaching a man on the other side of the room. The last time they talked, Emma wasn't in a relationship, saying her job kept her too busy. She placed more importance on her career than getting married and having children.

Now, her friend shows up at the gallery with a mysterious man and no explanation. Sarah would wait a couple of days before she called Emma. She didn't want to pressure her friend, but that didn't stop her curiosity.

Sarah saw her mother, Paolo and Chelsea across the room and made her way over to them.

Elated, Chelsea got the news that three paintings had sold already.

Sarah hugged Chelsea. "Congratulations. Looks like your showing is a big success."

"I'm thrilled people love my work, but I can't wait to get out of these Spanx."

Everyone laughed except Paolo who didn't get the joke.

"Seriously, it's been quite a while since I last cared what I look like. I've been happily ensconced in my home for the last two years. I don't dress up much anymore. Going out to something formal is my idea of torture."

Maggie agreed, "I know what you mean. But if you sell lots of paintings, I think it's worth it."

Paolo offered an apology that his sister, Ciara, couldn't make it.

Sarah jumped in. "Trevor is going to see his father. They haven't talked in a few years. Given the fact that Noah had a seizure recently, Trevor thought it best someone watch him while he's away. I think he's nervous leaving Noah, but I know Ciara will take good care of him."

Sarah could feel her mother's eyes on her. She was unsettled but tried to stay upbeat and positive for Chelsea's sake. Whatever Trevor was dealing with tonight, she hoped he would share it with her as soon as he was able.

When the evening was over, Chelsea had sold every one of her paintings. It was an incredible achievement for a new artist. Barbara Gregory, the gallery owner, approached the group with two thumbs up. "What a glorious evening. I hope you're as pleased as I am."

Chelsea introduced her friends to Barbara, and then thanked her for giving her the opportunity to display her work.

"My pleasure. If I can pull you away from your friends for a moment, I'd like to go over a few things with you before you leave."

Everyone except Chelsea, Paolo, Maggie, and Sarah had left the gallery. "Absolutely, I'll be right there."

Barbara excused herself. "Very nice to meet you all."

Chelsea sat on the sofa and pulled off her shoes, rubbing her feet.

"I'm exhausted. Who wants to come back to my place for a piece of Key Lime pie and coffee?"

Maggie raised her hand. "I know I want a piece. Count me and Paolo in. Sarah, what about you?"

"Are you joking? When did I ever pass up Key Lime pie?"

Putting her shoes back on, Chelsea asked, "Sarah, why don't you let your mother and Paolo go back in their car, and you can drive with me? I've got a few things to settle here, and I could use an extra set of hands to help me put stuff in my car."

"Sure. I'll wait for you at the front door."

Sarah checked her cell phone once again. She hoped that Trevor would get in touch with her, but as the hours passed, she had to accept that he wasn't ready to talk about it. She'd have to let him come to her in his own time. Until then, she'd try to focus on other things, and hope that when he did contact her, he would have good news.

Chelsea called Sarah to come to the back room where she had several smaller pieces of artwork she planned to make available if needed. She sold two of them, and six remained.

"Grab as many as you can carry and I'll take the rest."

Once they placed everything in the trunk, they got into the car and started for Captiva.

"You must be over the moon after tonight."

Chelsea smiled, "It certainly surpassed my expectations. I only wish my late husband, Carl, could have been there to see it. He always encouraged me to sell my work, but I thought no one would actually buy any of my pieces."

"I'm sure he can see your success from wherever he is. I've no doubt Carl is looking down on you and telling everyone in heaven about his talented wife."

Chelsea remained quiet for a few minutes before she spoke. "I'd give anything in the world to have Carl here with me. I miss him every day. We were married for twenty-eight years, and they were the best years of my life. The last few years were difficult, but not as much for me as they were for him. I didn't mind taking care of him. I guess that's what happens when you love someone so much, you'd do anything to make them happy."

Sarah didn't know what to say, but she understood what

Chelsea meant. She'd been with Trevor only a few months, and now, with Noah in his life, she could see how he would move heaven and earth just to make his son happy.

"Most aren't as lucky as you and your husband. At least in my experience. I think a love like yours is rare."

"Don't get me wrong, Sarah, there were times when we didn't see eye to eye. We had arguments, just like everyone else, but we'd never let them become more important than our marriage. Everyone struggles, but when two people come together as a team to tackle what life throws in their path, you only become stronger for it."

She thought about Trevor and how their relationship had progressed over the last few months. They teased each other at the start, but then a friendship developed, giving them time to learn about each other slowly. The attraction had been there from the start, but the romance needed time to grow. Now, with Noah in the picture, there felt an urgency to evaluate their closeness and what it meant for the future.

"Do you think Trevor is *the one*?" Chelsea asked, stirring Sarah from her thoughts.

Sarah felt uncomfortable with the question. She looked out the window and tried to come up with an answer for Chelsea. She didn't know what to say, but more to the point, she now understood the reason Chelsea wanted her to accompany her on the drive home.

"Did Mom tell you to ask me?"

Chelsea laughed. "I see where you're going with this, and the answer is no. Your mother has nothing to do with my question. I only ask because it feels like you might be in love with him, and I'm curious. I'm a hopeless romantic, Sarah. I like it when everyone is in love. But, you don't have to answer me if you don't want to."

Sarah thought for a minute before answering. What harm could it do to confide in Chelsea—at least if she promised to keep their conversation private?

"To be honest, I'm not sure. It's no secret that marriage and children have perplexed me in the past. I'm certain my mother has already told you that I don't want to get married or have children."

Chelsea nodded. "She might have said something about that."

"Uh-huh. I thought so."

"I promise not to say a word to your mother if you tell me not to. If you ever want to talk, I'm here. Just think of me as your second mother, without the nagging part. I'm a good listener."

"Thank you, Chelsea. I appreciate that. Don't be surprised if I take you up on that one of these days."

Chelsea pulled her car into the driveway, next to Paolo's car. "The gang's all here. Let the Key Lime pie eating commence."

Sarah couldn't be sure if her mother put Chelsea up to it, but she needed more time to work things out in her mind before she shared her thoughts with anyone, including Chelsea.

CHAPTER SEVEN

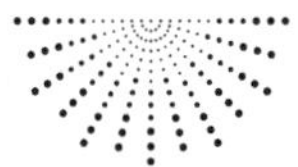

The next morning there was still no message from Trevor. Sarah couldn't stop thinking about him. Several times she found herself pacing the room, moving papers from her desk to the file cabinet. She kept looking at her phone for texts or emails from him, but there was nothing. The thought had crossed her mind that perhaps she should call him, but she decided against it.

The sound of a baby crying caught her attention. She couldn't imagine anyone in the office bringing their child to work.

She opened the door, and at her feet sat a car seat with an infant wrapped in a soft pink blanket inside. Sarah bent down and looked into the child's eyes. "How did you get here?"

The baby stopped crying and focused on Sarah. She pulled a taped envelope, addressed to Ms. Wheeler, from the handle.

Placing the car seat on her desk she opened the envelope. Just then, Ciara knocked on her door.

"I'm making a pot of coffee. Do you want a cup?"

Sarah turned her body just enough to show Ciara the infant on her desk.

"Well, hello cutie. Who does this little one belong to?"

"That's a good question. I have no idea. Someone left her in front of my door. Whoever it is wrote a note."

Sarah pulled the letter from the envelope and read the words aloud.

Dear Ms. Wheeler,

This is my daughter Sophia. She is three months old. I can't take care of her anymore. I want her to have a good life and I know that you will make sure she gets only the very best. I've watched how loving you are with the children who come to the Outreach center every week. You have a good heart. Please do what is best for Sophia. I'll be able to rest knowing she is in good hands.

God Bless you.

Ciara picked the baby up and, holding her close, rocked Sophia back and forth.

"I think I know who the mother is. I've seen this baby before, and the car seat looks familiar too. I could be wrong, but it doesn't hurt to check in on the mother just in case."

"Why would she leave her child in my care?"

"Let's not jump to any conclusions. Let me go to my office and look at my files. I'm betting it's Sharon Carter. She comes here every week for food. I'm sure this baby is Sharon's. I've wondered if there wasn't something seriously wrong with her. I'm not sure if she's in an abusive relationship or if she's ill. Either way, she's going to need our help."

Ciara handed Sophia over to Sarah. "I'll take a look at my records and be right back. If it's who I think it is, we should be able to drive to her place and talk to her. A while back I remember her needing someone to deliver food to her apartment. I can't remember the details, but I bet I have her address and record on file."

Sarah nodded and continued to rock the baby. The back-and-forth movement seemed to soothe her. Sarah looked down at the child and felt sorry for her situation. Every baby who comes into the world should be wanted and loved. Of course, Sarah had no way of knowing that Sophia wasn't wanted. A mother who would let her infant go so that she could have a better life, was someone who loved her baby very much.

Ciara returned quickly and confirmed her suspicions. "I'm certain this child is Sharon Carter's. I have her address. Grab your car keys and let's drive to her house."

Sarah placed the baby back into the car seat and the three of them headed out of the office. Fortunately, for Sarah, Ciara knew how to install a car seat. Once the baby was safely settled, they headed toward the south part of town. Ciara navigated while Sarah drove and within minutes they were in front of Sharon's place. It wasn't a house, as Sarah had expected, but an apartment complex.

Sarah got Sophia, and Ciara followed her up the stairs.

"It's apartment 2C on the second floor."

Reaching the door, Ciara knocked but no one answered. She tried a second time and could hear movement inside. It took a while, but eventually Sharon Carter came to the door. As soon as she saw Ciara and Sarah, Sharon tried to shut the door, but Ciara stuck her foot out to keep it open.

Sharon walked away and fell into a chair, a blanket pulled close to her. She looked terrible. Her face was gray, her body thin and frail. Sarah noticed the woman wouldn't look at her baby.

Ciara spoke first. "Sharon, why did you leave Sophia with Ms. Wheeler?"

Sharon's voice was soft and barely audible. "I can't take care of her. Didn't you read my note?"

"We read it. Why can't you take care of her? Perhaps we can find another solution. I'm sure you don't want to be separated from your baby."

"You don't understand. I'm dying. It's not a matter of finding another solution. I won't be here much longer, and I don't have any money to make things better. I don't want to die before I find a good home for Sophia."

She looked directly at Sarah. "Can't you take her? I've seen how you are with the other children. You always try to help people. I've watched you with them. You would be a good mother to Sophia."

Sarah's heart broke for the woman. Sarah didn't know how to tell Sharon that she couldn't.

Before Sarah could answer, Ciara stopped her.

"Sharon, where is Sophia's father?"

"He's dead, at least that's what I hear. He left me when I told him I was pregnant. We weren't married. He was a guy I met at a bar and dated for a few weeks. He told me in no uncertain terms that he wanted nothing to do with the baby. He gave me money for an abortion and said that was all he was willing to do. I never saw him again, but a few of the guys at the bar know him—knew him. They said he got himself killed in a fight. I guess someone knifed him. Serves him right."

Ciara had much more information about the area and what resources were available to Sharon, so she took the lead in making plans for the woman.

"We're going to get you the help you need to take care of Sophia for as long as you can. I'll contact the assisted care people and have someone come to see you. What have the doctors said?"

"The doctor said it won't be long. I've got cervical cancer and it's spread. They are saying without surgery it will be soon. Even with surgery and chemo, we're talking months. I can't afford any of it and I'm not sure I really want to go through chemo and radiation just so I can get a few more months. The only thing I care about is finding Sophia a good home. Then I'll be ready to go."

Sarah's heart broke for both Sharon and Sophia. Commendable as it was wanting to make a good home for the child before she died, Sharon wasn't dead yet. She needed to bond with her baby. Sarah spoke without thinking.

"We want to help you, Sharon. What I can promise is that I'll visit you and Sophia and take her for walks and do whatever you need me to do. As long as you're alive, you need to bond with your child. We can help you do that."

Sharon smiled. "Will you adopt Sophia?"

Sarah was careful not to make a promise she couldn't keep. "One step at a time, Sharon. Let's help you spend whatever time you have left with your baby. We'll help find Sophia a good home, I can promise you that."

Sarah's words seemed to calm the woman and she agreed to keep Sophia and accept whatever help was offered. Sarah took Sophia out of her car seat and placed the child in her mother's arms. She and Ciara watched as Sharon spoke to her daughter through tears. It was a bittersweet victory that they were able to return the child to her mother. No one knew what the next weeks or months would bring, but they each were committed to doing the very best for the little girl.

A call to Hospice was in order. Ciara said she would handle that. What Sarah could do was to look into what the options were for Sophia's care. A foster home would be necessary with eventual adoption but that wouldn't be as easy as Sharon had hoped. Finding a proper home for the baby meant working with the department of social services in their state. The Outreach Center would help facilitate, but they didn't have the resources or the legal right to place Sophia with anyone.

Ciara looked at her cell phone while Sarah played with Sophia. Little fingers exploring Sarah's larger ones, seemed to fascinate the baby.

"You're good with children, Ms. Wheeler. Do you have any of your own?"

Sarah shook her head. "No. I don't."

"Are you married?"

"No. I'm not married." Sarah wondered if asking these questions helped Sharon assess whether she would be a good mother for Sophia. Surely, her not being married would give her pause.

"It doesn't matter. Lots of women have children without the father's involvement. I wish you were married because I do want Sophia to have a father figure in her life. It's not a deal breaker though. Someone as pretty as you must have a boyfriend."

Sarah felt uncomfortable talking about her private life with a stranger. Under normal circumstances, Sarah would ignore the questions and move on. But Sharon's fate made her the exception to the rule. Somehow, Sarah didn't mind telling Sharon about Trevor and her previously unsuccessful dating experiences.

"Sounds like you've got a real good person in Trevor. Don't they say you have to kiss a few frogs before you find your Prince? I think Trevor must be your Prince."

"Sharon, have you had anything to eat today? I can make you something before we leave."

Looking into the refrigerator, Sarah found a few cans of soda and a pizza box with one slice in it. Surprisingly, no baby formula, or the bottles, necessary for feeding a child. Had Sharon removed those items from the apartment, as their presence would be too painful? Or did she tell the truth when she said she didn't have money to make things better?

Whatever the truth, they would get to the market and buy food and items for the baby before they went back to the office. If nothing else, they would comfort Sharon and her child until the very end. It was the least they could do under the circumstances.

CHAPTER EIGHT

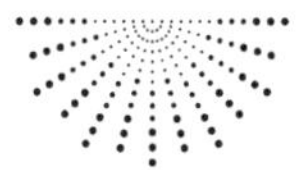

Placing two bottles of wine in his shopping cart, Paolo moved through the market wondering what other special items he should purchase for tonight's dinner.

He needed the evening to go as planned. No detail overlooked, he spent hours cleaning and twice he rearranged the living room furniture. Nerves weren't his only problem. He had little skill for sharing what was in his heart. He had so much to say but he'd let the food, wine and ambiance impress Maggie before he popped the question.

He had spent the morning making his mother's recipe for lasagna from scratch. He selected only the finest wine and his sister, Ciara, made a delicious tiramisu for the dessert.

Paolo's life changed completely the minute he met Maggie the year before. Since that day, nothing had been the same for either of them. Falling in love at his age shocked him. He had been in love before, but many years had passed since then, and he had given up hope of ever finding someone he considered his soulmate.

Paolo was certain that Maggie felt the same way about him. Until now, they had never declared their affection for one another. It was silly, really. He held back telling Maggie exactly how he felt because he didn't want to scare her away. Now, he couldn't wait to see her and get down on one knee. Tonight, he would tell Maggie everything he had been feeling ever since the day they met.

Paolo did his best to give Maggie the space she needed to find her place on Captiva and to recover from the events of the year before. Her husband's cheating and subsequent death shook Maggie to her core. Paolo never pressured her, but he was getting impatient. There was so much he wanted to share with Maggie. On the top on his list was a trip back to Italy, this time bringing the woman he loved with him.

Several years earlier, Paolo had left his family to accompany his sister, Ciara, on her move to the United States. He couldn't let his sister come to a new country by herself. Paolo saw it as his duty to watch over her.

Paolo and Ciara opened a plant nursery business. They called it *Sanibellia* and it was located on Sanibel Island. Together with his sister, they also worked for Rose Johnson Lane whose extensive garden needed personal attention. Ciara cooked and cleaned for Mrs. Lane, in addition to her job at the Outreach center in Ft. Myers.

Over the years when friends played matchmaker, Paolo politely met each woman he was introduced to. A date or two would follow, but nothing much would come of the relationships, and he ended things early so he wouldn't lead them on. He handled himself as a gentleman would, and in doing so, managed to stay friends with every woman he dated. It was impossible for him to get serious about anyone because his heart had been broken long ago, and he never got over her. A long-held memory of the woman he loved back in his hometown prevented him from moving forward with anyone else.

Daniella Russo was a childhood friend and the first girl Paolo ever kissed. Although he was only fourteen years old, and she was twelve, their families expected they would marry one day. Everywhere Daniella went, Paolo followed. As teenagers they were inseparable.

It was obvious to everyone that they were in love and were meant to be. No one was surprised when they decided to marry instead of going to college.

It wasn't that they didn't want to go, but they were poor and knew that only one would be able to afford it. Paolo was good with plants, and Daniella loved animals. They agreed to ask their parents for money to buy a piece of land and spent their days daydreaming of the life they would share as a married couple on their farm.

Their dreams were shattered one summer night after graduation. Their friends were having an end of school dance, and even though Paolo didn't really want to go, he indulged Daniella, who never was one to miss a party. Her dark brown hair framed the delicate features of her face. Her father came from Jesi, a town in northern Italy, and Daniella had inherited his fair skin and blue eyes. When she laughed, Paolo's heart skipped in his chest. He hung on her every word and would deny her nothing.

So, it wasn't a surprise that Paolo let Daniella drive the car to the event. She didn't have her driver's license for more than a week, and he was reluctant at first. She smiled at him and begged him to let her get behind the wheel. She was so proud of herself and wanted to show off in front of him. It was a decision that would haunt him for the rest of his life.

The accident was only two miles from his house, an intersection that had been the scene of many accidents before. A truck hit the driver's side of their car and killed Daniella instantly. Paolo had only minor injuries.

The Russo family blamed Paolo for not protecting their daughter. He agreed with them and couldn't understand why he was still alive. He didn't eat or sleep for days and the pain he suffered was more than he could bear. He had lost the love of his life, and it was all his fault.

In time, Paolo did move on with his life and eventually went to college in Rome. His sister remained with the family back in Gaeta. It was several years later that she decided to travel to America, and when she did, Paolo insisted on accompanying her. Paolo feared that something bad would happen to his sister if he wasn't there to protect her. It was this thinking that made him especially protective of Maggie.

Until he met Maggie, he assumed he would never marry. No one was more surprised than he at the instant attraction he felt for her when she walked into Mrs. Lane's garden. It was as if someone had sent her to him directly. He convinced himself that he had grieved enough, and that Daniella would want him to be happy. Tonight, he would tell Maggie all that she means to him. He couldn't wait to begin the rest of their lives together.

He asked Maggie if she wanted him to pick her up, but she insisted she drive to his home. At six o'clock, her car pulled into his driveway, and he ran out to meet her.

"I've been cooking for hours. You better like my food or I'm never cooking again."

They embraced and Maggie laughed at his words. "I can't believe in all these months you are finally cooking dinner for me. Why haven't we done this before?"

Paolo knew exactly why. He had planned when the time was right that he would propose to her over a dinner at his home. He needed complete privacy to share his feelings with her. He wanted it to be special, and so he waited.

"I can't take all the credit. Ciara made us her famous tiramisu. You will love it."

Paolo's home was directly across the street from the ocean. He wanted to buy a property right on the water, but at the time, the price was beyond what he could afford. After living on

Sanibel for several years, he had come to love his home and it showed in the way he decorated it.

The table was set with a beautiful linen cloth with pink and blue embroidered floral designs on the corners. "What a lovely tablecloth."

Paolo was proud of his Italian heritage and loved to show off items that were sent from his family in Gaeta.

"My grandmother embroidered this tablecloth. I have wonderful memories of her. I don't remember her ever not either knitting or sewing or crocheting. Her hands were always busy creating something."

Candles were lit and wine was poured before Paolo carried the lasagna into the dining room. His homemade pasta sauce coupled with freshly grated Italian Parmigiano Reggiano cheese tasted amazing.

"I'm sorry we never did this before. I had no idea what I was missing out on."

"I'm glad you like everything, Maggie."

"You're a very talented man. Your love of gardening and food makes us a perfect couple. I love gardens and I love to eat. We share my two favorite things."

Paolo tried not to appear anxious, but he wanted dinner to be over with so that he could ask Maggie to marry him. Once they finished Ciara's tiramisu, Maggie carried plates to the sink.

"Maggie, please, you don't have to do that. I'll clean up later. Let's take our coffee outside and enjoy the stars."

Several flowering plants adorned the patio. Carefully cultivated herb plants, especially large basil leaves, gave off an inviting scent and the lemongrass helped keep mosquitoes away. Paolo had strung white lights around the area and with soft music playing in the background, Maggie could easily imagine they were in his hometown in Italy.

They sat on the plush cushioned chairs and put their coffee on the table. Paolo took Maggie's hand in his.

"Maggie. I've wanted to tell you how much you have meant to me. I love the life we've created this past year. I think we make a wonderful team. Don't you?"

"Yes. Of course, Paolo. I feel the same. I enjoy our time together. Tonight, has been wonderful. What an amazing cook you are. I think we should have more nights like this."

"Maggie. I love you. I've been careful not to rush you and have kept my feelings to myself, but I can't anymore. I love you. I want to marry you."

Paolo got on his knees, pulled out a small blue box, and placed it on the table. "I think you know what is in that box. I'm going to let you open it and put it on your finger. If you do, then I'll know you want the same thing that I want. To spend the rest of our lives together as husband and wife."

Maggie looked at the box but could not take it in her hands. She sat motionless and struggled to find the right words to say. Her face told Paolo all he needed to know. He could see that she would not accept his proposal of marriage. He got up from the ground and sat back in his chair.

"Please, Maggie. You have to explain to me what is happening. I thought we felt the same way about each other. Have I misunderstood?"

"Oh, Paolo. You have no idea how much I love you. I wish I could explain how I feel but believe me when I tell you that I do love you with all my heart. I just don't think I can marry you."

Paolo pleaded, "Why? What is wrong?"

Maggie reached for him, but he didn't move toward her. "I don't know what's wrong. I only know that I don't want to lose you. I thought we would continue the way we've been. We enjoy our time together. We get along. I'm not sure what's holding me back. I only know that right now, I can't accept your proposal. I'm so sorry."

Maggie got up to leave, but Paolo stopped her. "Maggie. Wait. Would you please think about it? If you don't know what is keeping you from saying yes, perhaps you should figure that out. I can wait. Please, will you do that for me?"

All Maggie could manage was to nod her head in agreement. Paolo could see the pain on her face and the tears in her eyes. He hoped that given time to think things through, Maggie would come to realize that she loved him enough to accept his proposal. Whatever happened next, he couldn't lose his best friend and the person he loved most in the world.

CHAPTER NINE

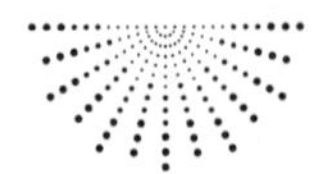

Maggie walked the beach, deep in thought. There was a mist over the ocean, and a chill in the air. As usual, she took solace in the sounds of the waves and the feel of her feet in the sand. No amount of cold wind would keep her from walking in the water. The surf teasing her ankles, it felt good to experience something other than remorse.

Had she made a mistake letting Paolo consume her heart all these months? He had become so important to her that the thought of him not being in her life caused actual pain in her chest. Nonetheless, Paolo's proposal had frightened her. She felt terrible that she wasn't able to say yes to a man she loved with all her heart. She needed time to think.

She didn't know what made her hesitate. Was it the thought of getting married again, or was it Paolo specifically she didn't want to marry? Either way, she needed to get to the bottom of her concerns, and quickly. It wasn't fair to keep Paolo waiting and wondering what the future would hold for their relationship.

"Riley said I'd find you down here. You know I can't start my day without one of your scones, or at the very least, a coffee. In truth, I shouldn't be standing right now. I hope you feel guilty."

As usual, Chelsea got a laugh out of Maggie even though she felt like crying.

"I'm sorry, I needed to clear my head, and you know me. When I need time to think, I always head to the beach."

"Mind if I walk with you? Before we get into anything serious, I'm officially reminding you that we have lunch-bunch this Friday. Rachel is hosting it this time. Don't you just love how we get to participate by video, and we don't have to do any of the cooking or cleaning? I know I do. Let's do the usual. You come over to my place and I'll turn on the iMac. That thing is almost as big as my television."

Maggie rolled her eyes. "I can't believe I forgot about lunch-bunch. I've got to start putting these things on my calendar. I'm surprised I can keep my head on straight these days."

"Well, I can give you advice if you want it, but I warn you, since I haven't had my coffee, there's no telling what I might say. I see your beloved isn't with you. Are the two of you having trouble? I've never seen you guys disagree on anything."

"Trouble? I'm not sure that's what I'd call it. But you're right, it is about Paolo. He asked me to marry him last night."

Chelsea let out a howl. "Oh, the cad! What a horrible atrocity."

Maggie always appreciated her friend's humor, but she didn't have the patience for it this morning. "It's not funny, Chelsea. This is a big deal."

Chelsea put her arms around Maggie and apologized. "I'm sorry. I didn't mean to make light of it. I assume you declined?"

Maggie nodded. "I think it was the right thing to do, although, I'm not sure why I think that. All I know is I feel miserable about it."

"Why don't we try to figure out why you feel miserable? Do you feel bad because you think you've hurt him, or do you feel awful because you think you made a mistake by saying no?"

Chelsea's question hit Maggie hard. She hadn't thought about it quite that way. "Of course, I hurt him, but that's not why I feel bad. I'm not sure I've done the right thing starting a relationship so close after Daniel. I came to this island to find my life. As silly as that might sound to someone else, you were there, you know what I'm talking about."

"I do know. I watched you struggle and I'm tickled pink every time I think about the woman you've become. You haven't lost anything by being in love with Paolo and you certainly didn't rush into anything. You've been honest with him all along. If anything, I've been the one pushing you to take things to the next level. But, my dear friend, it's hard for me to imagine you didn't see this coming?"

Maggie felt embarrassed by Chelsea's words. "I don't like to admit this, but you're right. I just kept pushing the thought of him proposing out of my mind. I figured as long as I was honest and clear about my need to take things slow, that was good enough. I even had the silly idea that if the day ever came when I would want to get married again, I'd be the one doing the proposing."

Chelsea laughed at Maggie. "Somehow, I can't imagine that. Look, nothing is set in stone here. You didn't break up with the man, did you?"

Maggie shook her head. "No, not at all. I just left it that I needed time to think. He agreed to give me that time, but there was no ultimatum. Although, if it's an emphatic no, I'm not sure what happens next."

Chelsea smiled and then rubbed her friend's back. "It's not too late to change your mind. But I also think that Paolo isn't going anywhere. He'll wait for your answer, whatever it may be."

"That's just it, Chelsea. He's waited for me already, and there's no reason to wait any longer. He's been patient but I think he's losing some of that patience because I can't give him a good enough reason not to marry him."

"Let's think about it. Why are you looking for a reason? Is it Daniel and what he did to you? Is it about trust? Are you concerned that what happened in your marriage to Daniel will happen with Paolo? What is it exactly?"

She couldn't answer. There was silence between the women for quite a while, before Maggie spoke. "I don't think my reluctance has anything to do with Daniel except this one thing. I love my freedom. Everything in my life with Daniel was all about him and the children. You remember how he was. He'd suck the life out of everyone in a room the minute he walked in. People couldn't help gravitating toward him. I've spent every minute since his death finding my own voice and I'm in control of all of it."

"And you're afraid if you marry Paolo, he will be the one controlling your life?"

Maggie nodded. "Unintentionally, of course. How many times do we hear stories about how relationships change the minute you get married? Everything is fine, until you sign that piece of paper that says, 'I belong to you.' The thought of that makes me cringe. I'm terrified of losing my autonomy after all I've been through. I'm completely head-over-heels in love with Paolo. He's the only man I want. But I love being alone too. I have a life I've always dreamed of, and I don't want anything to change it. There are moments with Paolo when I feel almost suffocated. I don't know how to explain it, but it's almost as if he's afraid I'll leave him and so he holds on tighter."

"Do you mean that he's controlling or that he's too possessive?"

Maggie shook her head. "Absolutely not. He never has issues with the way I live my life. It's deeper than that. It's coming from somewhere else, but I can't explain it. He holds so tightly I'm worried that I won't be able to have the freedom I've worked so hard to finally achieve. Does that make sense?"

Chelsea nodded. "It certainly does. All of what you are telling me is completely understandable. You've been through so much in the last couple of years. You've achieved more than you thought you'd ever be able to, and you don't want to lose it. You need to talk to Paolo about how you feel. This is something the two of you might be able to work through. It's going to have to be addressed whether the two of you marry or not. No relationship can survive without honest communication. In the meantime, how about you walk me back to the inn and give your best friend a cup of coffee and a delicious scone? After all, this advice deserves payment. I don't give out all this kind of precious wisdom for nothing you know."

The women laughed and carried their sandals close to the water to get their feet wet. They kicked up splashes as they continued arm-in-arm through the foam of the water. Maggie would talk to Paolo again. Chelsea was right about communication. Marriage or not, Maggie needed to share what was in her heart with the man she loved. No matter his reaction, she would do everything in her power to keep Paolo in her life. She couldn't bear the thought of any other possibility.

Maggie filled her garden basket with zucchini, tomatoes, eggplant, and spinach. Whatever Riley had planned for tonight's dinner, if it included these ingredients, she felt sure it would be delicious. She placed the basket on the kitchen counter. Riley had just finished cleaning the area to get ready for the dinner preparations.

"Thank you, Maggie. These look amazing. The garden is thriving thanks to you and Paolo."

"It's a labor of love for us, Riley. Next to digging my feet in the sand, there's no place I'd rather be than in a garden. It looks like you've got everything under control in here. I've got to get the blue room ready. I'll see you later."

Each of the six rooms at the inn were decorated with an ocean/beach theme. The blue room was Maggie's favorite guest room because it not only had an unobstructed view of the ocean, but it also had a constant salt-air breeze blowing through when you opened the window.

The crisp white linen covered with a tropical blue-green duvet cover adorned the bed and several beach-themed pillows on both the bed and corner chair added just the right accents. Blue hydrangeas sat on the corner of the dresser, and the lace curtains moved with every breeze. Ciara had the room perfectly prepared for the next guests, so there was little Maggie had to do.

She decided to spend some time sitting on the back porch swing that had recently been installed. Before she died, her friend Rose had left her journals to Maggie. She gained much strength and wisdom from reading them as she was beginning her life on Captiva Island. It encouraged her to write down her thoughts just as Rose did all those years ago.

The swing moved back and forth as Maggie thought about Paolo and his proposal. Memories of her marriage to Daniel popped up constantly. Nothing about her relationship with Paolo looked anything like her marriage to Daniel, but it didn't stop her from making comparisons, nonetheless.

Her husband cared about the optics of their union. Maggie often felt like an extension of his thoughts, his beliefs, and even his political views. Her life had been sculpted to match his own. Since Daniel's death, she had the kind of freedom she had always craved. No one could blame her for wanting to hold on to that freedom. And yet, she'd fallen in love with a man who asked nothing of her except her love.

For the last year, Paolo had put Maggie's dreams front and center. He had *Sanibellia,* and a home and life of his own, but he did everything he could to lift her up and support her dreams. He encouraged her at every turn to be who she wanted to be, to create a life she could be proud of. Never asking for anything to change, only that they grow old together, continuing to support one another in sickness and in health.

They weren't old. To think Maggie needed someone to look after her in her old age didn't carry much weight at present. What would marriage give them that they didn't have already?

Ciara stepped out onto the porch to join Maggie. "I'm glad someone is sitting on that thing. Ever since it was installed, I don't think I've seen one person sitting on it."

"I think I might make this a daily thing. I love it."

"I see you've been writing in your journal. Rose is looking down on you and smiling."

Maggie laughed. "I hope so. I miss her."

Ciara nodded. "Me too. I loved working for her. There were days when I thought I was too tired to drive over here, but the look on her face when I'd show up made it worth it. She made me feel like family. I think she thought of Paolo like a son."

"You must miss your family very much."

"Paolo and I try to get back to Italy as often as we can, but the last few years it's been difficult. Especially now, with our mother so ill."

Maggie was surprised to hear this news. "I'm sorry. I didn't know. Paolo never said anything about his mother being sick."

"She's not been in the best of health for a while. She's had Parkinson's disease for many years. I'm not surprised that Paolo didn't mention it to you. He's a very private person and I'm sure he probably didn't want to worry you."

Maggie didn't know what to say, so she said nothing.

"Maggie, I'm so happy that you and my brother have each other. I know he loves you very much. I think you love him too, no?"

Maggie smiled and nodded. "I do love Paolo. He asked me to marry him last night."

Ciara didn't look surprised by the news. "I know that he has wanted to ask you for a long time."

"I told him that I needed to think about it. I'm a little nervous to get married again."

"Of course. I can only imagine what you've been through with your husband, but I hope you know that Paolo would never hurt you. He understands only too well how precious life is. Has he ever told you about Daniella?"

Maggie shook her head. "Who is Daniella?"

Ciara shared every detail about Paolo's love for his childhood friend back in Italy, including the car accident. As Ciara spoke, Maggie's heart broke for Paolo. The loss of someone he loved so deeply changed his life forever. She understood the effect this trauma had on him and now their relationship, and it finally explained why he held on so tightly to Maggie. It also shed light on his desire to protect his sister as she traveled to America.

"Thank you for telling me all this, Ciara. I had no idea. It explains a few things. I need to talk to Paolo. Do you know where he is?"

"He's at *Sanibellia* all day. I don't think he planned to come to the island today."

Maggie hugged Ciara. "You have no idea how happy you've made me. I've got to run."

Uncertain of their future, Maggie began the day in contemplation and worry. Reconciling her love for Paolo with her fear of losing herself along the way, paralyzed her. Not able to move forward, she struggled to hold onto the joy of loving someone so completely. Ciara had freed her to accept Paolo's love and to not be afraid. Losing Daniella crippled Paolo for many years, and Maggie could finally understand her concerns were based on something that was easily overcome. Paolo entered her life when it was changing. That change brought her here to her new life, and to him. She knew where she needed to be, and she hoped when she got there, Paolo would be waiting with open arms.

CHAPTER TEN

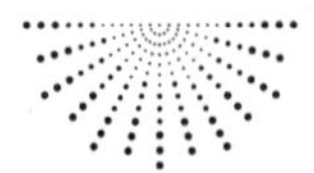

Sarah wondered if she had imagined her importance in Trevor's life. She'd had two major relationships, and they both ended badly. Perhaps she wasn't cut out for commitment after all. She'd been determined to stay single. After two failed relationships, and the events of the last day, she felt convinced there was wisdom in her decision.

Angry at herself for getting close to Trevor so quickly, she'd forgotten how fast things can fall apart in a relationship. Now, there was Noah. She wanted to be in his life as much as Trevor would let her. Only five, he had more loss in his life than most people. Whether she could make a positive difference in the little boy's life she wasn't sure. She'd need to find a way to be supportive, but at the same time not let herself get too close.

Sarah reached for her cell phone from the kitchen table. Her heart beat faster at the sound of Trevor's voice.

"I'm sorry I didn't call sooner. I was angry when I left my parents' house. It seemed a better idea to cool down before I got in touch."

"I understand. Do you want me to come over, or would you rather talk on the phone?"

"Noah is taking a nap and I'd really love to see you."

"No problem. Give me a few minutes to get ready and I'll be over within the hour."

Sarah had held little hope things would go well with Trevor's father, so she wasn't surprised to hear things didn't go well. Still, she supported his decision. She raced to get ready and made it to Trevor's place in record time.

Trevor whispered so that Noah wouldn't wake. "Hey, thanks for getting here so quickly. How've you been?"

Sarah wanted to tell Trevor about Sharon and her baby, but it could wait for another time. "I'm good. So, tell me. What happened?"

"I don't know what I was thinking going to see my father."

Trevor shared everything that transpired between the two men. "I'm afraid I made a mistake thinking we could mend fences."

Sarah put her arms around Trevor. "You had to give it a shot, otherwise you'd always wonder, and then you'd be angry at yourself for not trying."

"You're right, but now what do I do? I've got to create a better life for Noah. He'll be starting school in the fall. I need to be prepared for that. I have to check out the schools in this area. I'm clueless, but I've got to do something."

"Trevor, maybe I'm crazy, but what's wrong with things the way they are? You can always get a better house if that's what you want to do."

"I can't give Noah everything he should have. My pay alone is pretty abysmal. I can barely survive on it, there's no way I can raise a child on my salary. I'm talking about necessities—health insurance, clothing, a good education. I know I complain about my family, but at least they did provide for me and my siblings. We had the best their money could buy, and you know that's significant. I don't need that kind of money; I just need something to provide for my son. I don't mind going without, as long as he has what he needs."

The slam of a car door interrupted their conversation. "Who could that be?"

Looking out the window, Trevor saw his father standing in the driveway. Devon Hutchins looked up at the window and waited for an invitation from Trevor.

"It's my father."

Sarah cautioned Trevor, "Try not to let your anger control the conversation. The last thing you want is to wake Noah."

Trevor waved for his father to come up. He met Devon at the door.

"I'm sorry I didn't call, but I thought you might not want to see me. I'm sure you never expected me to show up at your doorstep."

"I admit, it is a bit of a surprise. Sarah, this is my father, Devon Hutchins. This is Sarah. My girlfriend."

"Hello, Sarah."

Sarah nodded but didn't move. She stayed on the other side of the room, leaving the two men to decide where to sit. Once they chose their chairs, Sarah offered to excuse herself so they could talk in private.

Trevor stopped her from leaving. "No. I want you to stay. Please."

Sarah watched Devon's reaction to Trevor's request. It was clear that Trevor wanted his father to understand Sarah's role in his life, and possibly Noah's as well. She sat in the corner chair and waited to hear what Devon had to say.

"I'm sorry about the other night. I was happy to see you, even if I didn't show it. Your mother and I have missed you terribly. I'm not sure you know that."

Devon appeared vulnerable. He didn't look anything like the man Trevor described to her only minutes ago. Something must have changed since their meeting. Gone was the tough guy attitude.

"You were right to feel that I didn't love any of my children. I was so focused on becoming a success that I never showed any of you the attention you deserved. I did what my father did to me. He left it up to my mother to show affection. He went to work every day and thought bringing home a good paycheck was providing all the love his family needed—that I needed. He didn't realize, and apparently, neither did I, that children want more than that. They need to feel loved. I failed you and your siblings. For that, I'm truly sorry."

Sarah could tell from the look on Trevor's face, that he was stunned at his father's apology. Devon wasn't the kind of man to apologize to anyone, much less one of his children.

Devon cleared his throat and turned back into his businessman persona for a moment. "Trevor, I know that you want to give your son everything you can. I'm aware of how you've spent the last few years, and I commend you for your humanitarian endeavors. However, I wonder if you've considered what the future looks like with regard to your work? How do you plan to provide for Noah?"

Sarah's heart started to race. If Trevor was put on the spot about his way of life, the conversation might become combative. She relaxed when Trevor didn't take the bait.

"Everything has been thrown at me in the last month. I'm not sure what I'm going to do. Noah's health is my first concern."

Devon's looked shocked to hear that Noah wasn't well. "Is he sick?"

"He has seizures, but the doctor said that sometimes children grow out of them. Every seizure is going to feel like the end of the world for all of us, so I'm taking it very seriously."

"Do you have medical insurance?"

"No."

"Trevor, I'm not here to tell you what to do. It seems I've done that for a very long time. I'm in new territory here, so have patience. I'm balancing giving you unsolicited advice with not telling you how to live your life. You are going to need financial stability. Of course, you know that whatever Noah needs, you can depend on your mother and me to provide any assistance. But I know you. You're going to want to provide for him yourself. I wonder if you will indulge me for a minute. I have a proposal."

In the past, Trevor probably would have already stopped listening to his father's words. Now, with Noah in mind, she was pleased to see that he let himself be open to any suggestion.

"I know you think every business decision I make has to make me tons of money. It's true, I don't volunteer the way you do, but I do get involved in humanitarian causes. I like to give back to the community that has supported me all these years. I've acquired a piece of land. One hundred-fifty acres to be precise. I purchased the land to build affordable housing. I'd like someone to oversee the project. I want you."

Trevor seemed shocked by the proposal.

"Me? What do I know about construction?"

"Construction experts I've got. I'm not looking for you to build the thing. I want you to be the person who makes certain that the project is done the right way—with the community's interest front and center. I know how to make money, Trevor. What I'm not good at is focusing on the little guy. I want to be sure that the people who will benefit from this project will be properly represented with you at the helm."

Sarah's heart beat fast in her chest. She wanted to jump up and down and tell Devon that of course Trevor would take the job, but it wasn't her place and she had to sit on her hands to keep from showing her excitement. Trevor looked over at Sarah for her opinion. Before either of them could speak, Noah, dressed in his pajamas, came walking into the living room.

Rubbing his eyes, he looked at Trevor. "Daddy, I heard noises."

"I'm sorry, buddy. I guess we were talking too loudly. Are you thirsty? Would you like something in your Sippy cup?"

Noah nodded, and then looked at Devon.

Trevor went to the kitchen and filled his Sippy cup with apple juice. When he returned to Noah, he decided now was as good a time as ever to introduce him to his grandfather.

"Noah. This is your grandfather. Can you say hello and it's nice to meet you?"

All Noah could muster was, "Hello."

Trevor realized Noah might not know what a grandfather was. "Noah, your grandfather is my father. Just like I'm your Daddy, he is my Daddy. That makes him your grandfather."

Devon smiled at the boy, and Trevor could see how happy he was to meet his grandchild.

"Hello, Noah. I'm very happy to meet you. I hope you will come to my house one of these days. I have a pool and lots of fun things you can play with there."

Devon looked at Trevor. "Maybe your Daddy will bring you for a visit?"

Trevor lifted Noah onto his lap. "I think we can make that happen."

Devon stood and turned to Sarah. "I hope you will come too."

"Thank you, Mr. Hutchins. I'd like that very much."

Trevor stopped his father before he got to the door. "Dad. I'll think about your offer."

Devon looked at Trevor. "Thank you, Son. Let me hear from you soon."

They watched Devon get in his car and wave as he drove out onto the street. Sarah was overwhelmed by the exchange and a lump had formed in her throat when she heard Trevor call his father, "Dad." She knew there would be bumps in the road, and that as much as everyone wanted to make amends for the past, there was still history to overcome and forgiveness to be had.

But, it was a start, and in some small way, it felt like a new beginning for Sarah and Trevor too.

CHAPTER ELEVEN

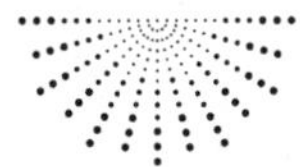

Maggie pulled her car into the *Sanibellia* parking lot and sat for a minute trying to find the right words. She knew what she wanted to say to Paolo, her concern was how she would do it. The nursery was packed with people shopping, and a steady stream of tourists walked across the lot from the Farmers' Market adding to the crowd.

She got out of her car and looked for Paolo, but she didn't see him anywhere. She pushed through the throngs of shoppers and headed for his office. The large windows made privacy impossible, but Maggie didn't care. She found him sitting behind his desk. She could tell that he already knew why she was there. The excitement in her eyes and the smile on her face gave away her mission. She didn't wait for questions or pleasantries.

"Yes. I will marry you."

Paolo came out from behind his desk and ran to her. Throwing his arms around her, he hugged her as tightly as he could.

He pulled away from their embrace and asked, "What made you change your mind?"

Maggie feared bringing up Daniella's name might upset him,

but she had to take that chance. She didn't want there to be secrets between them.

"Ciara told me about Daniella."

Her heart raced as she waited for his reaction.

"That was a long time ago, Maggie. I believe Daniella has blessed us and would want me to be happy. I am happy, Maggie. You have brought so much love and light to my life. I hope to do the same for you."

Maggie needed to explain what had been holding her back.

"Paolo, I've been scared I would lose myself if I got married again. You've never given me any reason to think that might happen. It's just that I've spent my whole adult life as a married woman. This last year, I've been single for the first time in my life. I love depending on myself for everything. I'm proud of who I am and what I've accomplished. I want to do more. I want you by my side supporting me, and celebrating every accomplishment with me, as my husband. I've never really had a partner before. Will you marry me and be my partner for the rest of our lives?"

Paolo went to his desk and found the little blue box he had presented to Maggie the night before. He opened the box and got down on his knee.

"I promise to be your partner in all things. I promise to be an honest, respectful, loyal husband for the rest of our lives. And one more thing. If you ever fear that you are losing who you are, or question your identity, you can come to me, and I'll remind you of the woman you have become. The one who can do anything she can dream. The woman who moves through the world by following her heart. I'm so blessed that heart found its way to me."

Paolo placed the ring on Maggie's finger. He got up from the floor, and pulled Maggie to him, wrapping his arms around her as they kissed.

Unaware that a crowd had gathered on the other side of the

windows, Maggie and Paolo jumped when they heard the applause and screams of congratulations. His employees stopped working so that they could witness the happy occasion. Paolo waved and thanked them all.

"Maggie and I appreciate your love and support. Now, everyone, get back to work."

With what little privacy they had left the couple committed to finding quiet time later when they could be alone. In the meantime, their families and friends needed to be told as soon as possible.

"How about you let me finish a bit of paperwork and we'll head back to the inn and make our calls to everyone?"

"Perfect. I want to walk around the nursery and see if there are any indoor plants for Sarah's condo."

"Maggie, before you go there is one more thing I need to say to you. As you know, Rose put the inn in my name before she died to avoid probate. We agreed it was the right thing to do, but you and I both know her wish was for you to own it outright. She wanted to give you time to heal and decide what you wanted to do with your life. In many ways, I've been waiting too, but there isn't any reason to wait any longer."

Paolo walked to his desk and pulled out a document.

"I've had a Quit-Claim Deed prepared so that the property is only in your name. I took my name off the deed. You now are the sole owner of the Key Lime Garden Inn and will be only yours for the rest of your life. It's a gift that you can pass down to your children."

"Paolo, this is silly. There's no need to do this. You and I are about to be husband and wife. We should own the property together."

"Listen to me, Maggie. This has always been the plan. Whether you and I married or not, the real estate is yours. That's the way Rose wanted it. I'm not going anywhere. I plan to be by your side for the rest of our lives, but the property is yours, and yours alone."

Maggie didn't know what to say. She felt embarrassed to admit, that it never occurred to her that anything financial needed to change, but she appreciated the gesture. Of course, they needed to discuss money. At their age they had many years of savings and investments earned before they ever knew each other. Paolo had done the responsible thing and started this discussion before they walked down the aisle. Maggie's desire to hold on to her autonomy in this marriage had given her great concern. Paolo understood that and this document was proof.

"I have already made a will and plan to leave Sanibellia to my sister, but I think in order for you to feel secure, we should prepare a prenup so that you can keep your investments and possessions safe for you and your children. It would be irresponsible for us not to prepare something at our age. You've already had the rug pulled out from you because of lies and secrets. I don't want there to be anything unsaid between us."

Maggie had tears in her eyes, and she threw her arms around him. Resting her head on his shoulders, it seemed impossible to love Paolo more than she already did, but in that moment their commitment to one another gave her the stability and security she needed more than anything else.

"Thank you, Paolo," she whispered.

They stayed in that embrace for several minutes and then she folded the deed and placed it inside her bag. She spent the next thirty minutes trying to look at plants, but she couldn't stop admiring the ring on her left hand. There was only one way to describe how she felt—at peace.

Sarah looked at the text message on her phone.

Come to Chelsea's house when you get home.

Her mother wasn't the cryptic type, and usually hated surprises. Sarah left her car in the driveway and decided the walk would do her good. So much had happened with Trevor and his father that she felt exceedingly pleased with the day. She wanted the feeling to linger and hoped whatever Chelsea and her mother had to tell her, would be good news.

She knocked on the screen door before entering the house. "Hello? Where is everybody?"

Chelsea called out to her. "We're in the kitchen."

Sarah was surprised to see Paolo and Ciara. Her eyes went immediately to the bottle of champagne on the kitchen counter.

"We wanted to wait for you."

"What's going on? What are we celebrating?"

Maggie walked over to Sarah and smiled. "Paolo asked me to marry him, and I said yes."

The news did not come as a shock to Sarah. Many times, during the past year she imagined an announcement just like this one. She wanted her mother to enjoy this moment and so she smiled and supported her decision, but she couldn't understand her desire to marry. Didn't she and Paolo have the companionship and intimacy they desired? Why wasn't that enough? Her parents' marriage wasn't perfect, but to Sarah it seemed a lie. Her father's infidelity, and her mother's forgiveness of his cheating ways convinced Sarah that marriage would never fulfill her need for stability.

Sarah hugged her mother and did the same with Paolo. "Congratulations to you both. I'm not surprised. I had a feeling this day would come. Let me see the ring."

Maggie waved her left hand in front of her daughter.

"Wow. It's beautiful." She reached over and gave Paolo a high-five. "Way to go!"

Sarah pulled a stool out from under the island.

"I guess that makes two things I'm celebrating today."

Chelsea poured the champagne and handed Sarah a glass.

"I'm always ready to hear good news. What else are we celebrating?"

"Trevor and his father seem to be on good terms. At least they're trying."

Maggie hugged Sarah again. "That is good news, honey. For everyone's sake, but especially for Noah."

Sarah agreed. "Mr. Hutchins—Devon, offered Trevor a job."

Everyone carried their glasses to the dining room table, where Chelsea had placed a charcuterie board.

Sarah continued. "Devon purchased several acres of land to build affordable housing and he wants Trevor to oversee the project. Of course, Trevor has no experience with construction, but apparently that's not what his father wants him to work on. He figures with Trevor's volunteer background he has a better understanding for the people these buildings will serve. Devon's not wrong. Trevor has natural philanthropic abilities. He hasn't said yes yet. He's thinking about it"

Chelsea raised her glass. "If I can interrupt the conversation? I want to toast my very dear friends and wish them every happiness in their marriage. To Maggie and Paolo."

Ciara raised her glass, and Sarah did the same. "To Mom and Paolo. I love you both. Congratulations."

Chelsea placed a cutting board on the table. She added a loaf of French bread and began cutting small pieces to go with the meats and cheese. "So, have you decided on a wedding date yet?"

Maggie looked at Paolo and shrugged. "Actually, no. We haven't talked about that. I guess we should pick a date. We're heading into summer and honestly having a wedding in the heat is too much for me. Not to mention, I doubt anyone wants to travel to Florida in the middle of summer. How about in the fall? September or October could work. It would give my kids enough time to schedule it around their work."

Chelsea liked that idea. "I think that is perfect. Planning a wedding takes time. I've got lots of ideas already."

Maggie looked concerned. "Whoa. Slow down. This is not my first rodeo you know. There is no reason to go crazy planning a wedding. We need to keep it simple."

Chelsea topped off everyone's champagne glass. "Well, just remember that we've got lunch-bunch tomorrow. I wouldn't be surprised if, when you tell them, they all say they're coming to Captiva for the wedding.

Maggie rolled her eyes. "I keep forgetting about the get-together. I'm glad you reminded me."

Sarah laughed at the image of the lunch-bunch ladies descending upon them. Pure chaos typically ensued whenever the women got together. It was hard to describe. One had to experience it for it to be believed. She could only imagine the kind of trouble they would get into on the island. Paolo Moretti would soon learn that he was not marrying one woman, but rather a group of very opinionated women. She sipped her champagne and then smiled at the thought.

Sarah was almost asleep when her phone buzzed with a text message from Emma.

Emma: Do you have time tomorrow to get together? Can you come to Naples for lunch? I'll make reservations at Baleen. It's right on the water. How about 1pm?

Sarah: That works for me. I'll see you then.

A thumbs-up emoji followed her response. She was looking forward to catching up with Emma. It had been a while since she was last in Naples. She loved the area, especially the shops on 5th Avenue.

It would give her plenty of time to get a few things done at her office, and then shop for baby items for Sophia. Ciara had already contacted Hospice, and, along with diapers had filled Sharon's refrigerator with food, and much-needed baby formula.

Sarah wondered how much time Sharon had left, but regardless, she felt an urgency they find a temporary foster home for the child as soon as possible. It pleased her that for now, Sharon was spending time with her baby, and that Hospice provided the company and support she needed. Sarah loved holding Sophia. The child's wide blue eyes staring back at Sarah warmed her heart. Perhaps when she brought the baby clothes over to Sharon's apartment, she would get another opportunity to hold Sophia.

Sarah took a sip of water and then turned off the lamp. She couldn't stop thinking about the events of the day. So much had happened, but she couldn't tell whether any of it was good or not. Was it awful of her to be suspicious of Devon's motives? She wanted to believe that everything would work out and that Trevor could have a healthy connection with his father, but only time would tell.

And what about his siblings? Trevor didn't elaborate on his interaction with them. If having his brothers and sisters in Noah's life made Trevor happy, perhaps those relationships might heal as well. If it helped Trevor to move forward, Sarah would choose to believe only the best.

Her mother's engagement continued to baffle Sarah. She tried to understand the necessity of a legal piece of paper. In her eyes, they were already married. She took comfort knowing that Paolo loved her mother very much. If the last year proved anything, Maggie loved Paolo deeply as well. For all Sarah's concerns, she didn't see any red flags, and that made her rest easy. In the next six months, if she changed her mind about supporting the marriage, she'd tell her mother. For now, she'd work with Chelsea to give her mother the best wedding ever.

CHAPTER TWELVE

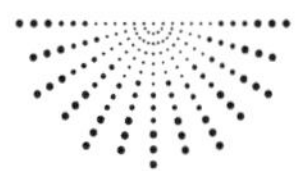

Maggie missed cooking when it was her turn to host the lunch-bunch ladies monthly gathering. She had to be content with spending time with her friends via Zoom. She hoped the ladies could get away and be with her on her wedding day, but a destination wedding wasn't always easy. She couldn't wait to tell them about the engagement and show them her ring.

It was practical to video from Chelsea's house but as soon as construction on the carriage house was complete, Maggie insisted they connect to the internet from her place. *Her place.* She hadn't given it any thought before, but where would Paolo and she live after the wedding? There was no way she could leave the inn. Not that she wanted to anyway, but she needed to talk to him about it.

Maggie promised to bring the Pinot Grigio and Chelsea grilled cedar-plank salmon to go with their salad.

Always up for adventure, Chelsea's eyes sparkled with mischief, "I don't think you should tell them about the engagement. Just flash that sparkler in front of the camera a few times and see who says something first."

Maggie laughed. “I can’t stop looking at it myself. It’s really beautiful, isn’t it?”

Chelsea hugged Maggie. “It’s so good to see you happy like this. I’ll never forget you trying to fix me up with Paolo last year. That man only had eyes for you from the first moment he saw you under Rose’s gazebo.”

Maggie smiled at the memory. “I can’t believe she’s been gone fifteen months. Did I ever tell you that I swear I hear her voice? Sometimes it’s when I’m in the garden, but a couple of times it was when I was in her reading chair. What’s really weird, is that I heard it the other day when I was upstairs in the loft area of the carriage house.”

“I have no doubt that Rose is hovering around the inn. There’s so much history in that place. I bet her spirit isn’t the only one either. What about Anne Morrow Lindbergh? I know she didn’t live there, but she might as well have, with all her books and shells around the property.”

Just then, a bell sounded from Chelsea’s computer. “That’s just my calendar telling me it’s time to get on Zoom. If you don’t mind, why don’t you pour us a glass of wine while I log onto this thing.”

Maggie opened the bottle of wine and got two glasses from the cabinet. She could hear Chelsea swearing as she tried to get into her computer. “I hate technology. I know it’s necessary, and I love that we can visit with our friends, but I just hate all the bells and buzzes. I feel like my computer is yelling at me.”

Rachel’s freckled face and wild auburn hair appeared first and soon the other women gathered around the monitor. Jane’s normally short blond hair had been styled in a pixie cut and looked adorable on her. Kelly was wearing her favorite blue topaz drop earrings and Diana, who was the spitting image of the actress, Rita Wilson, blew a kiss through the monitor.

Diana spoke first. “As usual, I’ve been up since four AM this morning. I know it’s only one o’clock, but it feels like midnight.”

Rachel rolled her eyes at Diana. "I guess you should have thought about that before opening a bakery. What did that guy with the mustache say? 'Time to make the donuts.'"

Jane came to the front of the others and twirled. "What do you all think of my new haircut? Do you think it's too short?"

Maggie shook her head. "Absolutely not. I couldn't pull it off, but it suits you. I love it."

Everyone agreed it was a perfect look for Jane. Chelsea decided to get the ball rolling on the latest news. "So, what's new with everyone? Anything exciting happen since last month?"

Kelly shared her children's latest accomplishments. Melinda's honor roll streak continued to make her parents proud. Jeremy had several three-pointers in his last basketball game. Chelsea bit her tongue trying not to announce Maggie's news, but she couldn't stand the wait a minute longer. She grabbed Maggie's left hand and pulled it into camera range. The gasps and screams came through the monitor like police sirens.

"I can't believe it. Paolo finally proposed. When? How did he do it? Did he get down on one knee?" Rachel asked.

Chelsea tried to control the narrative. "Oh, for heaven's sake. Let the woman talk."

Maggie gave her friends as much as she was willing to share. Her earlier ambivalence and concerns she kept to herself. "Yes, he got down on one knee to propose after he made me a delicious dinner. We're thinking the wedding will be in six months. We don't have an actual date yet because I need to call the kids first.

Jane spoke next. "Six months? Why are you waiting? If I were engaged to that handsome man, I wouldn't let him get away. I'd marry him tomorrow."

"June, July, and August in Florida can be brutally hot. There's no way I want my family to travel during the summer months. Waiting six months will give my kids time to organize their work schedules. At first, I thought October would be a good time, but I forgot about school. Maybe early September would be better. I don't expect you guys to fly down. I'd love it if you could, but you all have busy lives."

As usual, Chelsea had an idea. "Ladies, you all need to come down to Captiva and help with the wedding preparations. Don't you think that would be a blast? We haven't been together in so long. We could have a reunion as well as a wedding. What do you all think?"

Jane, Kelly, and Diana agreed a reunion on Captiva Island might be exactly what they needed. Jane felt burnt out from her job. Kelly couldn't remember the last time she took a vacation with her friends. Her husband and kids could fend for themselves for a week or two. Diana had plenty of people to run the bakery. She'd pack tomorrow if she could. Rachel was the only one who didn't respond. All eyes watched her and waited for an answer. When it came, it wasn't anything any of them expected.

Her voice was soft, almost a whisper. "Brian and I are getting a divorce."

Quiet fell over their meeting. Moments like this pained Maggie that she wasn't able to hug her friend. Living so far away, all she could do was offer her love and whatever help she could. "I'm so sorry, Rachel. Is there anything we can do?"

Rachel nodded. "You can all support me during the pregnancy."

No one said a word. Shock hit them all at the same time, but it was Chelsea who finally said what was on everyone's mind. "Honey, I thought Brian didn't want children?"

"He didn't. He doesn't. I'm forty-seven. He had a vasectomy. I never imagined I'd get pregnant. Well, I was wrong. Here I am, almost three months along. I want this baby more than anything. If Brian doesn't, then too bad for him."

Now, everyone talked at the same time. Soon, the sadness that dominated their get-together turned joyous and a reason to celebrate. Rachel continued, "So, Maggie. I won't be teaching school next year, but I can travel. If you don't mind a pregnant woman helping out."

Maggie's heart swelled with love for her friends, and for Rachel especially. "Are you kidding? I can't wait to meet this beautiful baby that you've waited your whole life for. It's a blessing for sure. The baby already has five aunts who love her or him."

Chelsea clapped her hands together. "Well then, that's settled. We've got a plan. As soon as Paolo and Maggie set the date, you ladies can purchase your plane tickets. I'm pretty sure between the inn and my place, you won't be needing hotel reservations."

For the next hour, the women talked non-stop about life in Massachusetts, and on Captiva Island. Jane checked in on Maggie's family whenever she could and promised not to say anything about the engagement. Maggie would call them later tonight to share the good news. She wanted Paolo to be in the room when she made the call.

It was an exciting time for both Maggie and Rachel. The love and support of the lunch-bunch did much to settle their nerves. Rachel would not go through this pregnancy alone, and Maggie looked forward to being with her besties in a few months. If she started to feel guilty about her good fortune, she'd remind herself that was the 'old Maggie' talking. For now, she basked in her blessings, and remained grateful for them.

As the sun set over the island, Maggie waited until her guests had finished dinner and the dining room was cleared of dishes. She helped Riley and Grace prepare the room for breakfast then did one last vacuum of the dining room before meeting Paolo in the carriage house.

So that she wouldn't have to make several phone calls, Maggie sent a text to Lauren, asking her to gather everyone over at the family home. Maggie took Paolo's hand. "Are you ready to do this?"

"Ready as I'll ever be."

Maggie dialed Lauren's cellphone using FaceTime. Lauren answered the phone on the second ring.

"Hey, Mom. We're all here. What's going on? You've got us worried."

"Nothing to worry about. Everything is fine. Paolo is with me."

Maggie turned her phone to face Paolo, who waved. "Paolo and I wanted to video with you all. We have news. We're getting married in the fall."

Maggie didn't know what to expect. Fortunately, her children seemed happy about their news.

Lauren was quick to react. "Mom, that is wonderful news. Beth and I actually predicted this would happen."

"Do you have a date for the wedding yet?" Beth asked.

"We were thinking sometime in the fall. I know the kids have school, but they wouldn't be absent for more than a day or two. We'll have it on a Saturday. Treat it like a long weekend. As a matter of fact, isn't there a holiday in October?"

Michael didn't want Paolo to feel out of the conversation. "Welcome to the family, Paolo."

"Thank you, Michael. We're looking forward to having you come to Florida. Your mother misses all of you."

"I bet Chelsea can't wait to organize everything. You've got a natural wedding planner with her," Lauren said.

Maggie explained how her lunch-bunch friends saw the wedding as a chance for a reunion. "I can only imagine what trouble they'll get into while they're here. With Chelsea at the helm, it could get interesting."

They spent the rest of the conversation catching up. It meant the world to her that her family supported her decision to marry again. They had all been through a terrible time with Daniel's death. It made perfect sense if any of them had lingering unresolved feelings about her moving on with another man. If they did, no one said a word about it.

She would call Christopher later in the evening when the time difference wasn't so inconvenient. He always defended her decisions, so she didn't have any concerns about his reaction. Maggie wanted to enjoy her engagement, and now that her friends and family appeared to be on board with her decision, she could rest easy and let the celebrations begin.

CHAPTER THIRTEEN

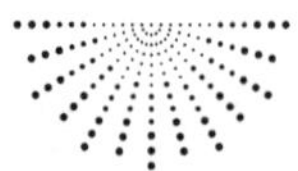

Captiva Island shops left little to the imagination. The usual tourist treasures, what Sarah referred to as "things a person would never buy if they weren't on vacation," dominated the stores. Important staples such as diapers, formula and bathing soaps and lotions she bought at the supermarket. She found it impossible to pass by the newborn section of the baby boutique and allowed herself the indulgence of buying two adorable one-piece outfits and a few soft toys for Sophia.

With an hour to spare before meeting Emma for lunch, Sarah made it to Sharon's apartment, just as a Hospice nurse was leaving.

"How is she doing today?"

"Are you family?"

"No. I'm a friend."

"Well, she'll be happy for the company. I think her spirits are good. I know taking care of her child helps considerably. Is there someone who will take the baby when Sharon passes?"

"Ciara Moretti and I are working on finding Sophia a good foster care situation."

"There's no father in the picture?"

"No. No father."

The woman looked up at the sky and shook her head. "What a shame."

Sarah didn't want to share too much about Sharon's personal life with the woman, but she needed some guidance on Sharon's medication.

"The decision to move the baby to another family will have to be made soon. Sharon doesn't appear to be in too much pain, but I assume that will change. She won't be able to care for Sophia once she is taking medication."

"That's right. As a matter of fact, she's just been given a prescription for morphine. She doesn't need it right now, but I expect she will soon. This way she'll have the pills if she needs them. I think we're at the point where Sophia might have to be cared for by someone else who could maybe bring the baby for visits. I don't think it's wise to keep Sophia away from Sharon in these last weeks, but you need to put something in place soon. Seeing that Sophia is cared for will give her peace."

Sarah thanked the woman and watched her drive away. She didn't want to talk to Sharon about the baby going to another family, but she had no choice. She wished Ciara was here. She could use the support. She took a deep breath for courage before entering the apartment.

Sharon was sitting up in her chair with Sophia in her arms.

"Look at the two of you. Let me get my phone. I want to take a picture."

Sharon smiled and looked down at her baby. Her face, normally tinged with gray, was bright and beaming with love. The hospice woman was right, no amount of medication could compare to the calm and euphoria Sharon experienced holding her child.

Sarah took a few pictures of them and shared the image with Sharon. "It's impossible to look at this picture and not see how much you love your baby, Sharon. You're a good mother."

Sharon looked at Sarah with tears in her eyes. "It's time, isn't it?"

Sarah wanted to cry. "Soon. Not this week, but soon. It doesn't mean that you won't see Sophia anymore. It just means that it will be difficult to take care of her while you are taking very strong medicine. I'll make sure that whoever takes her will bring her to see you as often as possible."

Sharon shook her head. "No. Wherever she goes, I'll be happy just knowing she's taken care of. Her life needs to begin and mine needs to end. I don't want her coming to my death bed."

She reached for Sarah and pleaded once more. "Are you sure you can't take her?"

The pull on Sarah's heart worried her. More than once, she had struggled with the idea of taking Sophia. What would it hurt to tell Sharon that she would be Sophia's mother? Regardless of the truth, if it gave Sharon comfort at the end of her life, why not?

All Sarah could manage was a whisper, "Let's not talk about this right now. I have baby clothes, toys, diapers, creams, and soaps as well as bottles and formula. I'm going to put these things away and visit with you and Sophia for a bit. I've got to meet someone in Naples, so I can't stay as long as I'd like. Ciara should be along soon though."

Sarah walked into the bedroom and put her hand over her mouth. She tried to compose herself by organizing Sophia's new clothes, but the tears she had been holding inside began to fall. None of this was fair. Soon, Sophia would be taken from her mother, and placed with strangers. The baby would be cared for, but her heart broke for Sharon's loss.

She wiped her tears, and called out to Sharon, as she entered the living room. "Are you hungry? Can I make you something to eat before I leave?"

"Can you take Sophia? I'd like to rest on the bed for a bit."

"Of course." Sarah took the baby in her arms and placed her in her bassinet. Sophia moved a little before settling back into a comfortable sleep. Sharon tried to get up from her chair, but Sarah stopped her. "Let me help you."

Sarah could feel Sharon's frail body against her own. They slowly walked to the side of the bed, and although Sharon weighed little, Sarah had difficulty lifting her.

"I'm sorry to be so much trouble."

Once Sharon was on the bed, Sarah placed Sharon's legs under the sheet, and covered her with the comforter.

"It's no trouble, Sharon. I can only imagine how tired you must be. I'm glad I can help. I'll stay a little until you fall asleep. Ciara should be here any minute."

Too weak to talk anymore, Sharon smiled and closed her eyes. Sarah walked to the bassinet and looked at Sophia. Bundled in a pink striped cloth, she looked so peaceful. Sarah didn't want to wake the baby but couldn't help touching Sophia's face. Her little pink mouth opened slightly. It closed and opened several times most likely reacting to Sarah's touch.

The apartment door opened, Ciara walked inside and started to speak. Sarah put her finger to her lips.

"They're both asleep."

Whispering, Ciara asked, "How is she today?"

Sarah shook her head. "Not good. She's so frail and weak. They're giving her a prescription for morphine. I told her we'd have to move Sophia soon. I hated to tell her, but we've got to be practical about this. I'm glad we've been able to give her some time with Sophia, but she can't take care of her like this."

"How did she take it?"

"She already knew before I even said anything. What's best for the baby is all she cares about. She understands the situation. I promised her that wherever Sophia goes, we'll make sure she comes to see Sharon as often as possible. I thought that would make her happy, but instead, she doesn't want Sophia here at her death bed. Once Sophia goes, Sharon wants that to be the end of them. It breaks my heart."

Ciara nodded, and then reminded Sarah of the time. "Don't you have to be in Naples to meet your friend?"

"Oh, gosh, I've got to run. Listen, I've already got a few ideas about a foster family for Sophia. I'll talk to you about it later. Thanks for coming over today."

"No problem. Careful driving."

Sarah took one last look at the baby. Sophia would never remember this day, or her mother, but Sarah would. She promised herself she would do everything in her power to keep Sharon's memory alive for her child, starting with today's photo. It would stay with Sophia for the rest of her life. Sarah would make certain of it.

Baleen restaurant sat just beyond the ocean at LaPlaya Beach and Golf Resort. The restaurant's reputation for outstanding food was well deserved. Sarah looked forward to spending time with her friend. The morning visit with Sharon and Sophia pained her and she wondered if she'd be able to think about something other than their fate.

Sarah could see Emma waving from her table on the far side of the room. She walked toward her while trying not to stare at the food on everyone else's table.

"I hope I haven't kept you waiting too long."

"I just got here. They said the table was ready, and they'd let me know when you arrived. It's so good to see you again. I'm sorry I didn't spend much time with you at the gallery, but I'm glad we're getting together today."

Sarah took the menu from the waiter. "Me too."

Emma ordered a glass of white wine, but Sarah decided on iced tea. She wanted to order their food before grilling Emma about her life. Once the waiter took their order it was Emma who spoke first.

"I've missed you Sarah-rah."

"Ah, well, I've missed you too, but not that nickname."

"Well, you did make an awfully cute cheerleader."

Laughing, Sarah admonished Emma. "I've worked very hard to forget that. Let's not bring it up again."

"Fine. It's in the past. Speaking of the other night, your mother looked beautiful, and that guy, Paolo? He's clearly in love with her. She knows that right?"

"As it happens, he proposed to her the other night, and she said, yes."

'Wow. That is news. How do you feel about it? I mean with your father passing away just last year. Do you think it's too soon?"

"First of all, I'm still not sure what they gain by getting married. Don't get me wrong, they're a great couple. Paolo is a wonderful man, and I don't have any issue with them being together. I should also tell you that right before my father died, he told my mother he was leaving her for another woman. He asked her for a divorce two days before he died."

"Oh, Sarah. That's awful. It must have been devastating to everyone. I'm so sorry. I didn't know. Christopher never said anything to me about that."

"Christopher? My brother, Christopher?"

"Yes. I guess he never mentioned it to you, but I saw him about six months ago when I was in Iraq on assignment."

"He never said a thing."

"I imagine so much has happened over the last year, he probably forgot about it. He told me that his father died, but he never mentioned the affair. He did tell me about your mother opening an inn on Captiva Island, and that you joined her down here. I was so glad to hear that you were in Florida. I figured it was only a matter of time before I visited my parents. It was a real surprise to see you at the gallery, but a happy one."

"Did you know that Christopher had a crush on you?"

"What? You're kidding."

"It's true. You didn't notice when he'd find ways to come into the room when we were talking? He made sure he was home every time you came to our house. I'm surprised you never noticed. He'd probably die to think I told you this."

"Your brother is a sweet guy. I couldn't believe it when he tapped me on the shoulder. I was taking pictures of the beautiful landscape when he came up behind me. How much longer does he have on his duty?"

"I'm not sure. I think only one more year, but then he has to complete two years of something else after that. I'm not exactly sure, and I forget what he said."

"Four years of active duty, and then two years of inactive duty probably. Any idea where he will be after he comes home?"

"No idea. I'm sure he'll tell us when he wants us to know. How long before you go back to Europe?"

Emma sighed and shrugged her shoulders. "I'm not sure. I decided that I am going back, I'm just not sure when. I love my work and the life I've built for myself, but it can be hard, dangerous even."

Sarah could tell there was something eating away at Emma, but unless she asked her directly, she wasn't sure her friend would confess.

"What is it, Emma? Why are you really in Florida?"

Emma had finished her wine and gestured for the waiter to fill her glass again. She took another sip and explained.

"I guess what you could say is that I'm having a crisis of faith. I've seen a lot of death and real anguish all over the globe. I knew that going in. As a matter of fact, it's what I've wanted to do most in the world. My dream has been to capture life in photos, not happy people posing with smiles on their faces, but real moments of living. Photos that capture life as it happens, the bad and ugly parts too."

Emma took another sip of her wine, and Sarah pushed for more.

"So, you're happy? You've got everything you've ever wanted. You reached your dream. You made it happen."

Emma nodded. "I have, for sure."

Tears started to fill Emma's eyes. Sarah waited for an explanation.

"I met a man. Timothy. We fell in love. He was a journalist writing about the war in Afghanistan. He was from Florida too. We spent so many hours talking about growing up down here. Timothy spoke of his love for the ocean and how he'd water ski and windsurf off Sanibel. He grew up in Tampa. I told him even though I grew up in Naples, I'd never been to Sanibel or Captiva. At least not until last week when his brother and I brought Timothy's body back to the states."

"Oh, Emma, no. I'm so sorry."

"There was fighting, he got caught in the crossfire. His brother, Oliver, came to get his body and we flew back a few weeks ago. That was his brother with me the other night at the gallery."

Sarah jumped out of her chair and ran to Emma, throwing her arms around her.

"Oh, Emma. How awful. I'm so sorry. What can I do? Please, is there anything at all?"

Emma held onto Sarah and patted her arm. "You're so sweet. Thank you. I'm just glad you're here. I've thought about getting in touch before this, but our lives seemed to be going in different directions. I'm happy we have this time at least."

"Emma, I know you love what you do, but are you sure you want to return? Maybe you need a little more time before you decide."

Emma shook her head. "No. I mean yes about taking a little

more time, but no, I know I want to return. This is who I am, Sarah. I couldn't do anything else. I'm living the life I've always dreamed of. I need time to grieve and mourn Timothy's death. But, when I'm ready, I'll go back. Right now, what I want to do is visit the places Timothy loved growing up. I want to walk in his shoes for a bit."

Sarah was proud of Emma. Her friend knew exactly who she was and had no doubt about where she belonged. Even in the face of terrible adversity, she stayed true to herself. Sarah admired such clarity.

"I'm renting a condo in Ft. Myers, and with my mother's inn on Captiva, we're close if you need anything."

"Thank you, Sarah. Perhaps I'll stop by, and we can spend some time together before I go back."

Emma raised her glass. "To Timothy."

"To Timothy, and to you Emma."

They ate their lunch and shared memories of college days, and family adventures. Sarah couldn't help but reflect on the fact that the day ended as it had begun, with tears. Even amongst the sadness, they found reasons to laugh. Sarah didn't voice her concerns about Sophia. She would save that talk for the next time they got together.

CHAPTER FOURTEEN

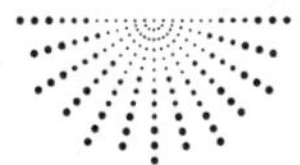

Sarah had scheduled a meeting with Ciara for the next morning. The Outreach Center had worked with the Florida Department of Children and Families for many years, and there were two possible families that were perfect candidates to take Sophia.

Ciara knocked on Sarah's office door. "Do you have a minute to go over this now?"

"Yes. Come in. I've been dreading this for days, but I know it needs to happen. Can I see the family profiles?"

Ciara laid out several papers on Sarah's desk. There were photographs along with extensive history on the two families.

"Honestly, Sarah, we can't go wrong selecting either one of these families. Both have already been fostering kids for about ten years and have impeccable reputations. They both have recently given up children for adoption after fostering them for close to eighteen months. They've got the room and the experience. I couldn't pick one. What do you think? Understand, that we don't really have any influence over the choice they make. My friend Meredith Carpenter shared this with me out of friendship."

Sarah agreed Sophia would be lucky to have such lovely people fostering her. She would be safe and lovingly cared for no matter which family they selected. She remembered the first time she saw Sophia. She could feel her little fingers wrapping around her own. Watching as her big blue eyes looked up at Sarah, wondering who this stranger was.

Ciara's voice startled her. "Earth to Sarah."

"I'm sorry. Yes, these are great choices. Why don't you call Meredith tomorrow and make the arrangements?"

"What's going on with you?"

"What do you mean?"

"What I mean, is that you're sitting in front of me, but you're not really here. At least your mind isn't. Are you upset about something? Is everything all right between you and Trevor?"

"Of course. Everything's fine. Let's move forward with this. Would you make the calls and let me know when we bring Sophia to them?"

"Sure. No problem. I'll get on it right away. As soon as I've got a date, I'll go over to Sharon's and let her know as well."

Sarah sat back in her chair, and watched Ciara walk out of her office. She knew what was wrong, but she couldn't bring herself to say the words out loud. She wanted Sophia to live with her. Ciara would think she was crazy, and she'd be right.

For days, Sarah had pushed that thought out of her mind, but it never left her heart. Giving voice to it now surprised her and felt bittersweet. She had nothing to give Sophia. She was a single woman with a full-time job, and a life she was building with Trevor. She barely talked about Sharon and Sophia to him for fear that her true feelings would come spilling out. Didn't they have enough to worry about with his job and Noah's health?

She'd never considered being a mother to anyone, but the moment she held Sophia in her arms, she knew they were meant to be mother and daughter. How could she hand Sophia over to another woman? It was the right thing to do, but it wasn't what she wanted, and she couldn't imagine herself capable of watching her drive away. She'd stay at the office and let Ciara assist Meredith in bringing Sophia to her new home.

A knock on her office door startled Sarah. Noah ran to her and jumped into her lap, leaving Trevor in the doorway.

"Oh, my. What are you two doing here?"

"He wanted to see your office. He wouldn't stop talking about you until I gave in. I told him you were busy."

Sarah hugged Noah. "I'm never too busy to see my favorite guys."

Trevor sat on the chair in front of Sarah's desk. "Are you too busy to let us take you to lunch?"

Sarah looked at the clock and couldn't believe the morning had slipped by so fast. "I think I can do that. Where'd you like to go?"

Trevor smiled, "Noah and I thought we'd take you on a picnic. I've got everything we need in the car."

Noah jumped to the floor and took Sarah's hands pulling her out of her chair. "Ok, Ok, "I'm coming."

When they got to the car, Trevor pulled a large basket and blanket from the trunk. They walked across the street from Sarah's office and to the right one block. Trevor found a small grassy area under a tree. Sarah helped him lay the blanket on the ground. Noah immediately fell onto it.

"How come you didn't bring Nessa for the picnic, Noah?"

"She's home taking a nap."

"Oh, I see. That's a good idea. Everyone should take a nap when they can."

"Do you take a nap?"

"Sometimes, if I'm really tired."

Sarah loved talking with Noah, and she felt relieved that he adjusted to having her in his life. She said so to Trevor, while Noah played with stacking rocks.

"Oh, I'd say he's more than adjusted, Sarah. He talks about you every day and always asks when we are going to see you again. Sometimes I think he likes you better than me."

They emptied the basket and gave Noah his sandwich and Sippy cup. They ate mostly in silence, letting the breeze rush through the trees and cool them off.

"So, are you ready to move into the condo tomorrow? I'm picking up the truck at nine o'clock. I should be at your place around nine-thirty."

"Ready as I'll ever be. I'm excited to get into my own place finally. I hope the truck isn't too big. I don't really have that much stuff. Mom is giving me the sofa from the carriage house. It's an antique and probably not at all my style, but hey, it's free. I mostly have my clothes and several boxes I had shipped down from Massachusetts. Once I decided I wanted to stay in Florida, I had my sisters gather my things and send everything down. Except for some clothing, I don't have much. I made Beth send me several things that she stole out of my closet. I wouldn't have known they were missing until I went looking to wear them. When I couldn't find them, I sent her a text, asking her if she had them. She acted innocent and said she took them because she assumed I didn't want them anymore."

Trevor laughed. "Your sister Beth sounds like a lot of fun. I hope I get to meet her, and the rest of your family."

"It looks like you will at my mother's wedding. Everyone is coming down for the weekend. Everyone, except my brother Christopher, of course."

"Which sister is Brea, the one who just had a baby?"

"No, that's my sister-in-law. She's my brother Michael's wife. They have three children now. Jackson is the new addition to the family. They have two daughters, Quinn, and Cora. Lauren and Jeff and their two girls Olivia and Lily will be here. Beth says she'll make it, but who knows with that woman. She almost always is either late or doesn't arrive at all."

Trevor took Sarah's hand in his. "I bet you miss them."

Sarah nodded and then looked down at their hands. She loved the way Trevor always reached for her when talking about things that mattered. He had come to know her very well, and that pleased her.

"I do miss them. Some days are really bad, and I call them just to hear their voices. It always makes things so much better. I used to do FaceTime and then later we'd get together using the Zoom app. We had Zoom parties pretty regularly when I first moved to Captiva, but..."

"But life got in the way, and people are busy? Is that what you were going to say?"

Sarah tried to hold back the tears that wanted release.

"Something like that."

"Maybe it's time you and your siblings try again. Look, if I can get in touch with my family, surely you can do it as well."

Speaking loud enough so that Noah could hear him, Trevor teased, "In the meantime, tomorrow is a big day, so we better eat our cupcakes and then get going so you can get back to work and we can finish our errands. I think Noah will go to bed early tonight. We'll need all our strength to help you move tomorrow."

Noah joined their conversation. "I'm going to help too."

"You are? What are you going to do? You can't carry very much and some of my things are heavy."

"Yes, I can," Noah insisted.

Sarah gave in and laughed. "Ok. We'll see. I'm sure there's some things you can carry."

"You do realize after about five minutes of carrying things, he'll be asking us to do something more fun?"

"I know. He loves Ciara and she'll be there. If he gets fussy, I'm sure they'll have some play time."

"Speaking of Ciara. I've hired a nanny to look after Noah when I'm at work. I can't keep asking Ciara to babysit all the time. She's spread too thin as it is."

Noah finished his sandwich and began munching on a cupcake.

Searching inside the basket, Sarah said, "I see you've packed a very healthy lunch for us. Are there any more cupcakes in here?"

She found two chocolate cupcakes and handed one to Trevor.

"We better have snacks tomorrow or none of us will have any energy to move the boxes."

"That's already taken care of. Did you really think Ciara and Chelsea would do any physical labor without food? I'm pretty sure the plan is to order pizza."

At the word pizza, Noah stopped eating his cupcake. "We're going to have pizza tomorrow?"

Trevor laughed at Noah. "That's the plan. Is that all right with you?"

Noah nodded and continued to eat his cupcake.

Sarah didn't want to say too much about it today, but she planned to surprise both Trevor and Noah by giving Noah her spare bedroom. Although a practical decision, Sarah loved seeing his things when he wasn't there. She felt it would help Noah to have as many places to call his own as was possible.

Sometimes, Noah liked to hide from the adults in the room. Having a secret hideout meant no one else could find you. It gave Noah a place to call his own. The fact that he'd have to go to Sarah's apartment to find it, suited her just fine.

CHAPTER FIFTEEN

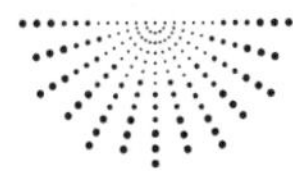

Sarah took the last of her belongings out of the bedroom and walked down the stairs to the kitchen. The noise from the construction made it impossible to sleep, and for once she felt grateful her mother blocked out reservations for the day. No guest would be happy about the noise, let alone the dust that seemed to be everywhere.

As usual, an assortment of scones sat on top of wire racks on the counter. Freshly brewed coffee and hot water for tea sat beside them.

"What time did you get up this morning? You must have been baking since six."

"Pretty much. You know me, I've already walked the beach too."

Paolo came into the kitchen to get another cup of coffee. "Good morning, Sarah. Today's the big day. You must be excited."

"Hey, Paolo. I am, but I feel a little sad leaving this place."

Her mother sneaked behind Sarah and hugged her. "You're hardly leaving. You're not that far away. I bet I see you even more than I do now."

Chelsea and Ciara finally arrived, followed by Trevor and Noah backing the truck up into the driveway.

Chelsea couldn't wait to get her hands on a scone. "Maggie, I'm so glad you made these for everyone. We need our strength to move Sarah, and I know I can't do anything on an empty stomach."

Sarah laughed, "You'd think we're moving tons of furniture. There are so many of us 'helping' we should be done in two hours. Seriously, people. I don't have that much to move. I think you all just want to see my apartment and swim in the pool. Tell the truth, how many of you brought your swimsuits with you?"

No one would make eye contact with her, "Uh-huh, I thought so."

Noah came forward, munching on a scone. "Can I have more?"

Sarah smiled and said he could but first he had to say hello to everyone.

"Everyone, this is Noah. He's going to be a big help today."

Maggie bent down to talk to Noah. "Nice to meet you, Noah, I see you like my scones."

Noah nodded, and Sarah introduced her mother. "Noah, this is my mother. She got up early this morning and baked these. Pretty good, huh?"

Noah was too busy eating his scone to say much. Sarah poured milk into his Sippy cup and coffee for her and Trevor.

As soon as they all finished their breakfast, they packed the truck and two cars filled with Sarah's things. The only item that gave them any trouble was an old sofa from the carriage house that Maggie wanted Sarah to take with her.

"You always say how much you love this sofa. I thought you'd like to take it with you—something to remind you of the inn."

"Thank you, Mom. I love it."

Watching Paolo and Trevor move the sofa down the stairs of the carriage house, Sarah laughed. "It's a good thing I bought a new bedroom set and kitchen table. You two look like you're struggling with that thing."

They got the sofa into the truck and Trevor agreed with Sarah. "Fortunately, they don't make furniture like this anymore. No one would be able to move if they did. This thing weighs a ton."

Paolo wiped his forehead with a wet cloth, "I think that's the last of it. We should be ready to go."

Sarah, Noah, and Trevor got inside the truck and the cars followed behind. When they got to the gated community, Sarah punched in the security code, and each car that followed did the same.

She laughed, telling Trevor, "You should have heard Mom when I gave her the code. She loved the fact that you can't get in here without it. Having a guard at the gate didn't hurt either."

"I'm with your mother. I like knowing you'll be safe here."

Everyone piled out of the vehicles and began carrying items into the house. Sarah made sure that Noah had a small item that he could carry, so she placed two small books into his hands.

"Are you ready to work? Just follow me ok?"

Noah stayed close to Sarah and walked to the front door. Everyone carried boxes, leaving the sofa until the end. Once again, Trevor and Paolo struggled with the piece, and were grateful that this time, there were no stairs to deal with.

When all had been carried inside, Chelsea went to the kitchen and opened the cooler, placing the items inside into the refrigerator. "Anyone interested in some homemade lemonade?"

Noah ran to the kitchen, being the first in line for the drink. "Where's your Sippy cup, Noah?"

"Chelsea, we left it back at the inn, can you pour a small amount into a regular plastic cup instead?"

"So, you're going to have a big boy cup? Well, I guess that's ok because you look like you're growing up. Would you like that?"

Noah seemed pleased with his new cup and held it close to his body.

Sarah's earlier suspicions were correct. Everyone brought a swimsuit and beach towels. They all jumped into the pool with Trevor and Sarah staying close to Noah to keep him from going in too deep. However, just like the ocean, Noah didn't go very far into the pool, staying on the stairs. His aversion to water worried Sarah, and she suspected there had been a traumatic event in his life that had made him afraid of it.

Chelsea ordered pizza and turned up her speaker, playing music from her cell phone. She danced around the pool, finally putting her hand out to Noah.

"Do you want to dance with me, Noah?"

Trevor and Sarah watched as Noah accepted the invitation and began to dance with Chelsea. They were surprised how much he seemed to like music. Sarah made a mental note to play music more often when she was around Noah.

By the end of the day, everyone had more than enough sun and food. They said their goodbyes and left Trevor, Noah, and Sarah alone at the apartment.

Sarah reached for Noah. "Noah, I have a surprise for you. Come with me, and I'll show you."

Trevor and Noah followed Sarah into the spare bedroom. When she opened the door, a twin bed and dresser along with a short, plastic basketball hoop and basketball appeared.

"This is your room. We can buy a few things at the store to make it just the way you want. Do you like it?"

Noah ran to the basketball and held it in his hands, not knowing what he should do with it. Trevor took the ball from Noah and threw it into the hoop. "This is a basketball, and that's a basketball hoop. You throw it in the hole. Do you want to try?"

Noah imitated his father's movements and placed the ball into the basketball hoop. Everyone clapped and laughed, and it made Noah happy that he had accomplished a great thing.

Trevor put his arm around Sarah's waist. "Thank you for this."

"I want the two of you to think of this place as your home. I'll miss you both when you're not here but looking at Noah's things will make that easier."

They watched Noah having fun with the basketball, and before long, he looked tired and ready for a nap. Trevor thought it best that Noah rest while Sarah and he relaxed in the living room. Noah seemed pleased with the dinosaur-designed comforter and kept his basketball close as he fell asleep in his new bed.

Trevor looked for a bottle of wine he brought for the occasion. He waited until everyone had left, and they were alone. He poured the wine and walked out onto the lanai.

"And now, I have a surprise for you."

He handed Sarah her glass and opened the two boxes of white lights he had tucked away in the corner.

"Oh, Trevor. I love it. These lights are going to make the lanai even more beautiful at night. Let me help you."

Trevor climbed the small ladder he brought for the move and began stringing the lights along the wall. Sarah held the strands, walking around the pool as Trevor stapled each cord. When he was done, the lanai glowed with the lights reflecting off the water.

"Thank you for doing this. It looks amazing."

The outdoor furniture had been furnished by the owner so they could enjoy the warm evening air and their wine. Crickets and tree frogs were the only sounds from the backyard, and in the quiet, Sarah decided it was time to tell Trevor about Sharon and Sophia.

Trevor had so much to deal with between his new job and reestablishing a connection with his family, not to mention, worrying about Noah. She didn't want to add anything else for him to think about, but Sharon and her baby had become very important to Sarah, and she wanted desperately to share with him what she had been going through.

Trevor listened to everything Sarah said about Sharon and her baby and didn't say a word until Sarah finished talking.

"Maybe I'm hearing something you haven't actually said, Sarah, but are you thinking you want to adopt this child?"

Sarah shook her head, "No. I'm just thinking out loud, that's all. I'm not sure what I'm saying to be honest. You know what my life is like. Adopting an infant isn't something I planned. More than anything, what I want is to give Sharon something to hold onto. I'm probably the last person in the world who should be adopting a child."

Trevor looked confused by her statement. "Why do you say that?"

Sarah paced around the lanai as she continued. "I don't know, it's just that I've never seen myself as someone's mother, that's all. I'm not really all that great with kids."

"What are you talking about? Don't you know how much Noah loves you? To be honest, you're a natural with him. I don't know what you've been through in your life that's made you feel this way, but I think you'd be a wonderful mother for any child."

Sarah worried she had overstepped and had confused Trevor about her feelings for Noah. "I love Noah, Trevor. Please believe me when I tell you that he means the world to me. You both do."

Trevor walked to Sarah and put his arms around her. He held her close and stroked her hair.

"I know you love Noah. It's obvious in everything you do. But this baby—It sounds like you're growing attached to her."

It seemed impossible to explain her feelings when she struggled to understand them herself. For now, she only cared that she made Trevor aware of her ambivalence around the idea of motherhood.

"I don't want Sharon to die thinking I won't be in Sophia's life. If it's the only thing I accomplish from all this, then that's good enough for me. As far as being Sophia's mother, for now, I think it's best she goes to a foster home."

Sophia deserved the best family she could have, and as much as Sarah loved the little girl, she didn't think she was the best. The tug on her heart had been relentless. Perhaps once the final decision had been made, and Sophia was settled into her new home, those feelings would fade. At least she hoped so.

CHAPTER SIXTEEN

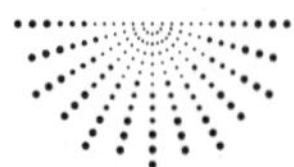

When Trevor walked into his father's office building, it was like he had been working there for years. Everyone seemed to know who he was. The security guard smiled and said, "Good morning, Mr. Hutchins." Greetings from several office staff surprised him as he walked toward his father's corner office.

Two men sat in front of Devon's desk. As soon as his father saw Trevor, he asked the men to leave.

"Trevor. I'm glad you stopped by. Can I get you a coffee or anything from the kitchen? We've got everything you can imagine in there. It's a way to keep the employees happy but also our clients when they're here."

"No. Thank you. I'm fine."

Although he had been in Devon's office many times over the years, Trevor felt uncomfortable and out of place. He tried to ignore the awkward feeling and instead focused on his reason for coming to see his father.

"I've decided to accept your offer to work on the affordable housing project."

Devon embraced Trevor. "This is wonderful news. I can't tell you how much this means to me. It will be great. You'll see. Come, let me show you to your office."

Devon and Trevor walked across the open office, passing the receptionist. Trevor's office looked much like his father's. With floor to ceiling windows and dark mahogany furniture, it reminded Trevor of a library.

"Well, what do you think? Nice, right?"

"It's fine, Dad. Thank you."

"Listen, I've got to finish my meeting, but I wanted to go over some things with you about the project. How about you look around the place, enjoy your office, and then we'll drive over to the site?"

"Sure. That would be great."

His father could barely contain his excitement. Pointing to a hat sitting on the desk. "Make sure to bring your hard hat. It's required."

Trevor nodded, as his father walked out of his office.

Left alone to explore, Trevor shook his head at the size of his office. He didn't know its square footage, but he imagined it must be larger than his house on the beach.

A fake palm tree leaned against the corner wall. Trevor ran his fingers over the green plastic leaves. At least it was dusted. Several shelves of books he would never read rested on two large bookcases.

Black leather chairs with silver metal frames sat around a large coffee table. Real estate magazines covered the table, and a small remote rested in the middle. He pressed a button on the remote, and a liquor cabinet opened. Several bottles and crystal glasses filled the space. The refrigerator underneath held water, beer, and white wine. He grabbed a bottle of water, pressed the button again to close the cabinet, and sat back on the leather sofa.

Staring up at the ceiling, he wondered who had this office before him. Devon never mentioned anyone, and there were no personal items or clues as to its previous occupant.

He could walk the halls of the firm, and visit the aforementioned kitchen, but his legs would only carry him as far as his desk chair. He sat and put his head in his hands. Was this the right choice? He questioned his decision. For only a brief moment he let these thoughts dominate his thinking before remembering that none of this was for him—it was all for Noah, and that was good enough.

His brother, Clayton, leaned against the door frame.

"You do realize he's been holding on to this office just waiting for you to take your rightful place as the next in succession to the throne?"

Trevor looked at his brother and sighed, "Clayton, I don't have time for another go 'round with you. If there's something you want to say to me, say it, and then get out."

Clayton smirked and shook his head. "I just don't get it. How is it possible you don't see what's going on here? Are you that clueless, or is it all an act? By the way, congrats on being a dad. Is this your only child or do you have more scattered around the globe? I'm just asking because eventually, we're going to have to divvy up the pot and I'd like to know just how little I'm going to get now that you're back in the King's good graces. It's a little like royalty. I thought I'd be next in line, but it looks like I've been bumped, at least by two. What's his name? Noah?"

Trevor got up so fast and with such force, his chair rolled back across the room. He walked toward his brother, his hands forming fists, his jaw set.

"I don't want to hear you even whisper my son's name. If you talk about him one more time, it'll be the last thing you talk about. Do you understand?"

Just then, Devon entered the room and Clayton slithered back to his office. Devon watched Clayton walk down the hall, and then looked at Trevor.

"What's going on?"

Trevor shook his head. "Let's go."

He grabbed the hard hat and stormed out of his office, his father following behind.

There was little need for a hard hat. At this stage of the project, the open area had only foundation construction underway.

"So, what do you think? It's a fairly large piece of land. We're ready to move forward after several months of struggle. We've worked with planning boards, architects, and have done the necessary traffic studies, and we're finally ready to get this show on the road. There were a few bumps in the road, mostly in the form of resisting neighbors, but we were able to overcome that."

"Looks like I've showed up at just the right time."

Devon laughed. "You've no idea. The plan is to build 256 one-, two-, three- and four- bedroom apartments. We'll have computer and fitness centers, a library, laundry facilities, two pools, and two playgrounds—one on each end of the property. We've added grilling stations, community gardens and the best part is where you can be a real help. I want to make available after-school programs, English literacy training, and computer labs. There needs to be more than just putting up some buildings. You've got to ask yourself; how can we help the community at large?"

Hearing his father talk about his plans for the city, and specifically for the people who struggle to make ends meet, impressed Trevor. For the first time, he felt excited about his involvement in his father's business.

"That's what interests me about this project. I've spent the last several years finding solutions for people who don't have the money or resources to improve their situation. A few years ago, I worked with a community to build a church, and then an elementary school. There's nothing wrong with sitting behind a desk looking at blueprints but looking into the eyes of the people whose lives you've positively changed forever is where it's at for me."

Devon continued, "That's why I hired you, Trevor. I understand what you're saying. Basically, what we're doing here is helping people thrive. Did you know that over 10% of all elderly households in Florida live at or below the poverty level? It doesn't take much for a person or a family to lose everything. Many are only one paycheck away from losing everything. Surely Sarah understands this. Talk to her and explain what we're doing here. Maybe there are people in her world who might need a place to live—one they can afford."

Trevor agreed. "Sarah has a big heart. I bet she'll know exactly what you're talking about. She sees people hurting every day, and she's trying to make a difference in their lives. I love that about her."

"Sounds like a man in love."

Trevor never imagined he'd be talking about his feelings for Sarah with his father, but he felt comfortable doing so. Only a week ago, he wouldn't have given his father the time of day. Now, he noticed a subtle, albeit cautious change in their conversations.

"Coming into my life and now Noah's has been a blessing. It's easy to be happy about Noah coming to live with me, but I have to remind myself that I don't know what trauma he's experienced. Losing his mother, with no real understanding of why, has to be terrifying. Sarah is wonderful at recognizing his vulnerabilities and takes things slow with him. She answers his questions better than I do. I'm not sure Noah and I can get along without her."

"She means a lot to you, doesn't she?"

"She does. More so now with Noah. We'd only been dating a few months before I found out about him. When I told Sarah, she could have politely ended things before they progressed further, but she didn't. Instead, it feels like we're a family now. Something I never expected."

"Speaking of Sarah. Why don't the two of you come for dinner tonight? Bring Noah too. We'd love to have him meet all his family."

The exchange with Clayton fresh on his mind, Trevor felt it best Noah stay home this time.

"I'll call Sarah and ask her, but I'd like to have Noah meet the family some other time. Too many people all at once could be overwhelming for him. I've got to check with my friend also to see if she can watch Noah before I accept. Let me talk to Sarah and Ciara and get back to you."

"Great. I'll get in touch with everyone as soon as I hear from you. I'm sure Carolyn and Wyatt would love to see you."

Trevor couldn't remember the last time he had dinner with his family. He wasn't sure tonight was something to look forward to, but he was certain it would be entertaining. He only hoped Sarah would see it that way.

CHAPTER SEVENTEEN

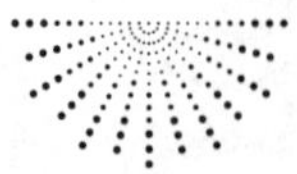

After she hung up the phone with Trevor, Sarah told her mother and Chelsea about the call. Chelsea couldn't resist sharing her opinion on the subject.

"Well, you know what this means, don't you? When you are invited to meet his family, it can only mean one thing."

Maggie joined in, nodding her head. "Listen to Chelsea, Sarah. She's right. Especially with Trevor's family. It's not like he's had a close relationship with them. I think he's serious about you and wants them to know it."

Sarah quickly shot their comments down. "Their opinion of me means very little to him. If he was close and ran everything by them, then I'd be worried. Will the two of you listen to yourselves? Ever since Mom got engaged, you've been high on romance. It's skewed your perspectives."

Maggie didn't miss a beat. "What do you mean you'd be worried?"

As usual Sarah said too much. She'd have a hard time getting out of this conversation if it wasn't for a guest walking into the kitchen.

"I'm sorry to interrupt, but I need to get my cranberry juice. I left one in the refrigerator."

Maggie smiled. "Of course. You're not interrupting. Can I get you anything else?"

"No. Thank you. My husband and I are about to take a catamaran. I'm hoping we see dolphins."

"Oh, that sounds like fun. I've taken that trip before. I'd be surprised if you didn't see several dolphins. Have fun."

"Thanks, we will." The woman scurried out of the room and met her husband who was waiting at the front door.

Sarah didn't allow her mother and Chelsea another shot at giving their opinions on Trevor's intentions. "Well, ladies. I've got to get ready for my dinner. I'll talk to you later."

Maggie got the last word in. "Make sure you tell us all about your evening as soon as you get back."

Sarah ignored her mother and ran out of the room.

Several cars parked in front of the Hutchins' home meant Trevor and Sarah would probably be the last to arrive. Trevor kissed Sarah and rubbed her shoulders.

"Are you nervous? You seem tense."

"Not nervous for me. I think I am a little for you though."

Trevor understood Sarah's meaning. "I'm hopeful the evening will go well. You already know what to expect from Clayton. Wyatt, Carolyn, and Jacqui, I'm not so sure."

Sarah tried to ease Trevor's worries. "I'm sure everything will be fine. Let's try to enjoy the evening."

Sarah was right about them being late. Several people with drinks in their hands, gathered in the great room. All eyes were on them when she and Trevor entered the room. Devon rushed to meet them.

"Trevor. Sarah. Please come in. Everyone's here."

Trevor put his arm around Sarah's waist and spoke first. "Hey guys. This is Sarah."

Eliza Hutchins extended her hand to Sarah. "Welcome to our home, Sarah. I'm glad you could join us." Trevor hugged his mother. "Hello, son, you're looking well.

Wyatt approached Trevor, pulling him into a hug. "Hey, Brother. It's good to see you. Sarah, very nice to meet you."

Carolyn was next. She gave Trevor a punch to the arm.

"I do own a phone, you know. You could call once in a while. Hey Sarah. Welcome."

Jacqui hugged Trevor and whispered in his ear, "I'm glad you came. Do you think you might have a few minutes to talk? Not here."

"Of course."

She then turned to Sarah. "Nice to meet you, Sarah."

Clayton stepped forward and didn't say a word to Trevor. "Welcome to Maison Hutchins, Sarah. Don't know much about you except that you're a very brave woman to get hooked up with this guy."

Sarah defended Trevor by standing her ground. She put her arms around him and pulled him close.

"Oh, I don't know about that. He's pretty special."

As expected, the tension in the room started to build. Trevor squeezed Sarah's hand and then reached for two glasses of white wine.

Of the five siblings, Clayton was the shortest with slick black hair and brown eyes. You could tell that Wyatt and Trevor were brothers as they looked so similar, one might mistake them for twins.

Carolyn had long light brown hair and blue eyes, and stood taller than Clayton, which Sarah could only assume, annoyed her brother.

Jacqui's curly short light brown hair framed her face, and like Sarah, had freckles on the bridge of her nose. While her sister

Carolyn dressed conservatively, Jacqui's style was more bohemian and wilder. Not afraid to expose cleavage, Jacqui delighted in shocking her parents with her appearance.

Sarah whispered in Trevor's ear, "Do you think there is time to tour the property before dinner?"

"I don't see why not." He guided Sarah through the open door leading to the pool. Outdoor furniture surrounded a long rectangular pool. "Can you see what's at the bottom?"

Sarah leaned over the pool to get a better look. "Is that the Beatles?"

"You win the prize. Yup, my father loves the Beatles, so when they were building the pool, he wanted an underwater mural painted with their image. Liking the Beatles myself, it's one of the designs in this house I actually love."

They continued through to a beautifully landscaped flower garden with lush tropical foliage passing a waterfall and leading the way to the koi pond and banyan tree.

Back inside, they climbed the stairs to the second-floor bedrooms, where Trevor spared her the opulence of his parents' room, walking directly to his old room.

Nothing had changed since he last slept in his bed. The room still had old posters on the wall, and tennis trophies lined the bookcase.

"I didn't know you played tennis."

"For most of my childhood, that's where you'd find me. I don't get to play much anymore, but maybe when Noah is stronger, I'll teach him."

"Teach me, too. I can play, but not as good as I'd like to. Maybe the three of us can find a tennis court nearby."

Sarah laughed when she looked out the window. "Um, I guess finding a tennis court wasn't much of an issue for you?"

Trevor pulled her into his arms and kissed her. "This house has everything and anything a kid could want, except one thing."

It hurt Sarah to see the sadness on Trevor's face when

describing his childhood. Even now, after all these years, he still felt the pain of what was missed.

Eliza called out to them. "Dinner is ready, you two."

"Be right down."

Trevor kissed Sarah again. "Are you ready for this?"

She nodded. "Lead the way."

They walked into the dining room and Sarah let Trevor select their chairs. The table setting looked exactly as Sarah imagined. The crystal and China place settings were stunning. A long shiny silver centerpiece filled with pink and white peonies lay before them. Sarah wondered if it had been designed for their visit or if such decorations were regularly displayed.

They talked a little about the affordable housing project, but the discussions turned to Wyatt's hedge fund and Carolyn's children's boarding school.

Clayton stayed unusually quiet. Devon took over the conversation and focused on Sarah.

"Sarah, Trevor told me a little about your work, but not much about how the two of you met. How did that come about?"

Sarah could feel everyone's eyes on her.

"Let's just say that your son and I didn't quite hit it off."

Clayton added his two cents, "Why doesn't that surprise me?"

Sarah ignored him. "I don't know what it was about Trevor that rubbed me the wrong way. I guess I thought he was arrogant and so sure of himself. At least he seemed confident enough to hit on me only five minutes after we met."

Trevor took exception to that statement. "You think I was hitting on you? If I remember correctly, I thought you were in Florida for vacation and probably didn't know the meaning of hard work, and I told you so."

Everyone laughed at that, and it felt good to break the tension. Jacqui decided it was her time to tease Trevor. "Trevor never had any trouble getting girlfriends. Keeping them, well, that was something else entirely."

"What's that supposed to mean?"

"You know what I'm talking about. At least you didn't date more than one girl at a time. I don't remember anyone thinking you were arrogant though. I wonder what made Sarah think so?"

Sarah looked at Trevor and smiled.

"Even though our first meeting didn't go well, it didn't take long before I got to know what a kind and giving person he was. It might have started out somewhat contentious, but we found common ground soon after."

Trevor pushed Sarah's hair from her face to the back of her ear. "Sarah is the best person I know. The truth is, I can't see a future without her."

The room was quiet. Sarah stared at Trevor. Maggie and Chelsea were right. In bringing Sarah to meet his family, Trevor wanted everyone to know how important she was to him and his future. Her heart raced at the thought, and it surprised her that she wasn't scared at all.

Sarah could feel everyone's eyes on her. Eliza didn't miss the significance of Trevor's words and began asking Sarah questions about her family life. "Tell us about your family, Sarah. Did you grow up here?'

"Oh, no. I grew up in Massachusetts, but every year, we came down to Florida, Captiva, actually. My parents had their high school class trip here, fell in love with the island and even honey-mooned here, It's been the place where we spent our yearly vacation."

"How many brothers and sisters do you have?"

Sarah laughed at the question and the coincidence, "Just like your family, there are five of us. Lauren, Michael, me, Beth, and Christopher, who is the youngest. He's in the military, in Iraq. He was in Afghanistan for a while, but now he's in Iraq."

Eliza pressed further, "and your parents?"

"My father passed away last year. After my father died, my

mother and I came to live on Captiva Island. She re-opened the Key Lime Garden Inn."

"I'm sorry to hear of your father's passing. That must have been difficult on your family, especially, your mother."

The last thing Sarah wanted to do was to get into the details of her parents' marriage, and so, she just nodded her head and continued to eat her dinner.

Under the table, Trevor's hand rubbed her leg. She wanted him to hold her and keep her from reliving the nightmare that was her father's death. For now, his hand on her leg would have to do. Later, when they were alone, she would let him hold her and comfort her. No matter how many months had passed since his passing, her father's death still brought tears to her eyes. She had to accept such things because no one ever truly gets over the death of a loved one, no matter how much time passed.

CHAPTER EIGHTEEN

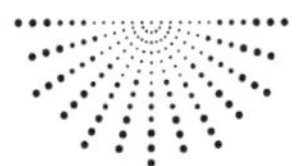

Trevor had never spoken with Ava's parents. Her brother, Cameron Barclay, contacted him only after Ava died. So, it shocked Trevor when the voicemail on his cellphone insisted he contact William Barclay as soon as possible. The man left no other information except that he was Ava's father and needed to speak with Trevor right away.

He had thirty minutes until his next meeting. That would be plenty of time to hear what he had to say. Trevor dialed the number.

"William Barclay."

"Yes, hello, Mr. Barclay. This is Trevor Hutchins returning your call. What can I do for you?"

"You can give me my grandson, that's what you can do for me."

"I'm sorry, but I don't understand. Mr. Barclay..."

William Barclay didn't let Trevor finish his thought.

"Do you still live at 2324 Seashell Lane, Sanibel Island?"

"Yes, that's my address, but I don't understand what that has to do with your call. Mr. Barclay, I wish you would explain yourself. My understanding is that you and your wife wanted nothing to do with Noah. What gives you the right to call me like this?"

"I've seen the house, if you can call it that, where you live. That, coupled with the phone call I received telling me that my grandson isn't being cared for properly. My wife and I only want the best for our grandson, and it appears that you are not the best."

"Mr. Barclay…"

Once again the man interrupted Trevor.

"You'll be hearing from my lawyer. I intend on taking you to court to gain custody of my grandson."

The click on the other end of the line ended the call, and there wasn't anything else Trevor could do, but walk into his father's office for advice. Unfortunately, his brother, Clayton sat on their father's sofa while Devon finished his phone call.

"All hail, Trevor has arrived."

Trevor had no patience for Clayton's usual poke-the-bear statements, and Clayton noticed it. "What's got you down dear brother?"

Trevor tried to ignore him, but when Devon hung up the phone, Clayton continued his goading.

"Well Dad, it seems my brother is having a bad day."

"Seriously, Clayton. Give it a rest."

Devon got up from his chair and walked over to Trevor. "What's this?"

"I just got a call from Ava's father. He wants custody of Noah. Apparently, someone contacted him and said I wasn't a fit father. He mentioned the house that I live in as not being suitable for Noah. Who could have called him, and why?"

Devon tried to calm his son, but Trevor couldn't stop pacing the office floor. "Listen to me, Trevor. They don't have a leg to stand on. Noah has us now. He has a family who loves him and will do anything for him. Not to mention the obvious financial situation you find yourself in. Is it possible that this has nothing to do with wanting Noah, and more that they are trying to get money out of you? This idea of taking you to court to gain custody is a lie. They want a settlement. That's what they're after."

Trevor nodded his head. "Yes, I suppose you're right. Ava's brother told me they didn't want Noah. Right from the start they had a chance to raise him, and they didn't want that. Still, it bothers me to think that someone would go out of their way to contact him. I didn't think I had any enemies, but I guess I do."

Clayton got up from the sofa and started to walk out of the room. Trevor stopped him. "It was you, wasn't it? You did this. You hate me that much?"

Anger showed on Devon's face. "Is this true? Did you call William Barclay?"

Clayton put his hands in the pockets of his pants. "I didn't know the guy didn't want Noah. I thought he'd be better off with them."

Trevor couldn't believe what Clayton was saying. "I don't believe you. You don't care about Noah any more than you care about me. You did this because you can't stand the fact that I've come back home. You are so consumed with jealousy, that you'd do anything to get back at me. For what? For some stupid perception that I'm Dad's favorite? You would take my only son away from me, just to satisfy your ego?"

Devon wouldn't listen to one more word from Clayton. "Get out, and when I say get out, I mean leave this building and never step foot on this property again, or I'll have you arrested."

Clayton's arrogance diminished, and he suddenly looked like a little boy. "Dad. You don't mean that."

"I do. I've never hit any of my children. Get out of here now before I do something I'll probably regret later."

Clayton looked at Trevor and then back at their father. His head down, he walked out of the office and down the hall. Trevor sat on the sofa and put his head in his hands.

"What am I going to do?"

Devon sat next to Trevor and rubbed his son's shoulders. "I tell you what we're going to do. We're going to get in touch with my lawyer and explain what has happened. If we have to pay these people off, then that's what we'll do. I promise you, Son, they will never get Noah. They'll have to come through me to get to anyone in my family."

Trevor looked at his father. "Including Clayton? Dad, you've got to do something about him. He's still your son, but he's lost his way big time. He wants your love and approval so much, he'll do just about anything to get it. Can't you see that?"

Devon nodded. "He's not the only one. Jacqui is giving me nightmares too. Have I been such a terrible father that my children can't communicate with me in any normal way? I feel responsible, but I don't know how to fix any of it."

"I guess we deal with one crisis at a time. If there is anything I can do, please tell me. Truthfully, I'd love to be closer to my siblings. It hurts me to see Clayton so angry. I don't think he'll listen to me though. It's got to come from you."

Devon stood up and walked to his desk. "My whole life I've written checks to solve problems. Even with my children I've given them money instead of my time and love. I created this mess."

He looked at Trevor and continued, "Maybe between the two of us, we might be able to clean it up. We can't go back, but I'd like to think we could start fresh."

Family had come to mean everything to Trevor. Joining his father in an effort to heal the wounds of the past would prove difficult. For now, he could only focus on Noah. Losing his son scared him more than anything. He hoped his father was right, and money was William Barclay's only motivation.

~

Eliza Hutchins never visited her husband's office. She enjoyed her home, her travels, and her clubs. She had a large group of woman friends and kept herself busy with interests that were as far away from the interests of her husband as she could get.

She had little in common with her husband. Never wanting to marry, she focused on her education She loved to write and published several articles about the British Government Code and Cypher School called Bletchley Park. Getting lost in the pages of her stories gave her a purpose, and her plans to write a novel were foremost in her mind.

She met Devon Hutchins on a cruise ship leaving Miami. They were young and neither were seeing anyone exclusively. Their attraction kept them in each other's arms throughout the vacation, and when it was over, they were in love.

Devon talked about his plans for the future and how he would build the largest and most successful real estate business in Southwest Florida. She agreed to marry him after three weeks of dating.

Her focus on making his career a success along with raising their children left little time for writing, and so she gave it up. Before long, the space between them grew and their differences became insurmountable. On more than one occasion, she tried to write, but her day-to-day responsibilities made it impossible to have any meaningful time to herself.

Over the years, they settled into a comfortable life with Devon going his way, and Eliza going hers. They could have divorced, but for the sake of their family decided against it. As long as she had the freedom to do what she wanted, their marriage could stay as it was. For some, their arrangement might have seemed sad, but for Eliza, it provided her with the life she craved. She could afford to do as she pleased, and that satisfied her.

Her decision to visit the office today surprised everyone. She walked through the halls looking for Trevor's office. When she found it, she didn't knock on the door. She could see through the glass that he was alone.

"If you don't mind my saying so, you look incredibly uncomfortable behind that desk."

"Mother. This is a surprise, and you're right. I must look as uncomfortable as I feel. I'm sure it's the suit."

She hugged her son, and then walked to the window overlooking the canal. "So, why don't you say something to your father about it?"

"Because I don't need another confrontation. I've already got too much to deal with."

Eliza nodded, "I heard about Ava's father calling you."

"Is that why you came here today, to talk about Noah?"

"Actually, I'm here to talk about you."

Trevor could never tell what was on his mother's mind. She kept much to herself, so when she spoke, her words carried weight.

"Is this job really what you want to do with your life?"

Trevor wondered what would make his mother question his choices.

"What makes you ask that?"

"Of all my children, you've always been the most sensitive. That sensitivity created in you a desire to help those who can't help themselves. I know your father wasn't happy when you left, but I secretly admired your decision."

"Secretly? Can I assume that means you never told him how you felt?"

"Your father knows how I feel. For a long time, I didn't say a word. Eventually, I had to speak up. I told him it was a brave thing that you did. That's why I'm worried about you. I support you no matter what you do. I'm not sure this is what you want."

Trevor appreciated that his mother had his best interests at heart and had been on his side all these years. What didn't surprise him was her ability to anticipate his worries. That talent kept him from keeping anything from her growing up.

"Mom, you know how important it is to make sure your children are safe and cared for. You've always wanted the best for us kids. I don't have to tell you that sometimes being a parent means that you've got to forget about what you want and do what's best for your children. That's what I'm doing now for Noah. What's wrong with that?"

Eliza got up from her chair and hugged her son. "Nothing but take it from someone who gave up her dreams a long time ago. You won't be helping Noah if you're unhappy."

Trevor had never heard his mother speak about her life this way. "I'm sorry, Mom. I had no idea."

"Oh, don't go feeling sorry for me. I'm perfectly happy with my life. I wanted to come here today to say that you'll be making a big mistake not creating the life you want. I'm not saying you have to quit this job. Maybe there's a way for both you and your father to get what you want. Just think about it. I know you've got a lot on your plate right now. Do what you have to but promise me you won't forget what I'm saying."

Trevor hadn't needed his mother for many years, but it didn't stop him from feeling grateful to have her support.

"I promise. I won't forget."

Eliza walked toward the door and turned before leaving.

"One more thing. I'm so happy to have you home, and I can't wait to meet Noah. You're a good father, Trevor. I'm proud of you."

He watched his mother walk out of his office and felt sorry for not having her in his life these last few years. Once again, she could read his emotions, and this time, he was grateful for it.

CHAPTER NINETEEN

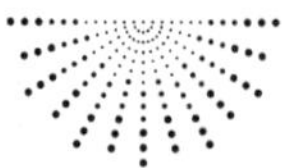

Maggie closed her laptop and sat back in her chair. "This is impossible. I can't find a wedding dress. I need something that says, 'older woman getting married for the second time'. Everything I see looks like it's for someone younger. I'm afraid I'll look like I'm going to the prom if I buy any of these."

Chelsea laughed and filled Maggie's coffee mug. "No one will mistake you for a high-school senior. You're approaching this all wrong."

Maggie had no idea what Chelsea meant. "What are you talking about? Are you telling me there's a right way to do this?"

"Of course. You're looking at wedding dresses. What you should be looking at is Mother of the Bride dresses. That way you get something appropriate, and you'll have lots to choose from."

Maggie opened her laptop again. "Ok, I'll give it another try."

"What color are you going for?"

"You know how much I love pink. Maybe a very light pink. What do you think?"

"That's perfect. Look, on this website, there are tons of

Mother of the Bride dresses. Not only that, look at all the colors you can choose from. This is fantastic. Maybe I'll get something from this website since I don't have a dress either. Oh, and they have matching shoes too."

Maggie and Chelsea spent the better half of the morning shopping online before Chelsea realized she was late for a meeting.

"I've got to go. I have to bring one of my paintings to a buyer. This guy bought my favorite painting the night of my showing, but he never showed up to get it. He wasn't even at the gallery. He called the gallery and bought it sight-unseen. Can you believe that?"

"That is weird."

Chelsea put her coffee mug in the sink. "Do you want to come with me? I could use the company. Who knows who this guy is? I mean he could be a serial killer."

"A serial killer who buys paintings. I don't think so. But I'd love to go. I want to see this mystery man."

Chelsea lifted the already wrapped painting into the backseat of her car. "Thank heavens this one is smaller than the others. If he'd bought one of the larger ones, I'd insist he come pick it up."

Maggie seemed annoyed. "What makes this guy so special that he can't come to the gallery anyway? I mean it reeks of arrogance if you ask me."

"Yeah, money usually does that to people."

Sebastian Barlowe's home sat on the farthest end of Captiva that one could get to by car. To reach the houses beyond, a ferry was needed. The light, teal-colored home, surrounded by palm trees, seemed too big for one person. A woman dressed in a nurse's uniform answered the door.

"Hello, Mrs. Barlowe?"

"No. I'm Mr. Barlowe's nurse. Please come in. He's been expecting you."

Chelsea and Maggie entered the house and stood in the foyer waiting for the owner to greet them. They were surprised when a handsome gentleman in a wheelchair came into the room.

"Ms. Marsden, thank you for bringing my painting. I appreciate you extending yourself. I must admit, I could have had my assistant pick it up, but I wanted to see the famous Chelsea Marsden in person."

Maggie watched her friend blush at his comment.

"It was no trouble at all, Mr. Barlowe."

Then realizing she wasn't alone, Chelsea remembered Maggie standing there. "Oh, I'm sorry, this is my friend, Maggie Wheeler."

"Lovely to meet you, Ms. Wheeler. Please won't you come into my home. Can you stay for lunch? I've had my cook prepare something for us."

Chelsea gave Maggie a look that convinced her to accept his offer. "Of course. We'd be happy to stay."

"If you don't mind, I'd like to look at my painting."

They unwrapped the painting and held it up for him to see. The painting, a country landscape with a shepherd tending his sheep, moved Sebastian. "It's beautiful. I reminds me of the Pennsylvania farm I grew up on."

Chelsea seemed smitten with Sebastian, and Maggie wondered why he was in a wheelchair.

"My family had a dairy farm in York, Pennsylvania. I loved playing with my brother in between the work we had to do. I wasn't always in this wheelchair. I was hit by a car about ten years ago. It was after my wife died. I had a rough time for a while after the accident. With Shelly gone, and then not being able to walk, I didn't have much desire to continue living."

Chelsea put her hand on his. "I'm so very sorry. That must have been a terrible time for you."

Maggie noticed Chelsea's embarrassment as she watched her friend quickly remove her hand.

"It was difficult, but I'm a very spiritual man. I believe in God and as much as I wanted to leave this earth, I realized that my life wasn't mine to take. I had no right to do that to my family. My children would suffer more than they already had. I couldn't do that to them."

His words moved Maggie. Although she had never contemplated suicide, she could understand how deeply in grief a person can go before reaching that point.

Sebastian continued, "Once I made the decision to keep on living, I got about the business of trying to walk again. Two years in therapy, and I managed to improve some. Now, I'm able to walk with the help of a special brace and poles. Most of the time it's just easier to use the wheelchair, but I get better circulation when I walk. I have a nurse who comes in to massage my legs. After the massage, I try to walk around the property a bit. I'm sorry for bending your ear. I didn't mean to ramble on like that. Come, let's go outside and see what the cook has for us."

They spent an hour visiting Sebastian Barlowe and listening to his stories. When their lunch was finished, Chelsea had a date for dinner scheduled with him for the next night.

Maggie smiled and couldn't help teasing Chelsea. "I've seen you go gah-gah over a guy before, but never that quickly."

"What are you talking about? I didn't go gah-gah over Sebastian. I think he's incredibly interesting, don't you?"

Maggie nodded and continued to poke fun at her friend, "I agree, he is an interesting man. I don't think it hurts that he's incredibly handsome either. Maybe you didn't notice that though."

They got in the car and Chelsea turned to Maggie.

"Ok, maybe I noticed that, but he's had an exciting career. I don't think I've ever met a Minerals Exploration Geologist before. Not to mention all the countries he's traveled to. He's worked all over the world studying rare earth deposits. It's incredible. I can't wait to see him tomorrow."

Maggie could see the excitement in Chelsea's eyes. Even with her latest accomplishments with her paintings, nothing could compare with the giddiness she felt meeting Sebastian.

She felt happy for her friend. It had been a long time since her husband, Carl, passed away. Chelsea had spent her time with friends and activities, but not with anyone special. Although Sebastian seemed able to get around, he still depended on a nurse to help with his circulation. She didn't want her friend to begin a relationship with someone she had to care for, just as she had done for her late husband.

Maggie decided to stop by the coffee shop on the way to Sarah's condo to see if she needed any help unpacking her boxes.

"How's my girl doing? I've brought your favorite iced coffee."

"Oh, I love you. About five minutes ago, I thought, 'wouldn't it be great if a nice ice-cold coffee from my favorite coffee shop showed up', and here you are. Thank you so much."

"You're very welcome. It looks like you've emptied most of these boxes. You must have been up all night."

"I did go to bed late. I wanted to get this place looking presentable before Emma's visit. She's going to come by after I get home from work tomorrow night."

"I'm glad the two of you are getting together. She's a sweet girl. So, I couldn't ask you yesterday when we were moving you. How did dinner with Trevor's family go?"

Normally, Sarah didn't share too much information about Trevor with her mother, but today she felt ready.

"It turned out to be a very nice visit. I got to meet his brothers and sisters as well as his mother. Every member of that family is unique. Except for the fact his brother Wyatt looks so much like

Trevor. I find them all fascinating. Well, everyone except Clayton."

"What's wrong with Clayton?"

"Pretty much everything. He's an angry guy, but he's also so vulnerable. I don't know how to explain it. Something about him seems so sad to me. He's definitely hurting, and impossible to get close to. I'm afraid he may remain a mystery. I could see myself getting close with his sister Jacqui. Carolyn seems nice, but we didn't talk to each other much. I really like his mother."

"Liking the mother is a very good thing. I loved my mother-in-law."

"Mom. Please. There you go again. No one said anything about marriage. Do you always have to go there?"

"Sarah, my love. Are you blind? Trevor is deeply in love with you, and it's only a matter of time before he asks you to marry him. I know you. I know what you've said about marriage and children, and no one is pushing you. But, at the very least, you're going to have to confront this one way or another. I don't want to see your relationship with Trevor fall apart because of some misguided judgments about marriage. We've had this conversation before. I always felt that you and Luke were not a match, and I concluded as much about you and Ben, but Trevor is another matter altogether."

"What does that mean?"

"It means that initially I had my concerns about you getting too close to Trevor because of Noah. I can see that you love that little boy. I didn't want you to commit to someone because you wanted to be there for the child."

"And now?"

Maggie didn't waste a minute telling Sarah exactly how she felt. She took Sarah's face in her hands and said what was on her mind.

"And now, I believe you love Trevor very much. The two of you belong together. No relationship is perfect, Sarah, but I'm certain that Trevor is perfect for you and you for him. Don't you think it's time you admit it to yourself and open your heart?"

Sarah's eyes filled with tears. She grabbed her mother's hand and squeezed. Her voice a soft whisper, she answered, "Yes."

They hugged and Maggie felt Sarah's head rest on her shoulder. It meant everything that Maggie could be with her daughter when she needed her most.

CHAPTER TWENTY

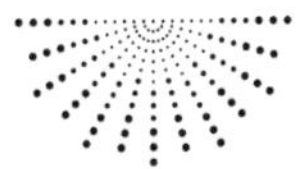

Sarah knocked on the Adoption Center Coordinator's slightly ajar door. Meredith Carpenter smiled and waved Sarah inside.

"Please, come in."

The woman stood and extended a hand. "You must be Sarah Wheeler from the Outreach Center?"

"Yes. Thank you for agreeing to meet with me."

"Of course. What can I do for you?"

"The Outreach Center, well, I have taken an interest in one of our clients personally. She's dying of cancer and doesn't have very long to live. In fact, she's currently in Hospice care. I believe you've already spoken with Ciara Moretti from our office about her—Sharon Carter."

"Oh, right. That's the woman with a newborn child and no other family members, is that correct?"

"Yes, that's the one."

"You needn't worry, Ms. Wheeler. Sophia will be placed into a good home until we find a permanent situation for her. I already gave Ciara information on the two families we are considering. Did you not see their bios?"

"Yes. Yes, I did. They certainly have had lots of experience with foster children."

"Oh, my, yes. I think the Clarkson family has been taking foster children for the last ten years. The Gallo family is equally experienced. Both families have relinquished their recent foster children for adoption so Sophia will have plenty of dedicated care."

"Yes. That's great. I'm not concerned with the families. Either one will be fine. My question is whether I might be able to visit Sophia once she is placed. I realize that someone from your organization makes regular visits to see that the child is being cared for, and if the family needs any assistance, but this is personal for me. You see, the mother is very concerned that I stay in touch with Sophia."

"Oh, I see. I'm not sure..."

"I realize it's unusual, but it's the mother's wish. I want to promise her that I will stay in touch and check in on Sophia now and again. I don't want to lie to her, but I need to give her peace about this. If I make this promise to Sharon, then I have to keep it. Can you help me keep my promise to her, please?"

Sarah could see the woman struggled with following protocol and approving her request.

"If you were family, then it wouldn't be an issue, but you're not."

"Would it make any difference if Sharon told you that she wants me to adopt Sophia?"

"Are you saying that you want to adopt the baby?"

"No... I mean... I don't know."

Ms. Carpenter seemed to understand Sarah's struggle. "Why don't I give you information on adoption in the state of Florida. There are requirements. Are you married?"

"No. I'm single. Is that a problem?"

"No, not necessarily. It depends on the agency's requirements. You'll need to have several hours of adoption training. I'm giving you a few documents that you can look over to see if adoption is right for you. As far as Sophia goes, if you can get a letter from the mother on her desire that you be guardian to the child, that could go a long way in helping your cause."

Finally, there was something to give Sarah a bit of hope.

"Thank you so much. I'll look these over and get Sharon's letter to you."

Both women stood, and Meredith walked Sarah to the door. "I'm sorry about your friend. My husband is battling cancer. When I'm not in this office, I'm taking him to chemo treatments. It's so difficult for everyone involved."

"I'm so sorry. It's a terrible disease. I feel awful that Sophia won't know her mother, but if I have any influence at all, I'll make sure she does."

Sarah walked out of the office with a plan to visit Sharon in the morning to see what she could do about getting the letter written. Depending on Sharon's pain, Sarah might have to put it off for another day.

She decided to stop by Trevor's on the way home from the Adoption office. When she arrived, the look on his face scared her. "You look awful. What's going on? Where's Noah?"

"He's playing in his room. Try to keep your voice down. I don't want him to think anything is wrong, but we've got trouble. William Barclay, Ava's father, called me today. He wants Noah and plans to take me to court to get custody."

"How is that possible? I thought her brother said they didn't want him."

"That's what I thought too, but thanks to Clayton, that's all changed."

"What does Clayton have to do with this?"

"He called Barclay, and told him that I couldn't provide for

Noah, and that he was living in a dump, basically. He made it sound like I'm an unfit father."

"That's easily disputed, Trevor."

"Of course, but the fact that I'd have to go to court to defend myself, and put Noah through disruption in his life again, is unforgivable.

"Did you talk to Clayton?"

"I'm not sure talking is what we did. I wanted to hit him, and I would have if Dad wasn't in the room. When he heard what Clayton did, he ordered him out of the building, and told him to never come back. I doubt that will hold for very long."

Sarah slumped down on the sofa. "This is awful. There must be something we can do to prevent going to court."

"There is, and my father is handling it. He thinks the Barclays don't really care about Noah. They rejected him when they had a chance to claim custody of him when Ava died, that has to count for something."

"When you say handling it, am I to assume that means he plans to offer them money to walk away?"

"That's the plan. He thinks that's what they're really after. Money solves everything, doesn't it?"

Sarah felt Trevor's frustration, but he seemed as angry about the solution as much as the problem. "Why am I sensing you're not happy about your father's involvement?"

"I don't live my life this way, Sarah. Money complicates things all the time. If my family wasn't rich, this probably wouldn't have happened in the first place."

"Whoa, wait a minute. Are you forgetting the reason for the Barclays' involvement? This is about Clayton's need for revenge. He's a little boy in a man's body. He's jealous of you and used this situation to get to you. I think what your father is doing is a blessing. One that you should appreciate. I know you don't want to be like your father, and that it matters to you to carve out a life that's your own. I get that, but there's something you keep trying to do and you can't see that it's a useless effort. You keep trying to be someone other than a Hutchins. No matter how you live your life, Trevor, you are never going to rid yourself of that name, and your family."

"Sarah, you don't understand…"

Sarah interrupted Trevor. "I understand that there is a history I can't relate to, but if your choice is to move forward, you have to embrace who you are and who your father is—your siblings as well. You can't expect them to change just because you've decided to come home. You have to make peace with this if you want to be happy."

Sarah waited for Trevor to say something, but he was silent, thinking about what she had said. She returned to the sofa and ran her hand over his shoulders. She had more to say and figured this was as good a time as any.

"There's one more thing I want to say to you if you'll let me. I made a big mistake doing everything I could to please my father. I worked in a job I hated but did it to impress him. Because my job involved making lots of money, it became the only thing my father and I talked about, because that was his passion. I mistook that for interest in my accomplishments, but it had nothing to do with me. When I learned more about the things he did to my mother, and our family, it took the shine off his crown. I saw him in a different light. His power over me changed, and I felt free."

Trevor held Sarah's hand as she spoke.

"I listened to my heart when I came to Captiva with my mother. I didn't have a clue where my journey would lead, but I didn't care. I knew I'd find my way when I let myself be who I was meant to be, not what anyone else thought I should be."

"It's funny to hear you say this to me now. My mother said almost the same thing. You think I'm making a mistake working for my father?"

"I didn't say that. What I'm saying is that you need to stop listening to everyone else and be who you want to be. Carve out a life for you and Noah that works for the two of you. You love that little boy, and I've no doubt you will always do what's best for him. Just remember that you don't need to sacrifice who you are to do that."

"What I want is to give this a chance to work. I've just started and I'm not ready to throw in the towel just yet. But I hear what you're saying. I'm going to make this job work for me and the company. If I can't do that, then I will have to let it go, no matter how my father feels about it. You're right about the Hutchins name, too. All these changes in such a short amount of time, has me reeling. I do need a period of adjustment and give myself a break, but I'm scared. I'm scared I'll lose Noah."

They sat with their arms around each other for several minutes before Noah came out into the room. Sarah hoped he hadn't heard them talking.

"Hey, Noah. I thought you were sleeping?"

Noah went directly to Sarah's lap and rested his head against her shoulder. She held him tight and kissed the top of his head, slowly rocking him back and forth. When he started to fall asleep again, she walked him back to his bed, and placed him under the covers.

She thought his eyes were closed, but instead he was still awake. "Read me a story."

"I'll read to you, if you promise to go back to sleep." She found a small book at the foot of his bed. "This one?"

Noah nodded. Settling onto the side of his bed, she began to read. A grumpy monkey had lots to complain about, but in the end he found a way to be happy. Noah liked the book, and his eyes were closed by the time Sarah finished. She sat for a few minutes listening to his breathing, and then turned off the light before leaving the room. She prayed that Devon's money and power would keep Noah safe from the Barclays. If it didn't, she was prepared to do whatever was necessary to protect him.

CHAPTER TWENTY-ONE

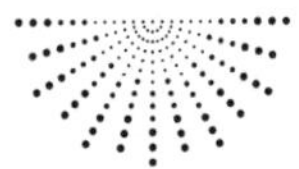

Grateful to have the day over with, Sarah couldn't wait to get home and prepare a few appetizers for her visit with Emma. She quickly made a couple of dips and filled two bowls with chips, and a smaller one with salsa.

Emma arrived at seven and she held two bottles of wine, one white and one red. "I couldn't decide, and I wasn't sure which you'd prefer, so I bought two."

"Come on in. I hope you didn't have any trouble getting in through the gate."

"Nope. The code worked just fine. I always laugh at these security boxes. I mean, how secure are they really when everyone gives out the code to family and friends?"

Sarah laughed. "Good point. I guess they figure our family and friends can be trusted. How about a tour of the place?"

"Lead on. The houses I passed on the way in are gorgeous, as is yours. How did you get to lease this one?"

"I'm going to assume that the landlord is wealthy. I met them, the husband and wife, who also are real estate agents. I think they own a few places for investment. Based on the beauty of this place, I can't imagine what their home looks like."

After they toured the inside of the house, Emma kicked off her sandals, and walked onto the steps leading into the pool. She sat on the side and dangled her feet in the water, admiring the lanai. "This place is beautiful. I'm jealous. My apartment looks like I'm living in poverty by comparison."

"I couldn't decide whether to buy a place or rent. When I signed the lease, it felt right. One year is all I can commit to for now. I'm going to give myself one more year before I sign mortgage papers. Maybe you'll do the same one of these days, although I'm not sure if you'd buy something in the U.S. or Europe."

Emma shrugged. "Either way, it would require me to settle in one place. I'm such a nomad, I don't think that will ever happen."

"Never say never. I'm learning that the hard way."

"What does that mean?"

"Before I get into all that, let me go inside and get a bottle of wine."

Sarah headed into the kitchen and got two glasses and a bottle of Sean Minor Pinot Noir. The timer for the lanai lights came on and reflected their glow on the water. She opened the bottle and filled their glasses. She sighed, wondering where to start.

"I'm not sure I've ever mentioned this to you, but after Luke cheated on me, I swore off getting serious with anyone ever again. That loss left a mark. I didn't plan on staying alone, just single. By the time Ben and I split, it was too late to maintain a friendship. We were together too long. He assumed we'd get engaged. I don't think that was an unreasonable assumption. I should have been clear about my feelings from the start."

"He didn't take it well, I gather?"

"No, and it's a shame because we were good friends. I'm sorry to lose that friendship. When I came to Captiva with my mother, the last thing I wanted in my life was another relationship."

"But then Trevor came along?"

Sarah nodded. "The first time we met, I didn't like him. Well, correction, the attraction was there, but he unnerved me somehow. I thought he was arrogant of course, but that wasn't the problem. I couldn't stop thinking about him. I found myself looking for him every time I came into the office. When I left work I'd look for him, and when I got home, I wondered what he was doing. When he did come into the Outreach Center, he kept needling me, trying to get me mad, but instead, we'd end up laughing. Over time, we got close. I came to realize that one of the reasons for the attraction, was his confidence. Sometimes, we'd have lunch together out on the lawn, and he'd tell me about his life and his travels. I hung on every word. I found myself falling in love with him. He tells me he knew he loved me early on."

"Sounds like it was meant to be. I'm sure there's a problem in here somewhere. What's the deal?"

Sarah took a sip of her wine. "The deal is that when we started to date, there was no Noah, at least Trevor didn't know of his existence. I've never thought of myself as anyone's mother. I like kids, but there's so much responsibility there. I never had that image in my head."

"What image?"

"You know, holding a baby in my arms, being pregnant, giving birth. None of that felt like me. But lately, I don't know..."

Sarah told of her experience with Sharon and Sophia, and how holding the baby had felt so natural. "I've fallen in love with three people. Trevor, Noah, and Sophia feel like my family now and I'm afraid of losing them."

Emma took a minute to gather her thoughts before she spoke.

"Sarah have you ever heard of The Camino de Santiago?"

Sarah shook her head, "No, I haven't. Sounds like it's in Spain."

"It is. It's a spiritual pilgrimage. They call it 'Walking the way of St. James the apostle.' The legend is that St. James' remains were carried by boat from Jerusalem to Spain and they buried him there. The cathedral is beautiful, and you can't help but be overcome with emotion when you kneel at the altar. Anyone can do the walk; you don't have to be Catholic."

Emma got up from her chair and went to her backpack. She pulled out a scalloped seashell, not unlike the millions that cover the beaches of Sanibel and Captiva.

"This shell is the symbol of the Camino de Santiago, and when you walk along the way you see posts with a yellow modern image of the shell to guide you. I'm not really sure why a seashell, but people who walk usually keep one like this displayed on their body or backpack. Timothy and I did the walk from Madrid to the church. It's five hundred miles and took us about a month to complete the walk."

"That's a serious hike. I could never do something like that."

"Timothy had done it before and wanted me to have the experience. There were many times when I wanted to quit along the way, but the fellowship with others who traveled on our path, along with Timothy's encouragement kept me going. I'm so glad I did it because when you reach the cathedral, somehow, your heart is overcome with gratitude and appreciation for your journey. I'm not a religious person, but you don't have to be to feel its impact. I remember I fell to my knees and cried when I got there."

Emma's words felt delicate, and Sarah didn't want to speak for fear of breaking their importance.

"I remember thinking that we were on an adventure together, something we would remember forever. Timothy gave me this seashell. I've held it close ever since. Before I go back to work, I'm going to do the walk again. It will feel different doing it alone, but it's something I need to do."

Sarah wondered why Emma wanted to share this story with her.

"After Timothy died, of course I felt anger, but I found comfort in thinking about all the adventures we'd shared. I laughed when I thought of his silly way of balancing a spoon on the bridge of his nose, or when he insisted we skip everywhere instead of walking. I have so much happiness from these memories. When I'm afraid that I will never love anyone again the way I loved Timothy, I think of our journey on the Camino."

Emma smiled through her tears when she said her next words. "Sarah, you have no idea how much the heart can hold. It can hold pain, and sorrow, but it can hold compassion and love at the same time. Open your heart and let in whatever is trying to reach you. I promise you won't regret it. If you want that baby, then you go get her. If you want to be Noah's mother, then let that happen too, and if Trevor wants to grow old with you by his side, welcome that as well. Never ignore your heart. No matter what anyone tells you, it's much wiser than your head because it's where the most important things live."

They sat in silence for a few minutes before Sarah let herself cry in Emma's arms. Each of the women had started as friends and roommates and for a brief moment, experienced their lives in the same place. But as the years passed, their journeys took them to different places in the world.

Crossing paths again had been an unexpected blessing. Sarah prayed they would have another opportunity to meet in the future. Until then, she would hold Emma's words close and live her life with an open heart and believe that when Emma reached the cathedral once again, Timothy would be waiting for her.

Trevor spent the morning in his office taking calls from various news outlets in the Ft. Myers area. The optics of the affordable housing project created the kind of attention Devon had hoped for, and Trevor hated.

Trevor had no problem working within the community in whatever capacity pushed the project forward, but he wasn't a celebrity, and the attention he got from the media made him feel uncomfortable. Somehow, creating houses for the poor wasn't as interesting as the personal life of the wealthy son of Devon Hutchins.

Everyone wanted to interview him, and each time a microphone appeared in his face, the questions inevitably turned to Trevor and his life volunteering around the world. Where had he been all these years? How does he spend his time when he's not working? Did he have a girlfriend?

The questions were endless, and as much as he complained about it to his father, Devon would brush it off saying it would die down in time and to ignore it. He loved the attention the project got because of Trevor's involvement.

He asked his assistant, Lori, to screen all calls to give him some time to think about the project. He'd had only a few minutes to himself when his cell phone rang. He never missed a call on his private line just in case it was the nanny. When he answered the phone, his sister, Jacqui sounded frantic.

"Hey, Jacqui. What's up?"

"I'm in jail, that's what's up. Can you come and get me out of here?"

"What the heck? What happened?"

"I'll explain everything when you get down here. It's on Widman Way."

"I'm on my way."

Trevor ran out of his office and to the elevators, stopping only long enough to tell Lori that he was leaving for the day.

He drove through town toward the police station and went directly to the officer at the desk.

"I'm Trevor Hutchins. I'm here to inquire about my sister, Jacqui Hutchins."

"Your sister, along with two others were picked up following a brawl outside The Whale on Ft. Myers Beach. It seems a customer made a rude comment to your sister, and she didn't like what they said to her. Instead of walking away, it appears that Ms. Hutchins threw water in the man's face. She backed away when the fighting started, but the others who were with her decided to keep the argument going. Before long, your sister and her friends managed to get a few punches in before the police arrived."

Sitting on a bench across the room, Jacqui could hear Trevor and the officer talking, and took issue with the officer's explanation.

"They threw the first punch, not us, and the jerk needed to cool down, so I threw water in his face."

"Mr. Hutchins, if you will sign this document, you can take your sister home. I have zero understanding of the kids today, but for some reason, no one is pressing charges, so my work is done here."

Trevor signed the paper, and then grabbed Jacqui's arm, pulling her to the door. "Let's go."

Jacqui forcibly pulled her arm back.

When they were outside of the police station, Trevor turned to his sister and shook his head. "Do you want to tell me what that was about? It's not like you're still in high school, so why act like a kid? What were you thinking?"

"The guy called me a name that I can't repeat. Let's just say it didn't flatter me. I'm sorry to have had to call you to bail me out, but you were the only person I could call. You're not like the rest of the family; you don't judge me."

Trevor pulled his sister into a headlock.

"Ow, cut it out."

"I'm going to hold you like I did when we were kids until you promise to start acting like an adult with some restraint."

"Fine. Now, let me go."

Trevor released his sister from his grip.

"Seriously, Jacqui, whatever happened to my little sister? You remember her? The one with all that talent? The most talented artist in the world? Do you still paint?"

Jacqui leaned against Trevor's car, and looking down at the sidewalk, shook her head. "What's the point?"

"What's the point? How about the fact that I've never known anything that gives you more joy than your art. The point is that I'd give anything to have your talent. Heck, most people would. How about you get back to it?"

"Dad thinks it's a frivolous way to spend my time. As soon as I graduated college, he already had plans for me to sell real estate. I gave it a go, but it's not me."

"So, you spend your time how? By hanging out with the wrong people and getting into fights in the middle of the day? How long do you think you can do this before you get into a serious situation you can't get yourself out of?"

Jacqui didn't answer him. In that moment, Trevor thought of Chelsea, and wondered if she'd be interested in talking to Jacqui.

"Get in the car."

Trevor made a note to call Chelsea later tonight to see if her spending a few hours with his sister might do Jacqui some good. After all, it might give her the motivation she needed to get back to her painting. After today's mess, it couldn't hurt.

CHAPTER TWENTY-TWO

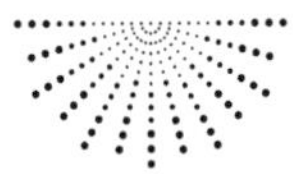

Trevor called Chelsea who agreed to see Jacqui the next morning. Jacqui resisted at first, but then warmed to the idea of talking to another artist.

"It's been a while. All I have are a few older pieces."

"That will be fine. I just want her to see your work, but mostly, I want you to have someone to talk to who understands what it takes to create a work of art. Chelsea is very talented. She had a showing at a gallery on Sanibel and it went quite well. She sold all of her paintings that night. I could see you doing something like that."

Jacqui shrugged. "You've always been a bit biased, but I'll take it. In our family, if you can get someone to show a little love and compassion, you can count yourself lucky."

They headed out to Chelsea's place first thing in the morning. When they arrived, she had already put out an assortment of pastries, fruit, and coffee.

After introductions, Jacqui didn't waste any time showing her snarky side. "My brother thinks I need to be reined in, and it looks like you've grabbed the short straw."

Never one to back down, Chelsea answered her, "Do you?"

"Do I what?"

"Do you need to be reined in?"

"Let's just say, I've had very few positive, female role models in my life."

Facing Trevor she asked, "Is Chelsea to be my muse, dear brother?"

Trevor watched Chelsea set his sister straight.

"I'm not sure you'd be worth the trouble, and I'm very busy. I don't think I've got the time." Turning to Trevor she apologized. "I'm sorry, Trevor, I hope you understand but my time is valuable, and I'm not interested in spending time with someone who can't act like a responsible adult, and I won't be a babysitter."

Trevor watched his sister's face. Jacqui's anger showed and he remembered when she was a child, her anger had been the impetus to any progress. He could see her trying to control her temper, and as he began to respond to Chelsea, she interrupted.

"I'm sorry to be so rude. I've got a lot of reasons to be angry, but you're not one of them. I appreciate you taking the time today. If you're still willing, I'd like to talk with you about painting."

Chelsea lightened the mood with an invitation to eat something. "Let's go out onto the lanai and have a bite to eat. Have either of you had breakfast yet?"

Trevor smiled and mouthed a silent thank you. "I'd love a cup of coffee."

They walked out to the lanai. A blank canvas sat on a frame in the corner of the space, oils and brushes lined a table next to it.

Trevor laid Jacqui's portfolio on the outdoor sofa, opening it to display some of Jacqui's work.

Chelsea looked at the paintings and then at Jacqui.

"You have talent. Trevor tells me you haven't painted in a long time. Why not?"

Jacqui took a sip of her coffee, and then shrugged. "It's always been a hobby only. A hobby that won't make me any money, so why bother?"

"Money isn't the only reason to paint. If it's in you to create something from nothing, then you should do it. Most artists make little money, but that doesn't stop them from creating. I don't think it has anything to do with money."

Pointing to the blank canvas, she continued, "I like to leave a blank canvas sitting alone out here for several days, maybe even weeks before I start any project. I walk by the canvas throughout the day and even at night with the lights on. At some point, it invites me, even compels me to begin. Until I get that feeling, I won't start painting."

She turned to Jacqui, and asked, "Money isn't the reason you don't paint. Something else is keeping you from painting. What is it?"

Trevor and Chelsea looked at Jacqui who seemed uncomfortable in her chair. "I don't know."

Chelsea sat in the chair across from Jacqui. "You've got to search your soul to find out what's preventing you from doing the thing you love. Your choices have to come from a place of conviction. You won't be able to commit to painting until you understand why you stopped in the first place. No one is going to force you to paint. It's a decision only you can make, but it has to be a decision that comes from deep inside you. I can spend all the time in the world with you, but until you reach that place in your heart, it won't do you much good."

Trevor knew he had made the right choice in bringing Jacqui to meet Chelsea. If anyone could reach his sister, it was her.

Jacqui sat up straight and took a deep breath. "My father never encouraged my painting. My siblings thought I had talent, and encouraged me, but my father called it my hobby. I still felt I could prove him wrong—that I was good enough to get the attention of people in the industry, so I kept at it. But then, I met a guy who acted jealous of the attention I was getting. He didn't like it that I was spending so much time away from him. When I'd paint, he'd get angry that we weren't together. Painting is a solitary endeavor, and he hated that I had something he wasn't a part of. We fought. He'd say awful things and I'd say things. As you can see, I'm not exactly shy about talking back. But then, he'd up the game, and finally hit me. I almost left him after that, but I didn't."

Trevor's heart broke at what his sister had suffered through. He wished he'd been around to be supportive, and deal with the monster who shattered her dreams.

"Eventually, I just stopped painting or doing anything that didn't involve Jack. It was easier to give in than get a beating."

Tears welled in her eyes, and Trevor reached for her, pulling her close to him. "I'm so sorry, Jacqui. I didn't know."

"How could you know; you were on the other side of the world…"

Trevor finished her sentence. "Taking care of strangers instead of you."

Now, Jacqui's tears fell, and she cried in her brother's arms.

Chelsea let a few minutes pass, before saying anything. Trevor wiped away Jacqui's tears and pushed her hair away from her face.

Her voice, soft and quiet, Chelsea spoke. "I'd say you've finally figured out why you stopped painting. Perhaps, now, together, we might help you find every reason why you should begin again?"

Jacqui smiled and nodded. "I'd like that."

Trevor couldn't have asked for a better outcome. He felt certain that Jacqui would come to find joy in what she loved, and in time, she'd let the world share in that joy. The light that was hidden, would shine again, and for that, he'd always be grateful to Chelsea.

~

Maggie's phone rang with a distinct ringtone that she assigned to her mother. She immediately stomped her feet, realizing she forgot to call her mother about the engagement to Paolo.

"Hello, mother."

There was no greeting from Sarah Rose McKinnon Garrison. Instead, her mother hit her with a direct question.

"Did you not think me important enough to be informed of your impending marriage?"

"Mom, I'm sorry. I planned to call, it's just that things are getting so busy around here, it slipped my mind. I'm sorry."

"Well, I guess congratulations are in order. Are you happy?"

"Yes, I'm very happy. The wedding is in October. The long holiday so that the kids won't miss much school."

"That's good. While Lauren is down there, maybe you can talk some sense into her."

"Talk sense? Lauren? What are you talking about?"

"For some reason your daughter is all up in arms about sending me to a retirement home. She's got some notion that I'm forgetting things and need a nurse to look after me. I told her to mind her own business. I think that girl is in her daughters' lives so much, she thinks she can treat me like a child. I won't have it."

"Mom, listen to me. This is the first I'm hearing about you going to a retirement home. Are you sure you understood her correctly?"

"You too? You think I'm so feeble-minded I can't remember or understand what someone is saying to me?"

Maggie tried to calm her mother down, but it seemed like the more they talked, the worse her mother got.

"Mom. Please calm down. I will talk to Lauren and find out what is going on. I'm sure there is a mix-up somewhere. On another subject, do you think you will come to the wedding? You don't have to. I know it's a long way to go, but you know you're welcome to join us."

"I'll have you know that I have every intention of being at my daughter's wedding. You can take that to the bank."

Maggie had never heard her mother sounding so angry. Maybe Lauren was right. Something had changed in her mother's tone enough to worry Maggie.

"That's wonderful. I'm glad you're coming. I've got to run now. We'll talk again soon."

"Don't forget to call Lauren. I'm tired of hearing that I need help."

"I won't forget. I'll talk to you later. Bye, Mom."

Maggie couldn't wait to hang up and call Lauren. She needed to get to the bottom of this right away. Lauren answered after the first ring.

"Hey, Mom. Is everything all right?"

"That's what I'd like to know. Your grandmother just called me all upset because you've been telling her she needs to go into a retirement home."

"Mom. That's not exactly what I said. The truth is that she is forgetting things all the time. The other day, she called me and asked if I would drive her to the market because she needs new glasses, and her eyesight was getting worse. So, I drive over there and she's in her bathrobe watching television. She had no memory of calling me to come get her. Not only that, but she was also angry because she thought I was insinuating that she had dementia and that I'm trying to put her in a home. I never said any such thing."

"That doesn't sound like Mom. Something's going on with her. Can you get her to her doctor if I make the appointment? She needs to be checked out. I don't like the sound of this."

"Sure, if she'll let me. The thing is that her bad moods come and go. I stopped in to see her the other day and she seemed happy and her usual self. I never know who I'm going to see when I get there."

"I'll call her doctor and get an appointment right away. I'll text you the details. Thanks honey. I'm worried that she does indeed have a bit of dementia starting. The best thing we can do is tell the doctor what's been going on and see if they can find the cause."

Maggie called the doctor. After describing her mother's symptoms, she booked an appointment for her the next day. She sent a text to Lauren with the details and asked her to call Maggie back after the doctor visit.

Maggie hated that she lived so far away. Taking care of her mother shouldn't be the responsibility of the grandchildren. With so much going on, it would be difficult, but not impossible to fly back to Massachusetts. If it became necessary, that is what she would do. For now, all she could do is wait for the doctor's examination.

CHAPTER TWENTY-THREE

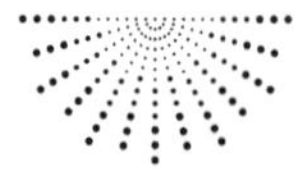

The next day, Maggie received a call from her mother's doctor. Fortunately, dementia was not her issue. A urinary tract infection had gotten so bad that it had moved to the kidneys.

"We've admitted your mother and expect her to recover and be released in a few days. I understand your daughter is the one I need to communicate with?"

"Yes, thank you. She'll call me and keep me informed. I live in Florida, so it's best to speak with someone living nearby. So, dementia isn't the issue? I only ask because my daughter said that my mother had been confused, forgetful and agitated."

"Those symptoms are very much like someone with dementia, but it's not unusual at all. There is no indication of dementia, and after she's had the antibiotics, her agitation and other symptoms should diminish."

"That's good news. Thank you, doctor."

"My pleasure, Ms. Wheeler. Enjoy the beautiful Florida weather. We've got rain here today."

As soon as Maggie hung up the phone, she called Lauren to let her know the good news.

"Hey, Mom. Have you heard from the doctor?"

"Yes. He just called. I asked him to call you to coordinate with Mom's care. She doesn't have dementia. She has a urinary tract infection which they are clearing up with antibiotics. You should be able to bring her home in a day or two."

"Oh, thank goodness."

"Yes, apparently, confusion and agitation are common symptoms of urinary tract infections in the elderly. Of course, they don't know Mom; she gets agitated over the smallest of things on a good day. She's angry at me for not telling her about my getting married."

"She did mention that to me. I'm sorry I didn't realize you hadn't told her, or I wouldn't have said a thing. By the way, why didn't you let her know?"

"Honestly, Lauren, it just slipped my mind. I had planned to let her know, but then I got overwhelmed with everything going on here, and I just forgot."

"You should have seen her. She was so mad, she said she didn't plan on attending the wedding. I suspect that will change."

"It already has. When I talked to her, she said she had every intention of coming to the wedding. Even in her angry voice, I was glad to hear she'll be here to celebrate with all of us. I need all my family here on the big day. It's important to me. I don't want to keep you. I know you've got to get to work. Keep me updated on your grandmother's situation. I'm going to wait until tomorrow before I call her. I think it's best to give the medication time to kick in."

Lauren laughed, "It's good to know that you avoid your mother on occasion. This way, you can't get mad at me if ever I need to do the same to you."

"Very funny. I'll talk to you later, honey. Give a kiss to the girls and say hello to Jeff. Love you."

"Will do. Love you too, Mom."

Maggie's mother had never been shy about saying what was

on her mind. No doubt, when the medication worked its magic, Maggie would have to work hers to keep her mother from feeling left out of the wedding preparations. It was a small price to pay, to have everyone she loved most in the world, be with her on her special day, even if it meant letting her mother vent now and then.

~

Ciara got the call from hospice to come to Sharon's apartment as soon as she could. Ciara ran to Sarah's office and knocked on her door.

"Hey, hospice just called to say we should get to Sharon's place right away. I think it's time."

Sarah grabbed her purse and followed Ciara out to her car. "We should contact Meredith Carpenter."

"Let's wait until we get there. I don't know what's happening. They didn't say anything more than for us to come to the apartment."

"I can't believe she is going so fast. I thought she'd have more time with Sophia."

"Sarah. There is never going to be enough time. This is all she gets. It's awful, but we have to accept it and do what's right for Sophia. You should prepare yourself because I think we're going to need to take Sophia out of there today. She needs to go to a new home where she can be the focus of a loving family. Sharon can't do that anymore."

"I know you're right, and I've always known this day would come, it's just so heartbreaking."

They reached Sharon's place in record time. The hospice worker met them at the door. "I'm sorry. She passed away about five minutes ago."

Sarah searched the woman's face, hoping she'd heard wrong,

but when she looked past her, she could see Sharon on the bed, and knew she was gone.

Sarah ran to Sophia and lifted her out of her bassinet, holding her tight. Sarah hurt for the child. Sophia had no idea that she now, was an orphan. Sarah sat in the chair, the spot where Sharon had many times before, lovingly held her baby, and wept.

Ciara sat on the bed next to Sharon, as the woman from hospice gathered her things, getting ready to leave. Sarah stopped her. "I'm sorry, I never got your name."

The woman smiled. "It's Kerry."

Through tears, Sarah whispered, "Kerry, thank you for everything you did for Sharon and Sophia."

Kerry nodded and walked to Sharon. She kissed two fingers and placed them on Sharon's forehead. She took an envelope out of her backpack and handed it to Sarah.

"She gave this to me the other day and said I should give it to you when the time came. I'm very sorry for your loss."

Sarah took the envelope, and watched Kerry leave the apartment. Ciara took Sophia from Sarah's arms and placed her in the car seat, leaving Sarah her privacy. Sarah opened the envelope and read the letter.

Dear Ms. Wheeler,

Thank you for everything you have done for me and Sophia. I'm so grateful to you for helping me have these precious days with her. I couldn't have done it without you and Ms. Moretti. I wish to be cremated. I don't have any particular desire to be buried anywhere, so I will leave it to you and Ms. Moretti to place my ashes wherever you see fit, and what is most affordable. I'm sorry I don't have any money to help with this.

As I mentioned before, it would be a blessing and make me very happy if you were to be Sophia's guardian. I don't know what your plans are for the future, but I wanted to give you a legal document explaining my wish just in case you ever decide to adopt Sophia. If you find that you can't, I know that she is in good hands with you, and that you will find the best family to love her as much as I do.

To whom it may concern:

This letter written of my own free will and with full understanding, is to convey my wish to grant Ms. Sarah Wheeler authorization to be the legal guardian of my daughter Sophia Eloise Carter if she so chooses to request. She is a wonderful person and loving caretaker, and honestly the best person I know to be my child's mother. I couldn't dream of anyone better.

Sincerely,

Sharon Elizabeth Carter

Sarah folded the paper, put it back inside the envelope, and held it close to her chest. The events of the last month slowly began to chip away at her belief that she couldn't care for a child.

Noah and Sophia had done what no one else had been able to do thus far, and that was convince Sarah that children choose their parents, not the other way around. Whether born of her body, or adopted, they would bless Sarah's life like nothing she had ever known before. Sharon's letter opened the door to a new world of possibilities for Sarah. The time had finally come to open her heart to a future she never planned, but actively ran away from.

Before she left, Kerry had signed and left the necessary hospice paperwork on the table. She had called the hospice doctor and the mortuary. There was nothing for Ciara or Sarah to do except wait for them to arrive. Ciara called Meredith Carpenter, who requested they meet her at the foster home with Sophia.

"I told Kerry last week that when the time came, they should move Sharon's body to Eternal Haven funeral home. It's close by. I didn't know what else to do without a family member to ask. I hope that's ok," Ciara said.

Sarah nodded. "That's fine."

They moved around the apartment in silence, gathering the baby's things. When the mortuary van arrived, two men put Sharon's body on a stretcher and covering her with a sheet, carried her to the vehicle. Once Sophia and Ciara were in the car, Sarah looked at the apartment one last time, and then closed the door.

~

They rode in silence for five minutes before Ciara asked Sarah about the letter. "What did she write?"

"She thanked us for taking care of her and Sophia and for giving her these last days with her baby. She wants to be cremated and has no particular interest in what happens to her ashes. The rest of the letter was addressed to the adoption agency, letting them know her desire for me to be Sophia's legal guardian."

Ciara took her eyes off the road long enough to see Sarah's face. "Is that what you want to do? Do you plan to adopt Sophia?"

Sarah couldn't imagine taking Sophia right now, at least not without talking to Trevor.

"I can't do it right now. I'm not settled, and I have no idea how Trevor would react to me suddenly having a baby to take care of."

Ciara laughed. "Oh, you mean like you had to adjust to the idea of Noah. Something tells me that Trevor will handle it just fine."

When they reached the adoption center, Meredith Carpenter, along with another woman, met them at the door.

"I'm so very sorry for the loss of your friend. This is a difficult time for both of you, I'm sure. When someone dies like this there are so many things you have to handle, at least you can rest easy about Sophia. She will be in good hands, I promise you."

Sarah reminded Meredith about her desire to visit Sophia at

her new foster home. She handed Sharon's letter to the woman, who read it and nodded in acceptance.

"This will do just fine. I don't see why you can't visit Sophia whenever you want. My only caution is that you do it at a time that works for the family. There can't be any disruption in Sophia's life or the lives of the foster family."

Sarah nodded. "I understand."

Meredith continued, "This is Ms. Porter. She'll take Sophia to the Gallo family."

"They're Italian?" Ciara asked.

"Yes, I believe they are. Why do you ask?"

"No reason. I'm Italian so I just wondered if they were as well. I wonder what part of Italy the family comes from."

"Perhaps Ms. Wheeler will ask them on one of her visits."

Ms. Porter headed for the door, but Sarah called out.

"Wait, please."

Sarah kissed Sophia on the cheek. The baby looked at Sarah and smiled. Sarah tried not to cry and made a promise to the infant.

"I will see you very soon, little one. Don't you worry."

She watched as the woman carried Sophia out of the office. She felt as if the child had been ripped out of her arms. The pain was unbearable, and in that moment, Sarah knew that Sophia Eloise Carter was her child, maybe not today, but soon.

CHAPTER TWENTY-FOUR

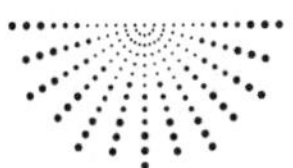

Sarah and Ciara had support from their families, and as soon as they heard about Sharon, were willing to help pay for the funeral.

The funeral home had been instructed to move as quickly as possible to cremate her and were told that there would be very few people attending the service. They were able to accommodate Sarah and the next day, everyone gathered together to support her grief.

Maggie, Paolo, Sarah, Trevor, Ciara, and Chelsea along with a few members of the Outreach Center sat in the funeral home with Sharon's urn at the front of the room. There were no flowers and no remembrances of the woman who had once been. The local parish priest said a few prayers and within minutes the entire celebration of Sharon's life was over.

Everyone went back to the inn to have something to eat, but Sarah felt removed from all of it. An overwhelming sadness engulfed her, and nothing except the thought of Sophia gave Sarah reason to smile.

The inn's chefs, Riley and Grace prepared a lovely buffet for everyone. Rather than upset Noah to be reminded of his mother's death, his nanny took him to the zoo.

Maggie sat on the arm of the sofa, and massaged Sarah's shoulder. "Sharon is at peace now, honey. You and Ciara did the best that you could for her and her baby. You can take some solace in that."

Sarah couldn't say anything but nod her head in agreement. The sound of other muffled voices in the room made her feel removed from the gathering. She thought of Sophia and how much Sharon loved her. She had visions of the two of them sitting in a chair, Sharon's arms cradling her child. She suddenly remembered the photo that she took of Sharon and Sophia. "Does anyone know how long it takes to get a photo developed once you send the file to the store? I've got a picture I want to frame."

"I think depending on their workload, they can do it right away," Chelsea said.

Sarah flipped through the photos on her cell phone and found the picture. She quickly sent the order online to the local store, and then grabbed the keys to her car.

"I'm going now to pick it up."

Maggie stopped Sarah. "Wait. You're going right now? Can't it wait? You haven't had anything to eat. At least have a sandwich before you go."

"I won't be long. Please, everyone, stay until I get back."

Sarah jumped in her car and drove to the store which was only a few blocks from the inn. She looked for someone to help her with her order. A young man behind the counter offered to help, but he couldn't find the order.

"I just sent it in, I know it takes a little time, but this photo is very important. Please, can you look on your computer?"

The boy found the order, which hadn't been processed yet. He looked at the clock and sighed. He acted as if she had interrupted his break but processed the photo as she asked.

He handed the picture to Sarah, who by now appeared frantic.

"Yes. That's it. That's the one. Thank you."

She stood looking at the photo for a minute before deciding to buy a frame. She walked the aisle until she found one that she liked and went to find the boy once again. "I'd like to buy this as well. Is it ok if I'm going to open it and put the picture in the frame?"

The boy couldn't care less what Sarah wanted to do. All he wanted was to get back to reading his magazine and head to the breakroom.

She paid for her items, got back in the car, and drove home. When she got inside the house, she was glad everyone waited for her.

Sarah took the framed photo and placed it on the table next to a bouquet of lantana and blanket flowers. Oranges and yellows dominated the spot, and breathed joy and new life into the room. Sharon had died, but her child lived on, and this picture was evidence of that. That was something to celebrate, she thought.

Sarah and Trevor returned to his house on the beach and waited for Debbie and Noah to get home. Noah had never seen the zoo before, so this would be a special experience for him. Sarah couldn't wait for them to get home to hear how the day went. They needed something cheerful to focus on.

When they heard Debbie's car pull into the driveway, Trevor and Sarah ran down to meet them. Noah had a new stuffed animal, this time a lion.

"Hey, buddy. It looks like you had a good time."

Sarah thanked Debbie and asked, "How did it go? Did he enjoy the zoo?"

"Yeah. He loved it. I don't think there was an animal he didn't like. You may have a future veterinarian in your family. We had hot dogs. I hope that was all right?"

Trevor laughed. "Is there a kid alive who didn't eat junk at the zoo, or amusement park, or the beach? Come to think of it, anywhere. "

Debbie gave Noah a hug. "I've got to go home now, Noah. I'll see you tomorrow."

Debbie pulled Sarah aside. "He started the day with lots of energy, but he's fading fast. I think a nap might be in order. I'm a bit worried though. His eyes did something right before we got in the car. I thought he was going to have another seizure. I sometimes watch another boy in my neighborhood who also has seizures, and almost always gets them when he hasn't had enough sleep. I'm sure Noah will be fine, but you might want to watch him closely tonight."

"Thank you, Debbie. I'll let Trevor know."

Debbie's words worried Sarah. Noah had been doing so well, even though the threat of more seizures was always there, they were hopeful he wouldn't have another.

Trevor's cell phone rang. "Sarah, can you get that? I want to put Noah to bed."

Sarah saw Devon's name and answered, "Hello, Devon. This is Sarah. Trevor is just putting Noah to bed. Can you hang on a minute?"

"That's fine, I just wanted to know if I could come over for a few minutes. I have information about the Barclays'."

"Yes, of course. I'll let Trevor know."

Trevor came out of Noah's room and grabbed a bottle of water out of the refrigerator.

"Who was that on the phone?"

"It was your father. It seems he has news about Ava's parents and wants to talk to you in person. He's on his way. There's something else."

"What is it?"

Keeping her voice low so that Noah couldn't hear, Sarah walked to the far side of the room, away from Noah's room.

"Debbie said that she thought Noah could have another seizure tonight. She said something about his eyes made her concerned. She babysits another little boy who has seizures too, and she recognizes the signs. Mostly, she said lack of sleep, and getting overtired is usually the cause."

"That's what the doctor said. He went right out as soon as I put him in the bed. It's possible going to the zoo wiped him out."

Trevor ran his hands through his hair. Two things were threatening his family, the Barclays and Noah's health, and he felt helpless to do anything about either one.

An hour went by before Devon arrived. By the time his car parked in the driveway, Trevor had been frantically pacing the floor. He imagined the worst and Sarah did her best to keep him focused on the good but was running out of things to say.

Devon shook Trevor's hand and hugged Sarah, who offered him something to drink.

"No, thank you, Sarah, I'm fine."

Trevor's impatience was palpable. "Well, what happened? Did you meet Barclay?"

Devon nodded. "I did. I like to look into a person's eyes when I'm talking to them for the first time. In this case, it was important to get a look at the man. His wife stayed home, so it was just the two of us. I insisted he come to my office, which he did."

"How much did you have to pay him?"

"Nothing."

"Nothing? What do you mean?"

"As I said, I need to look into a man's eyes to see what he's made of. This guy looked scared to me. He sounds a lot tougher on the phone, but in person, he looked weak. I told him that I had no intention of paying him a dime, and that if he ever tried to extort money from me again, I'd have him arrested."

"That's it? What did he say, and more to the point, how can we trust him not to come back?"

Devon pulled a small recording device from his pocket. "With this."

He played the recorded conversation for Trevor and Sarah to hear. Barclay admitted that he and his wife didn't really want Noah, but that a million dollars would help them walk away. They threatened to take Trevor to court to get custody of Noah but would look the other way if money were offered. It was all there on tape.

Devon put his hand on Trevor's shoulder. "Son, no judge in the world would give my grandson to these people. If I paid them money, in the court's eyes, I wouldn't be much better than the Barclays. You should have seen his face when I showed him the recorder. After that, I strongly suggested he leave the building before I had him thrown out. You won't be hearing from him ever again; I can promise you that."

Sarah beamed with joy. Trevor hugged his father. "Thank you, Dad. Thank you for everything."

Devon's love for his son and grandson proved to be a harbinger of things to come for the Hutchins family. Sarah watched Trevor and his father mend fences that had been created long ago. The wall of division would crumble over time, and it would be love that made all the difference.

CHAPTER TWENTY-FIVE

The summer months were not only hot, but busier than usual. The Florida heat didn't keep the tourists away. A steady flow of guests at the inn during the hottest months of the year, caught the eye of the local newspaper. An article and review of the Key Lime Garden Inn focused on the history of the property and Rose Johnson Lane. They interviewed Maggie to gather as much information about their friendship and Rose's decision to basically gift the property to her. The article drew interest from Floridians throughout the state and was the reason for several last-minute reservations.

Since many of the inn's guests during the summer months were residents of the state, Maggie decided to put money into advertising in a few of the local papers as well as several coastal living magazines. Five-star ratings were hard to come by, but in little more than one year, the inn had managed such a distinction. Every room had been filled from the start of the summer until the end, and Maggie couldn't have been happier about it.

With the carriage house construction complete, Maggie settled into her new space, spending hours decorating. Paolo decided to sell his home on Sanibel to his sister. Her place was smaller than Paolo's, so she jumped at the opportunity to close on his property right after the wedding.

At least once a week, Chelsea went on a date with Sebastian Barlowe. She had no problem giving Maggie every detail of their time together, and then some. Maggie often had to hold her hands up and yell, "TMI" but she was glad that her best friend had someone to share her life with again.

Maggie's wedding day was fast approaching, and other than keeping the inn's calendar closed to guests that week, there wasn't much to be done. At least that was how Maggie saw things. Chelsea had other ideas.

"Did you call the florist, and the photographer? What about music? And why are you waiting until the last minute?"

Maggie had been so busy with the carriage house and her guests, that a simple wedding on the beach felt like something she could easily throw together with her friend's help.

"No. I didn't call anyone. What's to plan? It's just the family and a few friends. We don't need to go crazy. Paolo already has Sanibellia employees helping out with the flowers. We've got Grace and Riley to prepare the food. We can use a Spotify playlist for the music, and I'm sure everyone at the wedding will be taking pictures with their cell phones, so why do I need a photographer?"

Chelsea rolled her eyes and put her hands on her hips.

"Are you kidding me? You think cell phone photos are the way to go, and Spotify? If I didn't know better, I'd think you were one of the kids planning a pool party."

Maggie's eyes grew big, "Oh, that's a great idea. We could use the pool. We can add extra lights around it."

Chelsea laughed at Maggie. She predicted that the days leading up to the wedding would be full of such revelations. For now, she'd remain the practical one.

"What about your dress? Did you finally decide between the two you showed me?"

Maggie's face lit up. "I did, and it already came in. Do you want to see it?"

"Are you kidding? You know what I'm like at Christmas. Of course, I want to see it, but don't put it on. I want to wait until the wedding day so I can be overwhelmed like everyone else."

Maggie ran to the bedroom closet and came back into the living room carrying a large white box with a champagne-colored ribbon around it. She opened the box and pulled out her dress.

Maggie looked stunning even holding the gown up against her body. The delicate lace halter neckline with front leg slit in the lightest pink complimented her tanned skin. Her cheeks were flush with excitement and made Chelsea's eyes water.

"Oh, Maggie, it's beautiful, and you're going to be beautiful wearing it."

Chelsea couldn't contain her happiness, and jumped up to hug Maggie, crushing her and the dress. "Oh, sorry. I guess you better put that back in the box."

Maggie returned the dress to the closet and suddenly felt hungry.

"What do you think about pizza? I don't want to bother the girls in the kitchen. How about we order one and enjoy it with a nice glass of wine?"

"That sounds like heaven to me. By the way, I really love how you're decorating this place. What does Paolo think of it? Isn't it a bit small for him? I mean, where is his man cave?"

"You've got a good point, Chelsea, because there isn't a man cave, at least not up here. He's already been eyeballing the downstairs area. This building hasn't been used since the late 1960's, and since then only for storage. Most of Paolo's gardening tools are in there. I've no doubt that he'll come up with some way to make it his alone."

Maggie couldn't wait for the day when she and Paolo were finally settled. Soon they'd be living together as husband and wife. *Wife.* Over a year ago that word had a very different meaning for Maggie, and trusting was not how she would define it. Now, knowing how life can change in an instant, she depended on only one thing. Paolo's love for her, and hers for him. Nothing had ever meant so much as that.

Trevor complained to Sarah that his job consumed so much of his time, that even when he left the office, calls into the night continued, leaving little time to do fun things with Noah. Toward the end of August, he brought Noah to the nearby school, to meet the staff there, and to register for fall classes. With little information about his pre-school history, combined with Noah saying he'd never been to school before, Noah would attend kindergarten in the fall. He would be six years old in February, so the age met the placement requirements.

Two houses had already gone up in the housing project, and just as Trevor had predicted, his brother, Clayton, had been welcomed back into the company. Whatever his personal grievances with Trevor, no one could deny Clayton's business savvy.

Trevor did his best to avoid interacting with his brother, but he knew it wasn't a long-term solution to their problems. Clayton seemed unusually subdued, and said little to stir up trouble, but he also didn't apologize to Trevor for his involvement with the Barclays' attempt to extort money from the family. For now, the best they could do, is not cross paths unless absolutely necessary.

The plan to bring the family together, starting with Clayton and Trevor, stalled during the summer, and Trevor remained wary of his brother's motivations. Trevor accepted that healing would take time and left it at that.

Sarah kept her promise to visit Sophia and worked out an arrangement with her foster family to visit twice a month. She wanted more time with Sophia but respected the wishes of the family.

Since placing Sophia with the Gallos', the family brought a three-year old into their home, with plans for one more to join them in the fall. It bothered Sarah to think that the Gallos' would divide their time and attention among three children, instead of Sophia receiving their complete focus, but there was nothing she could do about it.

Content to see Sharon's child when she could, Sarah did what she could to educate herself on adoption policies in the state of Florida. By the time September rolled around, she felt ready to take the necessary hours of training required for anyone planning to adopt a child.

The fact that Sarah was single could make it harder for her to adopt but she would cross that bridge when she came to it. As much as she wanted to talk to Trevor about it, Sarah felt to do so might put pressure on him to propose, and that was the last thing she wanted.

However, just as she had changed her opinion about motherhood, Sarah often daydreamed about being Trevor's wife. She loved everything about him and about the life they were creating. She adored Noah and admitted to being fiercely protective of him.

Tonight, they had plans for a quiet evening alone. Sarah savored moments when Trevor put his work aside and made time to focus on their relationship. Sophia, Noah, and their workloads kept their calendars full, but they kept a weekly date night, which thrilled Sarah.

A delicious Italian dinner at Cibo's in Ft. Myers started their evening, with plans to lay on a blanket under the stars back at the beach. As the waiter filled their wine glasses, they looked over the menu.

Sarah loved Italian food, and Cibo's had an unusual menu item she couldn't resist. "I understand that the chef's mother gets up every morning and makes the ravioli. It's a surprise every day when she creates a unique blend of ingredients. They don't even list it on the menu, instead, the waiter will announce the ravioli of the day. I wonder what tonight's specialty is."

Trevor took a sip of his wine, and then closed his menu. "Well, that's it for me, then. I'm having whatever 'Mama' made this morning."

Sarah reached for Trevor's hand. "I've completed all the adoption hours required, and I've filled out every possible questionnaire they could throw at me. There's nothing left to do at this point."

Trevor squeezed Sarah's hand. "Except adopt Sophia, you mean?"

Sarah nodded, "Yes, except that."

"So, what's the plan? Are you going to adopt her?"

Sarah shrugged. "I'm not sure."

"Why go through all this, to not be sure? What exactly is holding you back?"

Sarah told herself that she didn't plan to have this conversation tonight, but she quickly dispelled that myth. She brought the subject up for a reason, and now that she had, it felt important to continue.

"Trevor, you've never once said how you feel about it one way or another. I know you've been busy with work and Noah, so I've assumed you weren't ready to talk about it. I hate to put it this way, and I'm perfectly willing to be a single mother if necessary, but..."

She wanted to say more, but having gone so far out on a limb, she felt vulnerable and embarrassed.

Trevor looked around the restaurant, as if looking for someone. He slid out of the booth, and walked closer to Sarah, getting on his knee. Now, all eyes were on the two of them.

"Sarah Wheeler, for as long as I've known you, you've been the rock that I've leaned on, my true north. You and I have a solid foundation to build the most beautiful life on. I can't imagine my life without the three of you."

Sarah was never good at math, but in this case, she understood the numbers. "You've never even met Sophia. How do you know…?"

"The same way I knew I couldn't live without Noah the minute I heard I had a son. The same way I knew I'd grow old with you that first day when you called me obnoxious. I already love Sophia because you do. I love her as much as I do Noah, and you. How about you and I get this family started? Say yes. Marry me."

"Yes."

Whistles and applause erupted from every table. Their waiter brought out a bottle of champagne as a gift from the owner.

"This makes the third time this month. Must be something in Mama's ravioli that makes a man get on his knees. Congratulations from all of us at Cibo's."

Trevor reached into his pocket and presented Sarah with a beautiful single oval diamond set in platinum. He placed the ring on her finger and then wiped the tear that fell down her cheek.

"It's beautiful, Trevor. It's exactly what I would have picked. I love it."

Trevor moved into Sarah's side of the booth and pulled her close to him. They kissed which started several attempts by restaurant guests clinking against their glasses for more displays of affection. In time, as guests started to leave their tables, the noise died down, and they enjoyed the rest of their meal in private.

Sarah floated her way through the evening. She couldn't have asked for a better response to adopting Sophia than Trevor had given her. So much had changed over the last six months that she found the old Sarah unrecognizable.

She would always be more than Trevor's wife, and Noah, and Sophia's mother, but nothing compared to the joy she felt when thinking of herself that way. She couldn't wait to share their good news with family and friends. *Her family.* Sarah could hardly believe it herself.

CHAPTER TWENTY-SIX

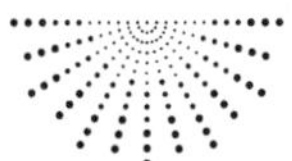

With only a little over a week until the wedding, Maggie had her hands full running the inn. Months earlier she had hired the daughter of the family friend who ran a catamaran business the next street over. Since she only worked part-time she had available hours to help with the laundry and cleaning of the rooms.

Becca Powell grew up on Captiva and had extensive knowledge of the island. In addition to helping keep the inn spotless, she proved to be a wonderful resource for Maggie and her guests. Becca told of Captiva's history and even had a few ghost stories to share, or as Maggie more accurately put it, "scare."

When necessary, Becca would check the new guests in and get them settled, but today, her family needed her to help with taking tourists out on the water. Maggie didn't mind the work. She loved meeting new people and getting details on where they lived and why they chose Captiva as their vacation spot.

A guest book sat on a table near the entrance. Maggie encouraged her guests to fill in any specifics about their stay at the Key Lime Garden Inn. A review of the inn was always welcome, and she thanked anyone who had something kind to say.

Maggie got the room ready just in time before her next guest arrived. A petite woman wearing a business suit and heels walked into the inn as if she had just come out of a business meeting. Nothing about her appearance indicated that this was a person on vacation. Maggie had to assume the woman planned to pitch a business opportunity to her, and stood ready to say, "thank you, but no thank you."

"Hello. Can I help you?"

"Yes, my name is Jen Laurier. I have a reservation."

Maggie smiled, thinking Chelsea would make fun of her mistake.

"Of course. Welcome to the Key Lime Garden Inn. I'm Maggie. Is this your first time visiting Captiva Island?"

"Yes it is."

Ms. Laurier was a woman of few words, and Maggie could already tell she didn't want to answer any questions.

"Do you need help with your luggage?"

The woman lifted a small overnight bag, carried on her shoulder. "No, thank you. I have everything I need right in here."

"Great. Let me get you your key and we can go upstairs to your room. Where are you coming from?"

"Massachusetts. Chatham to be exact."

"Oh, I love Chatham. I'm from Massachusetts myself. I lived in Andover for most of my life, but then came to Captiva about eighteen months ago to open the inn."

Maggie had become used to her guests' sharing stories about life back home, but something felt strange about this woman who traveled to Captiva, alone and with no desire to talk. Fearing she would irritate her guest, Maggie stopped asking questions, and let the woman settle in. If Jen Laurier wanted to talk, Maggie assumed she'd let her know. Until then, she'd leave the woman in peace.

"I love this room. If you open the windows, the breeze flows through and you can hear the ocean waves. This is one of the few rooms with its own bathroom. There is a card on the table with everything you need to know about the inn and the island. You're welcome to the kitchen any time, but we have set times for breakfast, lunch and dinner, if there is a need. Otherwise, consider the inn your home away from home while you're here, and if there's anything you need, please let us know. There's always someone downstairs that you can contact. Paolo and Ciara, as well as our chefs Riley and Grace and our housekeeper Becca can help you with whatever you require. All that information is on the card."

Patiently waiting for Maggie to leave, Jen nodded and thanked her. Maggie closed the door behind her when she left. Curious whether she might hear from the woman during her stay, she'd check with everyone else to get their take on Ms. Laurier.

Something about the woman made Maggie uneasy. She couldn't put her finger on it, but she felt certain two minutes in the room with Chelsea, and Jen Laurier's life would be an open book. Since her guest was here for three nights, she had plenty of time to get the two women together in the same room. She made a mental note to talk to Chelsea about it.

Maggie's family would arrive a few days before the wedding, but her lunch-bunch friends insisted they come down the week before to "help out." The inn's only guest was Jen Laurier, and she'd be gone in a few days. Otherwise, the rooms at the inn had finally been free for family members. A few rooms at the inn, coupled with two additional rooms at Chelsea's, and there was plenty of space for her friends and family.

Sarah stopped by to check on her mother and see if she needed anything. It took several attempts at flashing her new diamond in front of Maggie's face before her mother noticed.

When she did, she screamed. "Oh, my goodness, Sarah. When did this happen?"

"Last night. We went to Cibo's for dinner, and he proposed. He got down on one knee and everything. That's not all, though."

"What do you mean, that's not all?"

"How do you feel about being a grandmother again? Trevor and I are going to adopt Sophia."

Maggie put her hands to her face and started to cry. Though muffled, Maggie said what she had felt all along. "I knew it. I knew that little baby was going to be my granddaughter."

Maggie hugged Sarah and the two women laughed through their tears. "When is all this happening?"

"Good question. We're not exactly sure. There is so much we have to look into and people to talk to. We decided not to tell Noah until everything is in place with Sophia. I've taken the adoption course, but Trevor hasn't, so he'll have to go through that. We've made an appointment with the social worker to talk about next steps. We're very lucky that Sharon wrote the letter describing her wish that I adopt Sophia. Ms. Carpenter said it will go a long way in helping us adopt her."

"Sarah, honey, I'm so happy for you."

Sheepishly, Sarah had to admit her mother had been right all along. "Remember how you said that when the right person came along, I wouldn't be afraid to marry and have children?"

Maggie laughed at her daughter's memory. "Actually, that was your grandmother, but I agreed with her. I always felt you needed to make peace with all that. Not everyone should be married, or have children, and I was perfectly willing to accept that if it was truly what you wanted. Life has a funny way of throwing things in our path when we least expect it. By the way, there's something I've been meaning to ask you. I have a request."

"A request?"

Maggie took her daughter's hand in hers. "Yes. Would you be my maid of honor?"

"Oh, Mom. I thought maybe you'd ask Chelsea, being your best friend and all."

Maggie nodded and put her hand to her heart. "Chelsea is my best friend, but you're my heart. Nothing would make me happier than to have you standing beside me."

Once again the tears welled in Sarah's eyes and Maggie beamed with pride at her daughter. She was proud of all her children, but Sarah had walked life's journey with her these last eighteen months, and that bond meant everything to Maggie.

"I'd be honored, Mom."

"Wonderful. How about we have a cup of my famous tea to celebrate?"

Sarah laughed, "I wondered how long before you suggested tea."

"We've got to keep traditions in place so that you can do the same for your daughter one day."

Maggie couldn't believe that Sarah soon would be a mother. It was a dream come true for everyone, but secretly for Maggie, who worried she had done something wrong in her raising of Sarah to make her so fearful of marriage and motherhood. As silly as it sounded, she blamed herself and Daniel for Sarah's choices. She kept that to herself, but now could see that she needn't have worried. Sarah found her life by listening to her heart, and that was exactly what Maggie had prayed for all these months.

~

Maggie walked over to Chelsea's house after Sarah left. She couldn't wait to share Sarah's news with her.

"Oh, Maggie, that's fantastic. I had a feeling this would happen. All these months learning about adoption. Her visits to the Gallos' to check up on how Sophia was doing. You must have suspected it, didn't you?"

Maggie nodded. "Let's just say, I hoped. I'm just so thrilled that Trevor is on board with the whole thing. I think from the moment he met Sarah he knew she was the one. Noah and Sophia are icing on the cake—a ready-made family. Everything is falling into place."

"You do realize, Maggie dear, that as soon as you say that you jinx things."

"Chelsea! Don't say that. What makes you think anything will go wrong?"

"I didn't say that. I'm just reminding you that the quiet is about to fade into the nether. Have you forgotten what day it is?"

"I haven't forgotten. What time are the lunch-bunch ladies arriving?"

"Their flight gets in around two o'clock. They're renting a van. I'd say by three-thirty they should be here. We'll probably hear them the minute they cross the bridge. They can be a rowdy bunch."

Maggie laughed at the thought of their friends on a "girls' trip." With Jane as the ringleader, anything could happen. There would be tons of laughter and fun in the days leading up to the wedding. Already, Chelsea had been acting giddy at any talk of romance. Maggie made fun of her friend, who was a walking Hallmark Channel.

"You'd think you were the one getting married. By the way, is that in the cards with you and Sebastian, or is this just a dating/companionship thing?"

"Well, since you're the beacon by which I judge all things possible, I'd say, anything can happen, but I'm happy with things the way they are for now. He's my plus one whenever I get an invitation and I'm his."

Maggie winked at Chelsea. "I only ask because I want to torture you about getting married again, just the way you did to me all these months."

"Very funny. I promise you, if the day comes that Mr. Barlowe asks me to marry him, I'm going to tell him I need to talk to my best friend before I can answer him. By then, you'll have been married for a while and can tell me how it's going. In the meantime, let's focus on your big day. Is there anything you need me to do?"

"The rooms are ready. I don't think anyone will have to stay at your place unless they'd prefer to. Between the rooms here and the carriage house, we should be all set. I've still got one guest but she's leaving day after tomorrow. When she goes, whoever is in the carriage house with me can move to the main house. That way, Sarah and I will be the only ones in there getting ready the day of the wedding."

"Only one guest, not two?"

"I know. I don't usually have a single guest but she's on her own for some reason. She's from Chatham, Massachusetts. There's something mysterious about her. I'm not sure why I say that, but..."

"You get a weird vibe?"

"Honestly, I don't know what it is. She's probably here to get away from the stresses in her life. I can relate. It wasn't that long ago when I came to Captiva to get away from things I didn't want to think about."

"Yes. If I remember correctly, a very wise best friend dragged you down here. She's pretty smart, that woman."

Wrapping her arms around Chelsea, Maggie whispered, "She's the best."

CHAPTER TWENTY-SEVEN

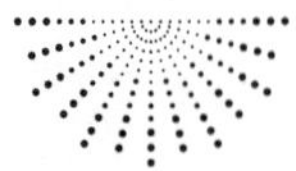

Trevor dropped Noah off at school, and then drove into work. He savored these early mornings with his son, but wished he had more time with Noah. The demands of his job had become a burden, and he wondered how he might better adjust his days around his son's needs. He had little time to talk with Noah's teachers, and Debbie, Noah's nanny, although helpful, was no replacement for a parent.

He'd spent countless hours thinking about the way his world had changed this past year. More than once, he found himself unrecognizable as he stared at the man in the mirror. No one demanded he cut his long hair, but everything under his chin looked like it belonged to someone else. How did he get here, he wondered?

He remembered his mother's words, "*You won't be helping Noah if you're unhappy.*" Soon, he'd be a husband and father to two children. He felt like his life was taking shape without his approval. Everything had moved so fast he didn't have time to think whether he was doing the right thing or the adult thing. After all, those two things went hand in hand, didn't they?

Pulling his car into his reserved parking spot, he took a deep breath and pushed his worries aside. He had a job to do, and he needed to stay focused on his work if he wanted to make the project a success.

He climbed the stairs to the main reception area, and when he looked down the hall, he could see Clayton in his office. Their relationship still on shaky ground, they did little to make things better. More than once, Trevor thought about approaching his brother, but hated the thought of another confrontation.

Walking toward his office, Trevor stopped, and turned around. He'd try one more time, and if nothing came of their meeting, he'd let Clayton come to him. He walked into his brother's office, and stood near the door, waiting for Clayton to acknowledge him.

"What's this? Have you lost your way to your office?"

Trevor closed the door and sat in a chair directly in front of Clayton's desk. "I thought maybe we could talk."

Clayton threw his pen down and sat back in his chair. "It must be something big for you to come in here. What do you want to talk about, or have I done something wrong?"

"How about we stop with the defensive rhetoric? I'm not here to fight with you. I'd like us to find a way to get along. Maybe even like each other again."

Clayton laughed and got up from his desk and looked out the window. "When did we last like each other, Trevor? Remind me because I can't remember when that was."

"How about we start by you telling me exactly what I've done to make you hate me so much? I remember when we were kids, you actually looked up to me. Did you forget all those times when you wanted to hang with me and my friends? You copied everything I did. What about those days? Did I imagine all that? What happened to that little kid who worshipped the ground I walked on?"

Clayton turned away from the window and faced Trevor. "I remember that little boy. I remember how he wanted to be just like you. Do you have any idea why that was? That's the part you don't get. If I wanted to be like you it was because our father loved you more. I figured if I did everything that you did, even wear the same clothes, and styled my hair the same way, he'd love me as much as he loved you."

Trevor sat motionless and felt his brother's pain for the first time. He never understood where the anger came from, and how far back in their lives it went. More than anything, he wanted to undo the damage their father had done.

"Clayton, what Dad did was terrible. I've always taken issue with the way he treated all of us, even Mom. Maybe in your eyes he loved me more, but I've never felt it. Not once. Is it possible that you and I suffered the same loss? I'd love nothing more than to fix this, but I can't do it alone. Dad and I have come to an understanding about some of this, but it's going to take time. If you and I are ever going to get past this, we're both going to have to work on it."

After taking a bottle of water from the refrigerator, Clayton held one up for Trevor. Trevor nodded, and Clayton threw the bottle to him. He walked back to his desk, took a swig of his water, and sat back in his chair.

"Did you know that I wanted your job?"

"What?"

"I did. Dad knew it, too. As a matter of fact, before you came home he had given me the job. They even put together advertising materials ready for distribution announcing my involvement with the new affordable housing project. It all got scrubbed the minute you walked into Dad's study. When you walked out of the house that day his mind went into overdrive, plotting and planning how he would pull you back into the family. You just made it easy for him with your need to create a stable home for your son."

"Clayton, I had no idea. I promise you, I knew nothing of this."

Clayton nodded. "I know. It doesn't change the fact that once again I got pushed aside in favor of you—his favorite son."

In that moment something clicked for Trevor. He had been played by his father once again. Whatever motivation he had for giving him the job, he still couldn't see the pain he had caused Clayton. If it continued, Devon's inability to empathize with anyone would crush this family forever.

"This has to stop. He has to understand what he's doing. I won't let him divide this family anymore."

Clayton shook his head. "You can't make him change, Trevor. This is who he is."

"I get that, but that's not what I'm thinking. This firm will survive Devon Hutchins. You and I will make certain of that."

"How are *we* going to accomplish this?"

"We're going to talk to our father, right now. Come with me."

Trevor and Clayton walked together, for the first time having a singular purpose. For Trevor, it felt good, but whether Clayton felt the same bond, they were about to find out.

Devon Hutchins was alone in his office. Trevor had timed this meeting perfectly. His father looked up when he saw his two sons standing before him.

"Well, what miraculous event managed to get the two of you in the same room together?"

Trevor spoke first. "You, Dad. You are what has brought us together. I should have predicted this actually, but the truth is I didn't see it coming. Just today, Clayton and I realized we have more in common than we thought."

Trevor didn't think it possible, but his father seemed uncomfortable in his chair.

"Why didn't you tell me that you first gave my job to Clayton?"

Devon looked at Clayton, and then back at Trevor.

"It was preliminary. We were going to throw the idea on the wall to see if it stuck—it didn't. We went another way."

"Don't give me that. Everyone knew he was the right person for the job, even you. He'd already been involved with the project from its inception. That all changed when I came knocking on your door. The ultimate plan to get me back into the company, and under your control. But this time you had a willing participant. You knew I was desperate to give Noah a stable environment, complete with an extended family. You used me, and you did it at the expense of your other son. And you didn't even blink an eye."

Red-faced, Devon's anger came to the surface. His voice raising, "What exactly would you like me to do about it?"

Trevor knew when he walked into his father's office what the answer was. Months of struggle and worry over his job, knowing he didn't belong behind a desk, lifted from his shoulders. He could finally breathe.

"Give Clayton his job back. You and I both know that he's the right person for this project. I've done everything I can to try to fit into a position I'm not designed for. I'm never going to be the guy behind the desk; I've tried, but it's not me. It never was, and you've known that all along, haven't you?"

"Son, you need to think of Noah."

Trevor wouldn't let Devon continue, "Stop trying to manipulate me. It won't work. Listen, Dad. I'm not saying that I want to leave the company. The truth is, that I think there is room for both Clayton and me. I'm sure between the two of us, Clayton and I can work something out. I know where my strengths are, and I plan to focus on that. I'm a community organizer at my core. He and I will figure out what my role will be, but you are going to let us take control of this project completely. Let the next generation run this place as a true family business."

Clayton agreed with Trevor, "He's right, Dad. This company

will thrive under our direction. Quite frankly, I think Trevor and I make a formidable pair."

Trevor turned and looked at his brother who smiled at him. Years of anger and resentment melted away. Trevor knew there would be adjustments and compromises, but it felt good to know that for the first time since returning home, he was proud of the Hutchins name.

CHAPTER TWENTY-EIGHT

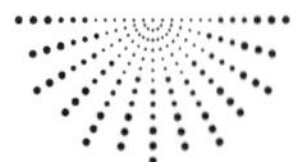

Maggie and Chelsea sat on the porch waiting for the lunch-bunch ladies to arrive. The van pulled up in front of the Key Lime Garden Inn at precisely four o'clock in the afternoon. Squeals of laughter and screams poured out of the van along with the women. Maggie raced to greet everyone, with Chelsea following closely behind her.

"Yay! I'm so excited. You made it."

Diana helped Rachel out of the van first. With only three weeks to go before her baby's due date, Maggie marveled that Rachel made the trip at all.

"My goodness, Rachel, you look like you're ready to deliver any minute. How in the world did your doctor let you fly?"

"He didn't. He doesn't know. I wouldn't miss this trip for anything. I had to come."

Typical Chelsea couldn't ignore Jane's new look. "I see there's been a visit to Dr. Campbell. Honestly, Jane, if you keep this up, we're not going to recognize you anymore."

"Oh, for heaven's sake, Chelsea, what's wrong with wanting to look my best? It's just a little Botox here and there. It wouldn't hurt you to try it."

Maggie interrupted the two before they got into an argument. "Now, ladies, enough with the plastic surgery talk. We're perfect just the way we are."

Kelly and Diana teased Maggie, "Maggie, dear, you're the only one of us who looks perfect. Look at that tan. Florida living seems to agree with you."

Paolo and Ciara came out of the house, and Maggie called them to join the group.

"Everyone, this is Paolo and his sister Ciara."

Jane clapped her hands. "Woohoo! We finally get to meet the groom."

The women swarmed around Paolo as Maggie made the introductions. Pulling him out from their clutches, Maggie put her arm through his. "What do you think of my friends, aren't they beautiful?"

Paolo seemed a bit overwhelmed by all the attention, but Maggie could tell he was happy for her. As much as Maggie loved her life in Florida, she missed her family and friends back home in Massachusetts. It meant the world to her that her friends traveled to Captiva to be with her on her wedding day.

"Why don't I give you all a tour of the place? Let's get your suitcases put up in your rooms. I do have one guest staying here, but she'll be leaving the day after tomorrow. Otherwise, we've got the entire inn all to ourselves."

Paolo helped carry the luggage into the house and placed them in the front hallway until the women were ready to come back inside. Chelsea walked back to her place to get dinner ready, leaving Maggie to give her friends a quick tour of the property, starting with the garden.

Rachel's ankles were swollen, and she needed to sit so Maggie walked her to the gazebo.

"Maggie, I'm sorry you've got a whale to deal with this week. I'll do my best not to be a burden, but if you see me waddling around looking for a chair, just swoop down and put one under me. I'll be fine."

"I love you, silly, and you are not a burden. Whatever you need, you let me know."

Maggie returned to the garden and guided the women from the garden to the carriage house, and then inside the main house. Telling them all about Rose and the history of the inn, Maggie felt proud that she had fulfilled Rose's wishes to restore the inn, and it showed. Diana was first to recognize Maggie's accomplishment. "You've done an amazing job with this place, Maggie. It's truly beautiful, and the gardens are gorgeous."

"Well, I've got Paolo to thank for that. Not to mention all the construction on the carriage house. I couldn't have done any of it without him."

"I'm going to get Rachel so she can unpack. Paolo and Ciara will help you all get your belongings into your rooms. Take a minute to freshen up if you'd like, and then we all can walk over to Chelsea's. Oh, wait, Paolo, I don't think Rachel should walk, would you mind giving her a ride?"

"No problem. I'll pull the car in front of the van. When you're ready to leave, just let me know."

Jen Laurier walked up the driveway. Maggie met her on the porch.

"Did you have a nice day, Ms. Laurier?"

"Yes. I spent a few hours on the beach."

"Well, you had a lovely day for it. Not a cloud in the sky."

The woman had a small plastic pail which she'd filled with seashells.

"I see you found our seashells. Captiva and Sanibel are known for them. I've collected more than a few over the years. Some, have more significance for me than others, but they're all beautiful to me."

Jen looked into Maggie's eyes and started to talk but stopped herself. It wasn't the first time that had happened since the woman checked into the inn.

"You know, Ms. Laurier, I came to Captiva right after my husband died. We'd gone through a lot over the years, and we never got the chance to say goodbye before he died. You can tell me to mind my own business if you want, and I know you're not here for a long time, but I'm a good listener, if you ever feel that you'd like to talk."

Jen nodded and started to walk away. She stopped and turned back to Maggie.

"I'd like that. When?"

"Well, my friends and I have a dinner to go to, so we'll be home rather late. Why don't we try for some time tomorrow?"

"Thank you. That would be great. I'll see you tomorrow then. Good night."

Maggie smiled, thinking that she might have met someone on the same path that she traveled only eighteen months ago. If she could make a difference sharing her experience with Jen, perhaps it would give the woman a comfort knowing she's not alone. Maggie looked forward to hearing what Jen had to say.

When everyone had unpacked and freshened up, they met out on the porch. Maggie found Ciara and Becca getting ready to leave for the day. "Why don't you ladies join us over at Chelsea's?"

Becca slung her backpack over her shoulders, "Thanks, Ms. Wheeler, but I've got a date tonight. Correction—blind date. I'm sure it will be a disaster, but I promised I'd meet the guy."

"You never know where these things can lead, Becca. Keep an open mind and have a good time. Ciara? What about you?"

"That's sweet, thank you, Maggie, but I've got a few things to do myself. Besides, something tells me it wouldn't be as much fun for me as it's going to be for you. You and your friends must have a million stories from your lives back in Massachusetts. Although, it would be fun hearing about them. You go on and have a good time. I'll see you tomorrow."

Paolo helped Rachel into his car, and Maggie gathered the lunch-bunch crew and headed out to Chelsea's home. As they walked, Maggie talked about her many visits to Captiva, pointing out various landmarks along the way.

Kelly stopped to take pictures of every flower she encountered. "Honestly, Maggie, I'm surprised you and Daniel came back to Massachusetts at all after visiting this place."

Maggie laughed at Kelly's suggestion. She had no idea just how close Daniel came to doing just that. There were moments when she allowed herself to reminisce about their past trips to the island. She compartmentalized those memories since she moved to Captiva permanently. They lived in a box with a neatly tied ribbon around it. She allowed herself moments here and there to take that box out and view its contents, but today was not one of those moments. Today was all about creating new memories with her dearest friends.

Rachel and Paolo waited for them at the foot of Chelsea's driveway.

Looking up at Chelsea's house, Diana's eyes widened. "Now this is the kind of place I'd buy if I lived here. I love all the pastel colors."

Paolo gave Maggie a kiss, and waved goodbye to the women. "Have fun, ladies." Then, whispering to Maggie, "I'll be back at the carriage house. I'm still trying to figure out what to do with that downstairs space."

Chelsea waved everyone inside. "Let's go, ladies. Key Limetinis await."

Jane couldn't get up the stairs fast enough. "I've never heard of it, but it sounds delicious."

Maggie and Rachel slowly walked up the stairs together.

"Chelsea invented it when I first moved down here. She calls it Key Lime Garden Inn's signature drink."

Rachel rubbed her lower back and found a chair to rest her legs. "No Key Lime-tini for me unfortunately."

Chelsea poured an iced-tea and brought it to Rachel. "Here you go. Not as exciting, but still, something to toast the bride. How about you follow me to the table?"

Everyone walked into the dining room. The white fabric-covered chairs had been placed around a table with a light pink table runner and coordinating place mats and napkins. A key-lime-green charger sat under each table setting with napkin rings of the same color.

"Oh, Chelsea, the table looks beautiful. I can't believe you went to all this trouble for me."

"Don't be silly, I eat this way all the time."

Everyone laughed, and Maggie hugged her friend. "Well, thank you, anyway."

Chelsea raised her glass, "To Maggie. The brightest light in our group. No one deserves to be happy more than you, my friend. If I could have wished for the very best life for you, I couldn't have picked a better place, a better life, and a better love than Paolo. Here is to all the love and laughter, now and forever more."

Jane, Rachel, Kelly, and Diana raised their glasses and in unison said, "To Maggie."

Maggie couldn't keep the tears from forming. "You guys are making me cry. Thank you all for flying down to be with me this week. I love you all so much."

Jane took a sip of her drink. "Are you kidding? We had to see your little slice of heaven in person. You and Chelsea might be stuck with us this week, but you can bet, we're coming back, and often. And, Chelsea, what the heck is in this drink? It's fantastic."

Chelsea finished her drink and poured another into her glass. "Sorry, ladies, it's a Key Lime Garden Inn secret."

CHAPTER TWENTY-NINE

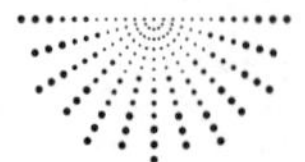

The evening at Chelsea's turned out to be a walk down memory lane. The women couldn't stop cackling, and Rachel laughed so hard she had to run to the bathroom at least a half-dozen times. When they were ready to head back to the inn, Maggie thought about calling Paolo to take Rachel back by car, but Rachel declined.

"I'm fine, Maggie. I could use a little fresh air, and so can everyone else I might add. That is, if they can stand up for any length of time. Whatever Chelsea put in those Key Lime-tinis must have been pretty strong."

Maggie wondered whether letting the women sleep at Chelsea's wouldn't be better. "Before we head back, what's the plan for tomorrow?"

Chelsea answered, "I thought I'd take everyone shopping and sightseeing on both Captiva and Sanibel. We can hit all the spots, with a dip in the ocean when we get back. How about you? Will you join us?"

"I've got so much to do tomorrow, Chelsea. How about we all meet at the inn when you get back? We can sit around the pool and relax or go to the beach. What about tomorrow night? I think it would be great to get together somewhere for dinner. Maybe Sarah, Trevor, Paolo, and Ciara can join us?"

Jane had more to drink than any of the other women and looked Maggie in the eye. "No can do, Maggs. Tomorrow night is the big night. It's your Bachelorette Party, don't forget."

"Jane! Nice going." Chelsea wasn't happy.

Kelly and Diana still had their wits about them and joined Chelsea in admonishing Jane. "Seriously, Jane?"

"What did I say?" Jane's drinking had not only wiped out the memory of Maggie's party being a secret, but she also apparently had no embarrassment about her mistake.

"Oh, Maggs doesn't care. She never liked surprises anyway."

Maggie laughed at her friends, and Chelsea did her best to explain. "Sorry, Maggie. You might as well know that we want to take you to that club on Ft. Myers beach. You know the one under the bridge with all the flashing blue lights? We thought we'd all go out for dinner at Doc Ford's first, and then for music and dancing after. Paolo knows about it and even offered to drive the van, but I told him no. So, you can expect the limo to pull up to the inn at seven o'clock."

Maggie couldn't believe what her friends had in store for tomorrow night. "Chelsea, we're not in our twenties. I don't know about you, but my days of partying at some club are over."

Chelsea wouldn't hear another word from Maggie. "Sorry, my friend, but I beg to differ. We're hardly old, and I have every intention of wiggling my behind on that dance floor. If you think your partying days are over, that's fine. You can consider tomorrow night your last hurrah. You're going and that's the end of it."

Maggie had no choice but to concede. "Ok. I'm in. Let's do this."

As excited as the women were about the bachelorette party,

they were too tired to pump fists about it. Maggie took control of the group and insisted everyone call it a night. Rachel wasn't the only one to walk slowly back to the inn. Maggie smiled thinking that if a few drinks were enough to exhaust her friends, there was little hope tomorrow night's party would get too out of hand.

~

As everyone trudged off to bed, Maggie checked on Paolo who had already gone to bed, and then decided to write in her journal, and also to read for a while.

She had filled a bookcase with Rose's books and journals, as well as several fiction books she promised herself she would read when she had more time. Maggie made a mental note to initiate a new habit of writing and reading before bed. It relaxed her, and helped her to take stock of her days, and find gratitude in her blessings.

She detailed her friends' visit to the island, and the dinner they shared. She wrote about her excitement about getting married in a few days, and the wonderful events in Sarah's life. When she finished writing in her journal, she took the last of Rose's journals and began to read from where she last left off.

December 28, 1974

These last few weeks, living in the house alone with my thoughts, I struggle to know how to proceed. Robert has given me very little choice but to consider divorce. Christmas came and went, and except for the celebrations on the island, there were little decorations on the house. Why bother? I have nothing to celebrate. Robert called to say Merry Christmas, and that he was worried I might be struggling during the holiday. He said he was having a difficult time as well. What does that mean? How am I supposed to feel sorry for him when I can barely get out of bed?

January 4, 1975

Robert sent me a letter asking for my forgiveness. What could he be thinking? I've read the letter several times, and even considered writing him back, but decided against it in the end. I'm much happier writing in my journal. At least there are no consequences for my words. I can say whatever I want to say in these pages, and no one can hear me.

I've put the letter away. I can't look at it anymore. Forgiveness? What is that? Should I forgive him for ripping my heart from my body? Should I accept his apology for letting my tears run so often that my eyes are dry? Can there be forgiveness when everything I believed in has been a lie? I have nothing left. Only my voice, a voice that shouts in the void, one that only I can hear.

If Robert wrote Rose a letter, Maggie couldn't find it anywhere. She assumed it must be tucked into the pages of one of Rose's journals. She opened every one, flipping through the pages, hoping an envelope would fall out, but nothing. She put the journals back on the shelf and looked over all the books that once belonged to Rose. Nothing about the books gave a clue as to the letter's whereabouts.

Maggie took every book from the shelf, opened each one and turned them upside down to wiggle the pages. An envelope addressed to Rose Johnson Lane from Robert Lane fell from a book entitled, *Seven Gothic Tales*, a book of short stories, written by Isak Dinesen in 1934.

Maggie pulled the letter out from the envelope and opened it.

Dearest Rose,

How do I begin to explain the irrational thinking of a man in times like these? That's the best way to describe the out of body experience that has been my existence these last few months. I feel somewhat possessed, as if my thoughts aren't my own. Regardless, my actions certainly are, and I make no excuse for the way I've treated you and our marriage.

When my heart hurts so much from knowing what I've done, I turn to my favorite thing, reading. I suppose I could fall into drinking or gambling or some other habit that could destroy me but reading brings me to a place no other behavior can. When I can't bring myself to say the words that plague me night and day, I look for others in books.

Without the ocean near me, I feel lost. Remember how we always talked about the healing properties of the sea? How whatever we struggled with, a walk on the beach cured what ailed us? I was reading a book recently by Isak Dinesen. Seven Gothic Tales is a book of short stories and one of the stories is titled: The Deluge at Norderney. These words jumped out at me:

"I know of a Cure for Everything: Salt Water...Sweat, or Tears, or the Salt Sea."

That is how I feel being away from you and our beach. Untethered, and without your love, I am nothing. I don't know if you can forgive me, but please consider it. I know it will take time for us to get back to where we were before, and maybe even if that's not possible, perhaps we can find a new beginning.

I don't think I can go on without your forgiveness. I will, of course, accept whatever you decide, but if my fate is in your hands, please know that my heart is as well.

Yours always,
Robert

Maggie could almost see Rose's tearful expression reading this letter. She knew that at some point, although not exactly when, Rose did forgive Robert. They grew old together, and she loved that flawed man until her death.

Maggie picked up the book and searched for the words Robert referenced in his letter. She found them, and putting the letter back in the envelope, placed it between the pages.

Rose never threw the letter away, and Maggie wondered how many times after her journal entry, did Rose re-read it. Knowing her friend, Maggie felt certain that as soon as Rose decided to forgive her husband, she never laid eyes on the letter again.

CHAPTER THIRTY

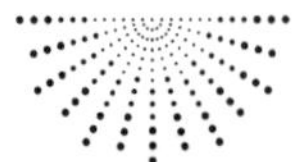

The next morning, Maggie and Paolo kept their early morning date, enjoying the sunrise on the beach.

Maggie slipped her arm in Paolo's and leaned into him. "Can you believe we'll be husband and wife in a just a few days?"

Paolo kissed the top of Maggie's head. "I'm excited to start the rest of our lives together, how about you?"

Maggie smiled and opened her arms, reaching to the sky. "I feel like I could fly." She twirled on the sand and kicked the water under her feet. "How is that for an answer?"

Running back into Paolo's arms, she couldn't believe how blessed her life was. "We're very lucky, Paolo. I don't ever want to take it for granted."

Paolo assured her, "We won't, I promise you. We've got much to be grateful for. By the way, we've not had a very important discussion."

"Important? How so? I'm certain we've got everything covered, and trust me, whatever we think we've forgotten, Chelsea's already taken care of it."

"How about our honeymoon? Did she take care of that?"

"Oh, my goodness, I hadn't thought about it. I figured since we live in paradise, there wasn't much sense in traveling anywhere else. What have you got in mind?"

"How about Italy?"

Maggie dug her feet in the sand. "Italy? Do you have any idea how long I've wanted to go there?"

Paolo smiled. "I do believe I've heard something about that once or twice. I'd love for you to meet my family in Gaeta. I hope you don't mind, but I feel it necessary to visit my mother since her health has deteriorated in the last few months. If I don't see her soon, I may never get another chance."

"Of course. We must go. I'm sure everyone can take care of things here. I bet Chelsea would love to help too. I'll ask her. How long do you think we'll be gone?"

"How does three weeks sound? There's so much of my country I want to show you. I'll get the tickets if you say yes."

"Absolutely, yes!"

Maggie couldn't imagine a more perfect honeymoon for them. There'd be no need to hire a tour guide or worry that she didn't know how to speak Italian. The added bonus would be a chance to meet Paolo's family, and to explore his world.

"Everything sounds wonderful, Paolo. Let's head back. I expect the others will be up and ready for breakfast soon. Also, I promised my guest, Jen, that I'd spend a bit of time with her today."

"About what?"

"I'm not sure, exactly. I think she just needs a woman to talk to. She's here alone and probably wants to ask questions about the island. Riley said she'd take the scones out of the oven. They must be ready by now."

They walked back to the inn and could smell the scones as soon as they reached the driveway. Jen Laurier was sitting on the porch swing, drinking her coffee, enjoying the early morning quiet.

"Did you see that sunrise?" Maggie asked her.

"I did. I'm glad I didn't sleep in."

"Can I get you anything? We have fresh baked scones that are probably cooling on the rack. Nothing better than warm scones right out of the oven."

Paolo excused himself, and left Maggie and Jen to talk.

"Is this a good time to talk, Ms. Wheeler?"

"Please, call me Maggie."

Maggie admired Jen's beauty. She had long, wavy light-brown hair, and her skin looked like it had never been in the sun. She had green eyes and long lashes that were free of mascara. She dressed in a relaxed white linen sleeveless summer tunic with pants and wore a turquoise and sterling silver necklace. Her earrings matched, with the exception of a small red coral stone in the middle. It reminded her of…of…

Maggie quickly got up from the swing and walked to the porch railing. The turn of her stomach, and panic in her chest, kept her from hearing Jen's words. She felt sick and thought she would vomit. She took deep breaths and steadied herself before turning to face the woman.

Jen Laurier. Maggie understood everything now. She knew in her gut that Jen was the woman Daniel was in love with when he died. He destroyed their marriage because of the woman sitting on her porch swing.

Maggie finally heard Jen's voice. "How did you know?"

"Your earrings. Daniel gave me those exact earrings a couple of months before he died…before he walked out on me…for you."

Feeling faint, Maggie leaned against the railing. "Why are you here? What do you want?"

Jen took a deep breath, and said one word, "Forgiveness."

Regaining her strength, Maggie felt anger. Anger at the gall of this woman to come to her home. Maggie couldn't stand the thought of Jen Laurier sleeping in her house, eating food from her kitchen, and drinking her coffee.

"Take your things and get out. Don't ever come back. Your money will be refunded to you, but I never want to see your face again."

Maggie couldn't believe Jen had the nerve to look shocked, as if Maggie had been unkind and unnecessarily cruel. Jen didn't move from the chair.

Maggie walked to the porch door and opened it. Facing the garden, she left no room for discussion.

Before leaving, the woman said the only thing she could.

"I know you don't believe me, but I'm truly sorry."

Jen walked inside and up to her room. She gathered her things, ran down the stairs and out the front door, driving as fast as she could off the property.

Maggie stayed on the back porch until the trees swaying on the side of the house were the only sound she could hear. Once Jen was gone, she ran up the stairs to the guest room. Pulling the sheets off the bed, she threw them on the floor. She removed the duvet cover and pillowcases and added them to the pile. She walked into the bathroom and pulled the shower curtain off the rod. Soaps and coat hangers were next, and before long, the room looked as it did before she decorated it months ago.

Maggie carried the collected items to the trash barrel and stuffed them down so far, she couldn't see them without bending to look inside. She wanted no evidence of Jen Laurier, and until she found a way to get her out of her mind, she'd at least keep from looking at anything that reminded her of the woman. She'd start today by joining her friends on their tour of the two islands. But first, she'd have to seek out Ciara and ask her to do her a very important decorating favor.

~

Chelsea wore the cutest Lilly Pulitzer dress and sandals; a summer striped tote over her shoulder, she looked like a tourist herself.

"Captiva and Sanibel tour guide at your service."

Maggie remembered the day Daniel died. Her lunch-bunch friends had gathered at her house only two days after he'd asked her for a divorce. Convinced if she could get through that day, she'd be strong enough to withstand anything. She smiled at her friend and pretended the moments with Daniel's mistress never happened.

"I'm going with you all."

Chelsea clapped her hands. "Fantastic. Now, where is everyone?"

Just then, Diana walked into the kitchen.

"I don't remember the last time I slept this late. That's the only drawback to owning a bakery—no sleep. I need coffee."

Soon the others stirred from the second floor, finally making it down to the kitchen. Diana leaned over the warm scones and breathed in the aroma.

"Too bad you don't still live in Massachusetts, Maggie, because I'd sell these at the bakery."

Taking charge, Chelsea stood at the doorway. "All right, ladies, finish your breakfast. We've got a big day ahead. You can take your scones and coffee with you. Maggie, you've got to-go cups, right?"

Maggie got busy pouring coffee and packaging up the scones.

Chelsea directed the women.

"Everyone, fix your coffee the way you like it, and let's get this show on the road."

One-by-one, the women packed up their breakfast and headed to the van. Chelsea being Chelsea, she had fun tapping each woman on the head as they passed. "One...Two...Three... Four...Five."

Walking slower than the rest, Rachel was the last to pile into the van. Maggie wondered how the pregnancy would impact Rachel's ability to walk very far. "How you are you doing, honey?"

"Oh, I'm fine. Don't worry about me. Just consider that there are five women and a beached whale in the car. I'll fit right in when we hang out at the beach tomorrow."

Maggie laughed and felt grateful for these women. They'd been with her through so much already, she'd keep the latest drama from them, and remind herself that Jen Laurier had no power over her. Maggie had already made peace with the past. This was just a blip, something to be ignored and forgotten. Nothing would spoil her time with her friends. She had much to be grateful for and lots to celebrate. Nothing was going to ruin her wedding, especially not Daniel's mistress.

~

Maggie stood in front of the mirror and put her hands to her face. Chelsea watched Maggie's reaction and Kelly patted Chelsea on the back. "You did good, Chelsea. She looks great."

"Doesn't she?"

A pearl-colored sash with the word BRIDE in pink bold letters draped across the front of Maggie's dress. Her friends all wore a similar sash only theirs displayed the words BACHE-LORETTE on the front and PARTY on the back.

Maggie didn't know what to say. Chelsea's efforts to make this night the best memory touched her heart, but she felt foolish to think people would see her trying to appear much younger than her age. All she could say was, "Oh, Chelsea."

"It's great, right?"

Not to hurt her friend's feelings, Maggie nodded, then turned and hugged her. "You are too much; do you know that?"

"Yes, I do believe I've heard that before, and don't make me cry. You have no idea how long it took me to get these false eyelashes on. I'm not responsible for what happens to them if I start blubbering."

Rachel's maternity dress hugged her body and ample breasts. "What do you think ladies? No chance a guy will approach me tonight. I look like I'm about five minutes away from being wheeled into the delivery room."

Jane's response to that made everyone laugh. "I do believe there are men out there who are only interested in pregnant women. If you think you're safe, think again."

Diana and Kelly twirled in unison to show off their outfits as well. Chelsea whistled. "I think we're six of the loveliest women on Captiva Island. Now, let's get going. The limo is out front already."

Maggie looked forward to a delicious dinner at Doc Ford's restaurant. The rest of the night, she wasn't so sure, but no matter what the evening presented, she needed the distraction. The events of the last twenty-four hours threatened to dominate her thoughts. Distraction was the best medicine, and she intended to make the most of it.

CHAPTER THIRTY-ONE

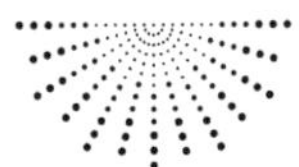

Maggie had only been in a limousine three times in her entire life. Once, for her prom with Daniel and a bunch of classmates, once, when her husband used it as a way to apologize for his cheating, and the third time was at Daniel's funeral. None were especially fond memories since she was pregnant two of those times and the final ride was one of the worst days of her life.

The tinted windows made it impossible to see what direction they were headed, but Maggie felt that something seemed off.

"I don't think this is the way to Doc Ford's." Turning to Chelsea, she asked, "Does he know where we're going?"

"He certainly does. Stop worrying so much and enjoy your champagne."

Rachel took a sip of her drink. "Thank you, Chelsea, for getting alcohol-free bubbly for me. This is delicious. I may buy some of this when I get back to Massachusetts."

Jane was already on her second glass. "Not me. I love the real stuff."

Maggie could almost predict who, out of the six of them,

would find herself unable to stand at the end of the night. The word moderation was not part of Jane's vocabulary.

When the limo stopped, Chelsea thanked the driver and handed him a tip. The women got out of the car and were greeted by a man who escorted them onto a dock.

Everyone yelled, "Surprise!" Maggie looked around and realized they weren't at Doc Ford's.

"What is this?"

Chelsea put her arm around Maggie's waist. "You've been talking about going out on a sunset dinner cruise ever since you arrived on Captiva. We thought it was time that you finally did it."

Maggie couldn't believe it. Her business had kept her so busy, that she never found the time to do more than go out to eat. Suddenly, her bachelorette party turned into a dream fulfilled. She didn't have to worry about getting out on a dance floor with her bridal sash after all.

"You guys are the best."

The captain welcomed everyone onto the boat, and a beautifully decorated table and bucket of champagne appeared before them. Their waiter opened the bottle and filled their glasses as the boat left the dock.

The waiter invited everyone to sit; he then placed plates of salad in front of each of the women. The main course, salmon with miso lemon, butter, and garlic with broccolini and risotto came next, followed by a delicious chocolate mousse.

When they were done eating, the music was turned up, and Jane and Diana began dancing. Along with the beautiful sunset, the waiter opened two more bottles of champagne and kept them on ice.

Maggie leaned forward on the boat's railing and gazed out at the sunset. The view calmed her but couldn't erase the image of Daniel with Jen. She wanted to scream out over the ocean but contained her anger for the sake of the party.

Carrying a new bottle of champagne, Chelsea stood next to Maggie.

"What's on your mind?"

"What do you mean?"

"I mean that you *seem* to be having a good time, but I can't tell whether it's an act or if there's something going on inside that head of yours.

"Remember my telling you about Jen Laurier? She's the woman who traveled here alone."

"You mean the mysterious single lady who gave you weird vibes?"

Maggie nodded. "She was Daniel's mistress. She's the one he left me for."

Chelsea turned and stared at Maggie. "You are not serious. Why is she stalking you?"

"She's not stalking me. She wants forgiveness."

"Forgiveness? That's fresh. What did she say, exactly?"

Maggie shook her head. "I wouldn't let her talk. I kicked her out of the inn and told her to never come back. Except now, I feel this pull to call her. I've got questions."

"I bet you do. I have a few of my own, like what the hell made her think you'd welcome her with open arms?"

"Come on, Chelsea. You have to give her some credit for coming here. I don't think I'd be that brave."

Chelsea poured herself another glass of champagne, and then filled Maggie's glass.

"You, my dear, would never sleep with someone else's husband. I'm not sure she's brave, but she's got some nerve. By the way, what questions do you have?"

"I want to know if Daniel talked about me, and what happened the day he died? I'm not sure you can understand this, but I've been holding on to an anger I haven't yet released."

"It's understandable that you'd be angry at what he did. The man lied to you for years."

"No. It's not that. I mean, yes, of course I was angry at him for cheating on me yet again, but my anger isn't about his affairs. I'm angry that he died."

Chelsea stayed quiet, and let Maggie get it all out. Soon, the other women gathered near the railing.

Maggie gulped the contents of her glass, took the bottle of champagne from Chelsea's hands, and filled her glass again. She took another sip of the bubbly and continued, this time in front of her friends.

"I mean, as long as he was alive I could stay angry at Daniel for cheating. I could tell everyone about the terrible thing he did. I would have shouted it from the rooftops that he was a lying cheat. I might even have ruined his career and his life, and no one would blame me. I'd be entitled after all. If Daniel had lived, I'd be at a lawyer's office taking him for every penny and I'd be justified."

Her voice, louder, she continued through tears.

"When he died, I lost my right to be the victim in all this. Instead, I sat there in that church and let everyone think Daniel was a wonderful man, a loyal and devoted husband and father. Even now, I feel like a horrible person for talking badly about a dead man. It's like once you die, not only are your sins forgiven, but you also get to enter sainthood."

By now, Maggie was pacing the deck of the boat like a madwoman. All her friends could do is watch and keep her from jumping overboard. It was Jane who shed light on the situation. Her words were soft but poignant.

"You're wrong, Maggie. Everyone in that church knew what loyalty and devotion looked like. They saw it in you and the wonderful wife and mother you'd been all those years. Everyone knew about Daniel's cheating, everyone but you, that is. The people in that church weren't there for Daniel. They weren't there to celebrate his life. They were there for you, and your children."

Maggie's mascara-stained cheeks were flushed. She leaned against the railing, stunned at Jane's words, not knowing what to say. She always wondered but had no evidence that anyone knew of Daniel's indiscretions. The reason she didn't know, was because everyone protected her from the truth.

Rachel's meek voice rose from the group. Standing in a puddle of liquid, she looked at Maggie. "My water broke."

For only a moment, everyone froze. Whatever drama the bachelorette party had so far endured, it was about to get downright chaotic. Chelsea ran to the bridge and banged on the window.

"Turn this boat around. A woman is about to have a baby and she's not having it on the deck of this boat."

The women gathered around Rachel, helping her into a chair. Maggie worried they'd never get her to the hospital in time. None of them had a clue how to deliver a baby. The captain came out from the bridge to assess the situation.

"I've called an ambulance to meet us at the dock. We should be there in about fifteen minutes. How is she doing?"

Rachel's contractions had already begun, and Chelsea's face looked pale. "Not good. Are you driving this boat as fast as you can? Because if not, I suggest you put it in top speed. Otherwise, you'll need to move over and let me drive."

The captain went back to the bridge and within ten minutes the boat reached the dock. There was an ambulance waiting for them when they arrived. As they helped Rachel into the ambulance, she called out to Chelsea.

"Will you stay with me?"

The EMT driver agreed that Rachel could have one of her friends in the ambulance to accompany her. The other women followed behind in the limo. At Maggie's direction, the limousine driver drove faster than usual. Jane, Diana, and Kelly tried to freshen up before reaching the hospital. Jane gave Maggie a tissue and a mirror.

"Oh man, why didn't someone tell me I looked like this?"

Jane answered, "I am, hence the mirror and tissue. If you need makeup remover to get the mascara off your cheek, just let me know."

The limousine made an abrupt stop, and Maggie almost landed on the floor of the vehicle.

When they got out of the limo, Maggie pulled Jane aside. "Thank you for what you said on that boat. I needed to hear it."

Jane nodded. "I never wanted to hurt you, Maggie. I probably should have told you all that a long time ago, but I'm not sure you were ready to hear it back then."

The four women walked into the emergency room and found Rachel sitting in a wheelchair, Chelsea by her side. Rachel felt terrified that she was about to deliver her baby at a strange hospital, and by a doctor she'd never met before. The nurse tried to reassure her, but it was Chelsea who came to her aid.

"Listen to me, Rachel. This is a wonderful hospital. My Carl was in here, and I can tell you that they took exceptional care of him. You are in good hands."

Rachel nodded and then asked, "Will you come into the delivery room with me? I've taken the Lamaze classes, so I know what to do, but I need a familiar face in there."

Chelsea panicked, "Me? I'm not sure I'll be much help. I faint at the first sight of blood. I don't think you want me."

Chelsea looked at the other women, "What about Maggie? She's perfect. Think of all the babies she's had. She'll know what to do."

Rachel pleaded with Maggie. "Will you, please, Maggie?"

Maggie ran to Rachel and leaned down to hug her. "Of course, I will."

Rachel and Maggie waved as they wheeled Rachel to the delivery room. Maggie turned back one last time and smiled at her friends. Chelsea formed a heart with her fingers, helping

Maggie to carry the love and protection of the lunch-bunch ladies with her into the delivery room.

Maggie held Rachel's hand and supported her back as she pushed. Between contractions, Maggie wiped Rachel's forehead with a cool wet cloth and helped her breath the way they taught her in Lamaze class.

It seemed like forever, but in fact it had only been an hour when they heard the baby cry. Rachel's little girl arrived in the world at seven pounds, seven ounces. Maggie cried with Rachel as they placed the infant on Rachel's chest.

Maggie looked at the doctor and asked, "Can we bring her family in here for just a couple of minutes?"

The doctor agreed, and a nurse went to get them. Within seconds the lunch-bunch ladies entered the delivery room.

Kelly touched the baby's little fingers. "She's beautiful."

Diana and Jane hovered over the baby.

"What's her name?" Diana asked.

"Everly Brooke Adams. Brooke was my mother's name. She's been gone so long now. I think it's been ten years. I know she's looking down from heaven at her first and only grandchild."

Maggie stared at the baby. "And Everly?"

"The Everly Brothers of course. They sang my favorite song. 'All I have to do is Dream'."

CHAPTER THIRTY-TWO

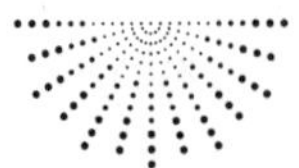

The next morning, Maggie felt on a mission. It was only seven o'clock in the morning when she decided to contact Jen Laurier. Jen picked up on the first ring.

"Hello. I wasn't sure I'd hear from you again."

"I'd like to talk to you before you go back to Massachusetts. Could you come now? I have guests and I'd prefer to talk before they get up."

"Yes, of course. I'll leave right now."

Maggie normally would prepare tea, coffee, and breakfast items, but this meeting wasn't a social one. There were things that needed to be said, and she wanted it over as quickly as possible.

When Jen arrived, Maggie directed her to the gazebo. She waited, letting Jen start the conversation. Remembering her request for forgiveness, Maggie wanted to hear what Jen had to say.

"I'm not sure what you know about me and how Daniel and I met."

Maggie stopped her. "Jen, I'm not interested in how you met. What I want to know is simple. What do you want from me? You asked for forgiveness, but I don't think you understand what you're asking."

"I do understand, but please hear me. Daniel wasn't the only one who was married. I was...I am married."

Maggie never considered Jen's marital status. She just assumed Jen was single and dating a married man.

"Can you please explain to me why people cheat? If you don't believe in monogamy, then why marry at all?"

Jen looked down at her hands. As she spun her wedding ring, she answered, "I think it's because something is missing, and I don't mean in the marriage. I mean inside the person. When you're constantly looking outside yourself for the solution it's a sign that you feel less than—not worthy of much. I can't speak for Daniel, none of us can, but I can tell you that he had little confidence in himself. It was something even our affair couldn't change."

Maggie could relate. "But Jen, many people feel like that at some point in their lives. Not everyone cheats."

"That's because not everyone looks to another person as a solution. Some look to gambling, some to alcohol, some never find it and give up living. When two people come together as Daniel and I did, it had nothing to do with my marriage, and everything to do with the fact that both of us suffered from the same malady. It was a perfect storm."

It shocked Maggie that she felt empathy for both Jen and Daniel. It helped to understand their motives, but it did nothing to erase the pain of betrayal. That she found a person in Paolo with whom she could trust, was a true miracle—a blessing she would treasure for the rest of her life.

"What will my forgiveness do for you?"

Jen smiled. "My husband took me back after my affair. I didn't think it possible, but he wanted to see if we could start over. I think we've made progress, but I still feel trapped in the past because I ruined your marriage. I hurt not only my husband, but you and your children as well. I haven't been able to get beyond that, and it's having a negative impact on my marriage. I know it's asking a lot for you to help me save my marriage, but that's what I'm asking when I say I need your forgiveness."

The irony wasn't lost on Maggie, but she also knew that more than anything she needed to close the door on the past, and on Daniel. The need to hurt Jen Laurier felt overwhelming the day before, but that impulse was now gone. What would it cost her to forgive this woman?

"Never in a million years did I ever think I'd be talking to you about my marriage to Daniel, but for what it's worth, here it is. I think I had been mourning the loss of my husband for several years before you, —before he died. Everyone thinks that I was blindsided. I thought so too, but that's not entirely true. Somewhere deep inside, I knew things weren't right between us. Given our history, I shouldn't have been shocked at his affair with you. All the signs were there, I just chose not to see them."

Chelsea walked the path toward the inn, and directly to Maggie and Jen.

The women got up from their chairs. "Jen, this is my friend, Chelsea. Chelsea, this is Jen Laurier. She's just leaving."

Chelsea didn't shake Jen's hand. "I'll be in the kitchen when you're done here."

Chelsea left Maggie and Jen to finish their conversation.

Maggie hesitated before speaking again.

"Jen, I've got guests, so I should attend to them. I do have one question. Is there anything about the day Daniel died, that you think I should know—anything he might have said?"

"Maggie. He didn't say anything after that, just your name. He just said 'Maggie' and then he died."

Maggie started to walk away but stopped. A lump in her throat made it difficult to speak, but she managed as best she could.

"You have my forgiveness, and I hope it helps you. I still

believe in happily-ever-after, in marriage, and in love. When you find it, hold onto it as tight as you can. I know that's what I plan to do."

~

Maggie found Chelsea sitting at the kitchen table drinking her coffee. She got herself a cup and joined her.

"I guess you and I are the only ones awake so far."

"Quit the small-talk, Maggie. I want to hear what happened between you and that woman."

Maggie reached across the table and took Chelsea's hand in hers. "Listen to me. I'm fine. Honestly, I'm better than fine. I feel released from the past, and it's about time."

"Honey, I'm glad to hear it, but just yesterday you scared all of us. I thought you had worked through everything about Daniel months ago. The girls haven't been around you for the last year. It came as a shock to me. If you've been holding on to unresolved issues, why didn't you tell me?"

Maggie sat back in her chair. "It's simple. Because just like everything else having to do with my marriage, I wasn't honest with myself. I was quick to forgive Daniel, but those were just words. As usual, I felt a need to protect my children from further trauma, and the truth is that I didn't want to look at it anymore. It was easier to go on a holiday with you and begin again. I pushed it all down deep and never really grieved the loss of it all."

"And now?"

"And now, I feel free. Jen coming here forced my hand. I had no choice but to face it. It's been painful to say the least, but I feel the weight off my shoulders."

Chelsea laughed, "Just in time, too."

"What do you mean?"

"What I mean is that you are about to get married again, and I'm a firm believer in not walking into something unless you are completely certain it's the right thing. So, I'll ask you, are you ready to marry Paolo?"

"I love you, Chelsea. You've always got my back, and I'm so grateful. Yes, I'm more than ready to marry Paolo. This time, I don't have blinders on. My eyes, my head, and my heart are completely open to this new journey. I know what I want my future to be. The best part is I get to create it all with someone I love with all my heart."

"Good. I'm ready to spend the day on the beach. How about you? Let's show these ladies how to collect seashells."

As if summoned, Jane, Kelly, and Diana walked into the kitchen. Jane still had her silk sleep eye mask pushed up on her head.

"Is there coffee? Once again, I might have had a bit too much of that champagne. I really have to cut back on that stuff."

Diana pulled a chair from the table and plopped down on it. "You'd think the trauma of childbirth would sober me up, but nope."

Chelsea laughed. "Well, it would have if you were the one giving birth. Except for Rachel, Maggie's the only one who isn't hungover, and I think she drank the most."

"Well in my case, I had a front row seat to the childbirth event. Nothing like watching a baby come into the world to wake a person up."

Kelly didn't seem too bad and poured herself a cup of coffee and grabbed a croissant. "You guys don't know how to handle a few drinks. Look at me, I'm perfectly fine."

Jane couldn't stand the smell of Kelly's croissant. "Do you have to eat that thing so close to me?"

Maggie couldn't wait to get their beach day started. "You guys will recover nicely laying on the beach all day long. You won't have to do a thing except sit up and take in some lunch in a few hours. Otherwise, you can sleep on a beach chair if you'd like."

A car door slammed and noise from the front of the inn caught everyone's attention.

"Hey, hey, where is everyone?"

Sarah, Trevor, and Noah came into the kitchen, and those of the lunch-bunch crew that could, screamed.

Kelly being the most alert yelled, "Sarah! Look at you, you're so beautiful. Obviously Florida agrees with you. Introduce us to these two handsome men."

Sarah made the introductions and Jane lifted her head off the table. "Sarah, my love. You look amazing. I had a bit too much to drink at your mother's bachelorette party last night. Nice to meet you, Trevor and Noah."

"Mom, I talked to Lauren last night. Everyone will be here tomorrow. They all decided to stay at the Marriott Sanibel Harbor, so they'll be close, but not underfoot. Besides, I think you have your hands full with your guests already. Beth kept telling me about her latest boyfriend drama, and I thought I'd never get off the phone with her. Anyway, they're all coming in on the same flight. It gets in about noon. They can't check in until later in the day, so they want to stop over here first and visit with you and everyone. How does that sound?"

"Sounds great to me. I can't wait to see everyone. What about you? When are you going to bring your dress and stuff to the carriage house?"

"I'll do it tomorrow. I'm leaving work early and plan to take a few days off. Trevor and I want to introduce Noah to everyone here, and then after the wedding, we plan to visit with Trevor's family. Only Trevor's father has met Noah. It's time he meets everyone."

"Oh, honey, that's wonderful. Noah, are you excited about the wedding party we're going to have? There will be lots of people but lots of fun too. You can jump in the pool and when you get out there'll be lots of cake and ice cream. Do you like those things?"

Noah nodded, and Sarah explained that he was a little shy amongst so many people. "I think it will get easier, the more exposure he gets from these functions."

Maggie's anticipation for the wedding and to see her family again made her teary-eyed. So much happiness and joy were welcome after a tumultuous week. Soon, she would be surrounded by everyone she loved most in the world. New memories were already being created. She'd come through a difficult time with a renewed sense of the love that surrounded her. Nothing was better than that.

CHAPTER THIRTY-THREE

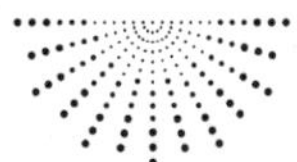

Maggie couldn't wait to see her family. It had been months of video and cell phone calls, so being with them in person was a dream come true. Jackson, who was twenty-six weeks old, would soon be in her arms, and she'd get to squeeze all of her grandchildren.

Chelsea and the lunch-bunch crew planned to see everyone tonight. The women had gone to pick up Rachel and Everly. They wanted to buy a few things for the baby, including a car seat, and then go directly to the hospital.

Sarah, Trevor, and Noah arrived at the inn at three o'clock and helped Maggie, Riley and Grace prepare a buffet for everyone. No need for a rehearsal, tonight would be a pre-wedding gathering of family and friends. Noah and Trevor hung out with Paolo in the carriage house. Paolo was reorganizing the bottom floor, and Maggie thought it was cute that her future son-in-law and grandson joined him in the pursuit of a man cave.

Maggie's cell phone buzzed, and she answered the FaceTime video from Lauren.

"Hi honey. Where are you?"

"We just landed, Mom. We're going to get our luggage and

then drop everything off at the hotel. We decided to rent two cars. Michael, Brea, and their kids, plus Grandma are in one car and Jeff, Beth, me, and the girls are in another. There's enough room for two cars right?"

"Plenty. Don't worry about it. Just hurry up and get here. I can't wait to see everyone. And don't eat anything. We've got a huge buffet of food here."

"Will do. See you soon."

Maggie walked through the garden and out the back gate. She wanted to look at the wedding arch. A trellis with flowers and twigs woven through branches and billowing white fabric had been installed an hour ago. It sat before several rows of white chairs.

Paolo came up behind Maggie and put his arms around her. "It looks beautiful, doesn't it?"

Maggie reached over her shoulder to touch his face. "How many more hours before we stand under that thing?"

"Nineteen hours, I believe. Nervous?"

Maggie shook her head. "Not a bit, you?"

Paolo kissed her neck and squeezed her tight. "I've never felt calmer."

"The kids are checking into the hotel. They should be here within the hour. How are Trevor and Noah getting on?"

"It's adorable to see that little boy so happy to be with his dad. He's a good kid."

"I'm so happy for Sarah. Trevor absolutely loves her. They're going to be a beautiful family of four. I can't wait to meet Sophia. Do you realize this will make me a grandmother of seven?"

"I guess that makes me a grandfather of seven."

Maggie turned to face Paolo. "I hadn't thought of that. How does that make you feel?"

"You mean other than old?"

Maggie laughed, "Hey, join the club, but don't worry, grand-children have a way of making you feel young again. One thing is for certain though. You'll definitely be a handsome grandfather."

Paolo kissed his bride and then Maggie buried her face in the crook of his neck, and whispered, "I love you, Paolo Moretti."

Paolo lifted an eyebrow. "I just realized something. We never talked about whether you would change your last name to Moretti. What do you think?"

"I honestly hadn't thought about it. I've been a Wheeler for so long I never imagined myself as anything else. Do you have an opinion one way or the other?"

She could tell that Paolo didn't want to dictate Maggie's choice, but she knew he was traditional enough to want her last name to be Moretti. Maggie didn't need time to decide. She felt ready to make the change, but she also wanted to honor her children.

"Would you mind terribly if I changed my last name to Wheeler-Moretti? Keeping the Wheeler name has nothing to do specifically with Daniel. I'm who I am today because of a lifetime of experiences, and I don't want to throw that away. I want to celebrate my journey—all of it, even the difficult times."

As usual, Paolo supported Maggie's decision.

"Maggie Wheeler-Moretti. I like the sound of that."

"Great. Let's get back to the house. The kids should be here soon."

They walked arm-in-arm back to the house. As they approached the inn, they could hear the crunch of the seashell-paved driveway under the wheels of two vehicles.

The cars stopped and her granddaughters, Quinn and Cora, came running toward her.

"Grandma!

They wrapped their arms around Maggie's legs and squeezed tight. Lauren and Jeff's two girls followed their cousins and ran to Maggie, hoping to get in on the group hug.

"Olivia, you look so grown up."

She and her sister, Lily, held out their hands for inspection. Their nails had been painted a pretty light pink.

"Oh, don't you both look so pretty."

Lauren hugged her mother. "They insisted they get their nails painted pink in honor of the wedding and your favorite color."

Jeff kissed his mother-in-law and shook Paolo's hand. "Congratulations, Paolo. Big day tomorrow."

"Thank you, Jeff. We're so happy everyone will be with us to celebrate."

Beth gave Maggie a big hug and handed her several photos. "I had these made for you. I decided to go around the house and the garden and take pictures to remind you of our house back home. I'm taking good care of it, Mom. You'll have to come north one of these days and see for yourself."

"Thank you, honey. What a sweet idea. And look at my garden. What's that in the corner?"

"Well, first, let me tell you that I've made friends with the woodchuck. As a matter of fact, I call him Chuck. That thing you see in the corner is my elevated raised bed. My friend Gabriel made it for me. I love kale and collard greens and Swiss chard, but Chuck loves them too. So, I decided I'd still get my greens and Chuck can't reach them by digging underground."

"Beth, that's brilliant. It certainly beats my coyote urine idea."

"Gabriel is really talented, Mom. He's got his own furniture-making business in West Newbury. You should see his work. I'll send you a link to his website."

Lauren made eye contact with Maggie and smiled. Maggie took that as a sign of approval from Beth's big sister.

Michael pulled Jackson from his car seat and carried him to Maggie. He placed the baby in Maggie's arms. "Mom, this is your new grandson, Jackson. Jackson, meet your grandmother." Michael's wife, Brea, beamed watching Maggie's face.

Jackson stared at his grandmother and reached for her finger. "Hello, Jackson. Welcome to our family." She turned to Paolo and showed him the baby. "And this man is going to be your grandfather. You can call him Grandpa."

Sarah introduced Trevor and Noah to her family and watched as her nieces made immediate friends with Noah. Showing her engagement ring, Sarah enjoyed the attention.

Maggie's mother walked over to Paolo and looked him in the eye. "Do you know what you're getting into marrying into this family? The Garrison women are very strong-minded, starting with Maggie Garrison-Wheeler. You best get used to that."

Lauren came to Paolo's defense. "Don't worry about her, Paolo. Her bark is bigger than her bite. She's actually a real softy. You'll see."

"That's what you think, Missy." She turned her attention to Maggie and gave her daughter a kiss. "You're looking well. Must be all that Vitamin D. Well, what do you have that I can drink? It's been a long day. How about a vodka tonic with lime? I don't care for those fancy drinks with the umbrellas in them—too much cream. I'm usually in the bathroom right after one of those..."

Maggie cut her mother off. "Why don't we all go inside. Riley and Grace have appetizers and drinks ready for everyone."

Her mother continued, "Your sister and brother send their love. I wish they could have come down, but you know your brother, he hates leaving California. And don't get me started on Elizabeth. That daughter of mine acts too high and mighty if you ask me."

Maggie hoped her mother's rambling didn't scare Paolo. She'd keep an eye on her and check with Lauren to make sure her mother had all her necessary medications. Another unscheduled trip to the hospital was the last thing Maggie needed.

Sarah hugged her grandmother and followed her to the corner of the room. "What is it, Grandma?"

"This Trevor you plan to marry."

"Yes?"

"What's with the long hair?"

Sarah tried not to laugh, but shrugged, "I don't know. I guess that's just who he is. I like it."

"Can't he be who he is with shorter hair? Last I heard, women were the only ones who wore ponytails."

Sarah was patient with her grandmother. To everyone else, her namesake seemed opinionated, but for Sarah, her grandmother's wisdom, more often than not, got to the heart of things.

"Do you remember what I told you about getting married?"

Sarah nodded. "I remember. You said when the right man comes along, I won't be afraid to marry and have children. You were right, Grandma. I'm not scared anymore."

Her grandmother patted her hand. "Good. Now tell that young man to cut his hair, or I'll do it for him."

Maggie loved hearing everyone talk over one another. In her mind she could see her children when they were little. Fighting at the table, and either Maggie or Daniel trying to get everyone to eat their dinner. By the end of the night, Maggie was always exhausted. Countless nights of homework, sport commitments and carpools dominated her life. She loved every minute of it. Looking around the table she felt enormous pride at the people her children had become. The only way the night could be more perfect was if Christopher was here.

Trevor put his napkin on the table, stood, and tapped his glass. He cleared his throat and the room quieted. "I'd like to say a few words if you will indulge me for a moment. As the best man, I feel it's my duty to share a few things about the bride and groom that many of you don't know. Now, I realize I'm the new guy around here, but that doesn't mean I can't be an authority where Maggie and Paolo are concerned. To claim knowledge of another person, you have to observe their behaviors very closely. For the last eight months, I've done that very thing."

Beth interrupted, "Please don't put something in our brains that we can't remove."

Everyone laughed and Sarah made a face at Beth.

"Ignore her, Trevor. Go on."

Looking at Beth, Trevor explained, "I promise you, Beth, this is something you'll want to stay in your brain forever. I've watched Paolo anticipate Maggie getting up from a chair or walking out a door—to take her hand and walk with her. I've watched him push a few strands of hair off her face and out of her eyes when she's at the sink, and her hands are deep in soapy water. I've seen him gently place a sweater over her shoulders when she's cold and have been blessed to witness the way he looks at her when she enters a room. I mention all this, because tonight, as we get ready to celebrate the joining of these two hearts, I pray that I can be half as loving to Sarah, half as good a man for Sarah, as Paolo is to Maggie."

Trevor raised his glass, "To Maggie and Paolo."

Cheers from around the table erupted as Paolo kissed his bride.

Sarah got up from her chair. "I guess it's my turn, as the maid of honor. Let's hope I can do this without crying. Mom, when you asked me to stand next to you on your wedding day, I kept thinking, 'Is this really happening? Is she asking me to be a witness as she tells her family and friends how much she loves Paolo?' I thought what an honor to be asked, but what my mother doesn't know is that tomorrow won't be the first time I've been witness to her love. Mom, you've shown me and all of your children what love looks like. You did this every day of our lives. It's a lesson we all will take with us for the rest of our lives. I love you."

Sarah raised her glass. "To Mom and Paolo."

There wasn't a dry eye around the table. No one could lighten the mood better than Maggie's dearest friend, Chelsea, who, at that very minute, walked into the Key Lime Garden Inn along with the rest of the lunch-bunch crew.

"For heaven's sake, Wheeler family. Don't cry. I'm here. Let's get this party started."

CHAPTER THIRTY-FOUR

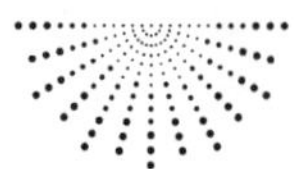

Maggie woke before the sun came up and reached for her robe at the foot of the bed. She walked to the window and looked down at the garden's bird bath. The sounds of birds chirping, the slow trickle of the small water fountain combined with the distant sound of ocean waves called to her. The wind chimes tilted back and forth as she watched the sun lift out of the ground reaching for the sky.

The morning of Maggie's wedding day looked like any other. Most of her days began this way. Except for this private moment alone, the coming hours would be filled with celebration and love. Today, she would join her life with Paolo's and forever share the early mornings with the love of her life.

She had selected an assortment of pink and white roses, and baby's breath surrounded by several green palm leaves for both her bouquet and Sarah's. The bouquets, boutonnieres, and table centerpieces would be delivered soon, and the musicians and photographer would arrive at eleven o'clock.

Soon, her friends and family would wake and gather in the dining room, sharing breakfast together. Paolo, Trevor, and Noah would get ready at Paolo's home. Ciara asked if she could bring her new boyfriend, Matteo, to the wedding. Maggie had to remind Paolo that Ciara was a grown woman and didn't need permission to date whomever she wanted.

Maggie could see beyond the garden to an area of several round tables covered in white linen. Just to the left, and closer to the water, a dance floor had been constructed. Smaller tables were placed around the pool with strings of white lights around it. The lights were also strung around the trunks of the palm trees, and although Maggie didn't want to rush the day along, she couldn't wait to see the lights when the sun went down.

Chelsea planned to arrive early to make sure everything had been done to her specifications. Maggie admired the way her friend took control and although she might rustle a few feathers, most everyone agreed that Chelsea's talent for organization was considerable.

Rachel and Everly would come by a bit later, giving the baby and her a chance to take their time getting ready. There was plenty of time before the ceremony, so Maggie decided to join her family for breakfast after she showered.

Her cell phone buzzed and although she didn't recognize the number, decided to answer it.

"Hello?"

No answer.

"Hello? Can you hear me?"

Maggie could hear static, but nothing else. She kept talking and listened for a voice at the other end of the line, but there was nothing.

She ended the call and threw her cell phone on the bed. Whoever it was would call back if it was important.

She made her bed and got into the shower.

Chelsea called to Maggie as she climbed the carriage house stairs to Maggie's apartment.

"Where's the bride?"

"I'm in the shower. I'll be out in a minute."

Maggie knew Chelsea would get here early, but this was ridiculous. She got out of the shower and toweled off as quickly as she could.

"Why are you here so early?"

"You know me. I've got to make sure everything goes according to plan. I'm fussy about these things."

"Fussy? I'm not sure that's the right word for it. More like unrealistic. I remember reading somewhere that the people who live the longest are able to go with Plan B when Plan A doesn't work out. You need to learn how to chill. Look at me. I'm the bride and I'm not worried about a thing."

Maggie's phone buzzed once again. She picked up her cell phone and pressed the button.

"Hello?"

Again, no one answered her.

"Can you hear me?"

Nothing but static.

She ended the call in frustration. "That's the second time this morning. Someone is trying to reach me, but all I hear is static. The first time I thought I could hear a voice but this time, only noise."

Chelsea didn't miss a beat, "Maybe it's Daniel calling from wherever he is to offer congratulations on your wedding day."

"Very funny, Chelsea."

Maggie finished getting dressed while Chelsea looked at her watch. "Can you tell whether anyone is up across the way?"

"I haven't looked actually, but if anyone is, it would be my mother. As a matter of fact, we should probably get over there before she says something inappropriate. When the kids arrived yesterday, they decided it would be best if Mom stayed here with us instead of the hotel. I think they just wanted to get rid of her. Can you imagine trying to get showered and dressed, get the kids ready and deal with her at the same time? No wonder they left her here."

"I love your mother. She's a hoot."

"Yes, a barrel of laughs all the time. Come on. Let's see if she's starting trouble already."

~

Maggie called it. When they entered the kitchen, her mother was instructing Riley and Grace on the proper way to make a pot of tea.

"I can't understand these restaurants that give you a cup of lukewarm water with a tea bag on the side. Who the heck wants a cup of tea like that?"

Riley looked at Maggie as if to say, "Help."

"Mom, why don't we go into the dining room and have our breakfast? Riley and Grace have prepared a breakfast buffet, and if you wait a few minutes, a nice pot of hot tea will be brought out to you."

Her mother agreed and Riley mouthed a thank you before they left the kitchen.

Before long, the rest of the lunch-bunch came downstairs. This time, Maggie noticed that Jane looked bright-eyed and wide awake.

"I'm very proud of you, Jane. I don't think you overdid it last night."

"You're right. I only had one glass of wine and then switched to water. I've noticed I do much better if I drink lots of water along with my alcohol."

Maggie's mother had to interject. "My husband had the same problem. He liked his scotch."

No one said much after that.

Sarah arrived, carrying her dress in her garment bag. "Morning everyone. Happy wedding day, Mom."

"Hi, honey. Why don't you hang your dress over in the carriage house?"

"Sounds good. I'll be right back. How long before the makeup and hair ladies arrive?"

"They said they'd be here at nine-thirty. Riley, do you think you and Grace can prepare a breakfast platter with coffee and tea, and bring it up to my place around nine-fifteen? I'll probably have butterflies in my stomach and the last thing I need is to pass out from not eating."

Grace gave a thumbs up and Riley said, "No problem."

Sarah came back and poured herself a cup of coffee. "I stopped by Trevor's place just before he left for Paolo's. You should see Noah's outfit. He wasn't dressed yet, but it looked adorable on the hanger. I can't wait to see him in it. Trevor said he talked with Paolo and the groom seems relaxed. I think everyone else is more nervous than the bride and groom."

Maggie laughed and pointed to Chelsea, "I know one person who's on pins and needles worried that there will be a glitch of some sort."

Sarah looked at Chelsea. "Really? I wouldn't have pictured you as a worrywart."

"There's a lot of things you don't know about me, Sarah. Fortunately, your mother doesn't talk."

Just then, Rachel and her baby arrived. Everyone got up from the table and ran to see Everly.

"So far, she seems to be a very content little baby. I'm sure before long, she'll be fussy and screaming her head off."

Kelly shrugged. "Not necessarily. My youngest was peaceful from the moment she was born, and remains the quiet, introspective one now that she's a college student."

Maggie's mother had her own opinion. "When my kids got too fussy, I'd just put a little whiskey on my finger and rubbed it inside on the gums. Worked every time."

Maggie put her head in her hands as everyone turned and stared at her mother.

Chelsea took Everly from Rachel and guided her into the

dining room. "Have something to eat. I want everybody's belly to be full by the time the ceremony begins."

"Mom, what time is everyone getting here from the Marriott?"

"Lauren said they'd have breakfast at the hotel before they got showered and dressed. I'm sure with her kids and Michael's, they've got their hands full getting ready. She thought perhaps they'd get here by eleven o'clock."

Maggie's cell phone buzzed, and Sarah reached for it.

"Mom, it's Christopher on FaceTime. Hey little brother, how are you?"

"Sarah, I didn't expect to see you. Where's Mom?"

Sarah turned the phone to face Maggie.

"Hey, Mom. Happy wedding day."

"Oh, Christopher, now the day is perfect. I'm so glad to see your handsome face. I wish it was in person, but this will have to do."

"Is everyone there? I tried to call you earlier, but it wouldn't go through, so I figured I'd wait to see if we could video."

Maggie turned her cell phone slowly around to give him a better view of the room. "Hey, Grandma!"

"How's my favorite grandson?"

"I'm good, Grandma. Michael must not be in the room, or you wouldn't be saying that."

Maggie looked at the screen. "They're all still at the hotel. They'll be here a little later. They'll be sorry they missed you."

Christopher looked tired. "Mom. You can tell them that I'll be seeing them sooner rather than later."

"What? How? When? Are you getting leave soon?"

"No. It looks like they're sending me home. Nothing to worry about but I'm in the hospital in Germany right now. There was an explosion near the mess hall. My leg got hit pretty bad, but I was lucky. Twenty-two were killed."

Maggie's hand reached for her throat.

"Mom. I'm going to be fine. Everything is fine. Please, don't worry. I have to stay here in the hospital for another week at least. After that, I'll be coming home."

Maggie could tell that he dreaded making this call. He knew how she would react, and she felt terrible that she couldn't mask her fear.

"Promise me that you are telling me everything. Don't try to save me from anything, Chris. I mean it. Do they have to take your leg?"

Christopher paused before he spoke again. "They're not sure. Maybe not, Mom. They think they can save it. I can't talk much more. I get tired pretty easily. I'm sorry I had to give you this news today of all days, but I wasn't sure when I'd get another chance."

Maggie did her best to hold back her tears.

Christopher's voice was soft and far away. "Mom, everything is going to be fine. I promise. I'll be home soon."

Sarah grabbed the phone from her mother. "You do what you have to do to get yourself back home. You hear me? I don't care what you have to do, you just do it."

Christopher smiled and nodded. "Take care of Mom, sis. Love you."

The screen went blue, and he was gone.

The room was quiet, and none of Maggie's friends knew quite what to say.

Sarah held her mother close and the two women, followed by Sarah's grandmother, walked into the living room. They sat on the sofa, and Maggie wiped her eyes.

"I'm going to him."

Sarah wasn't sure she heard right.

"What?"

"I'm going to Germany to see my son. Paolo and I were going to Italy anyway. How difficult can it be to stop over in Germany?

I have no idea what I'm going to find when we get there, but I have no choice. I have to see him."

Sarah nodded and Maggie's mother put her arm around her. "Of course, you do. Christopher needs his mother. You must go."

The makeup and hair stylists arrived, and Maggie did her best to compose herself.

Smiling at Sarah, she said, "Come on, let's go get ready. Time for a bit of glam."

Maggie and Sarah got ready in the carriage house, and through the window they watched as a crowd began to gather. Sarah helped her mother get into her dress and buttoned the back, straightening the lace folds. Maggie turned and looked at Sarah.

"Well, what do you think?"

"Oh, Mom. You look stunning."

"As do you my precious girl. I guess it's time. Are you ready?"

Sarah nodded. "Let's do this."

They reached the area where they were to stop and wait for direction from Chelsea. When everyone was seated, the music began. At Chelsea's direction, Sarah walked down the pathway to the beach. A few seconds more and it was Maggie's turn. As she turned the corner, Paolo and Trevor came into view. Maggie focused on Paolo, keeping her eyes fixed on only him, and her future.

After they finished their vows, and exchanged rings, the minister pronounced them man and wife. Maggie threw her arms around Paolo's neck as he wrapped his arms around her waist. Paolo dipped his wife as they kissed and the crowd went wild with whistles, screams and clapping.

They turned and walked toward the inn. The crowd followed and the music blared from the pool area. When they got to the house, Maggie turned and called out to Sarah as she threw her bouquet.

"Catch."

Even though she already had her own bouquet, Sarah managed to catch the bride's flowers.

Everyone clapped, and Sarah waved her engagement ring in the air. "Kind of a no-brainer, Mom."

Chelsea got her way and had hired a DJ to keep everyone on their feet. It turned out to be one of her better ideas. Maggie couldn't remember the last time she danced. Paolo proved to be a good dancer, and Maggie made a mental note to do it more often.

The rest of the night was a blur of excitement and joy. Maggie and Paolo thanked everyone for their love and support. She wanted to tell her new husband about Christopher but thought it best to wait until the festivities were over.

Maggie's heart broke for her son and in her mind she was already on the plane to be with him. But the most important events of her life taught her how to be strong no matter what. She had two men that needed her now more than ever. In that moment she remembered the words of a poem by Rumi. *"Your heart knows the way. Run in that direction."*

CHAPTER THIRTY-FIVE

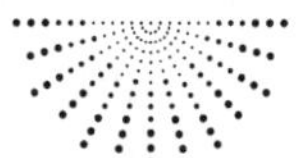

Two days after the wedding, the lunch-bunch ladies and Sarah's family returned to Massachusetts. Maggie and Paolo left for Germany, and she promised to update Sarah and the rest of the family as soon as there was more information about Christopher's condition.

Sarah took comfort in knowing that her brother would soon return home. She had no idea where that would be. Massachusetts had been his home all his life, but she knew her mother would have something to say about it. Sarah felt certain that before long Christopher would be living on Captiva Island.

Noah had done so well surrounded by a large, boisterous crowd at the wedding, that Trevor and Sarah felt ready to introduce him to his father's side of the family. Noah Hutchins would soon learn that he had many more people ready to love and care for him.

"So, what do you think? It's going to be really hot on Saturday. I think Noah would love to swim in your parents' pool."

Trevor agreed. "You're right. I think it's time. It's impossible to explain Clayton to him, so I'm not going to bother, but I think it might be a good idea to talk a little about his new family."

Noah was in his room playing with a new truck that Quinn and Cora brought him from Massachusetts. Sarah thought it sweet that her family welcomed Noah right away. The idea that there were additional toy-bearing family members in his life excited him.

"Noah, do you remember when my father came to visit us?"

Noah nodded his head but didn't stop playing with his truck.

"Would you like to go to his house and play in his pool? He invited us to come for a visit, but I told him that I'd ask you first."

Noah looked up at Trevor. "I want to go. When can we go?"

"How about in a few days?"

"I have to go to school."

"You don't have school on Saturday. We'll go then. You'll get to meet my brothers and sisters too."

"Who are your brothers and sisters?"

"You mean what are their names?"

Noah nodded.

"Well, my brothers are Wyatt and Clayton, and my sisters are Jacqui and Carolyn."

Sarah watched Noah's face light up. "I want brothers and sisters too."

Trevor looked at Sarah and smiled. "I tell you what, Noah, maybe one of these days we'll get you a sister. Would you like that?"

Noah nodded and went back to playing with his truck. "Ok, buddy, sounds like we're going to have fun this weekend."

Sarah and Trevor left Noah's room. Sarah whispered, "I guess we don't need to test the waters where Sophia is concerned. Looks like he'd love a sister."

"You're right, but don't be surprised if he then asks for a brother."

Sarah laughed, thinking about adding to their family. Soon they would get married, and Sophia would join the three of them—she couldn't wait.

Sarah watched Noah's face as they pulled up in front of the Hutchins home and got out of the car. The mansion would be difficult for anyone to take in, but for a little boy of five years old, it appeared massive.

"This house is big."

Trevor nodded. "You're right, it is. Is it too big?"

Noah wasted no time with his response. "Yes. It's too big."

Sarah couldn't wait to hear Devon's response to that statement.

Jeffrey usually greeted Trevor at the front door, but this time his mother met them.

"Hello, Mother."

Eliza kissed her son and then Sarah. She knelt down to Noah's level and gave him a hug too. "You must be Noah. I'm your grandmother, and I'm so glad you came to our house today. It's very nice to meet you. Would you like to go outside and meet the rest of the family?"

Noah didn't answer but looked up at Trevor.

"It's ok, Noah. Remember when I told you there was a pool? That's where everyone is. Let's go see them."

Noah held his father's hand and they all walked through to the back of the house. Devon got up from his chair the minute he saw Noah.

"Hey, you made it. I'm so glad you guys came. We've got a beautiful day for the pool and barbecue."

Noah watched as a boy threw a ball to a girl at the other end of the pool.

Sarah could see that Noah seemed shy and uncomfortable. She worried this might happen, and as soon as Trevor finished introducing Noah to the rest of the family, she suggested Noah get in the pool with her. Remembering Noah's fear of the water, she thought it best he leaned on her for support.

"How about we put these arm floats on?"

As Sarah put the floats on Noah, Carolyn's two children, Hannah and David, stopped playing with the ball and came over to meet him. At twelve and ten years old, Hannah and David, were old enough to think that Noah was cute.

"Hi Noah. I'm Hannah and this is my brother, David. Do you want to play with us in the water? We can stay in the shallow part so you can play with us if you want to."

Sarah stayed close to Noah but could feel his body relaxing. She was shocked when he let go of her and tried to swim. Splashing in the water, he laughed, and Hannah and David laughed with him. Sarah wanted to cry and wondered if this was how life would be for her going forward. With every milestone in Noah's life, be it small or major, she would probably shed more than a few tears. Hopefully, they would be tears of joy.

Clayton came outside to join them and made a point of saying hello to his new nephew. "Hello, Noah. I'm your uncle, Clayton. Looks like you're enjoying the pool. I don't go in the water myself."

Noah looked up at Clayton. "How come you don't go in the water?"

Clayton bent down to get closer so Noah could hear him better. "Well, I don't know how to swim."

"Are you afraid?"

Somewhat amused, Sarah and Trevor watched Clayton, a grown man, try to explain his feelings to a five-year-old child.

"No. I'm not afraid."

"Then come in the pool."

It was a simple request. Clayton could see everyone's eyes on him.

Clayton nodded. "Ok. I'll come in. I've got to get my swimsuit on first though. I'll be right back."

Everyone smiled and tried not to make eye contact with Clayton as he walked past his family and into the house.

Devon said what everyone was thinking. "Who would have thought that it would take Noah to knock Clayton down to size?"

Trevor responded, "We'll see. He hasn't come out of the house yet. Who wants to bet he never returns?"

They all laughed as Wyatt pulled out a twenty-dollar bill. "I believe I'll take that bet."

Sarah watched as Devon put money on the table too. It was wonderful to see Trevor's family come together after so many years of turmoil. Soon, these people would be her family too. Two years ago, her world looked completely different. She had to pinch herself to believe her new life was real. What she couldn't predict, however, was Clayton coming out of the house in his swimsuit, ready to prove that he too had changed for the better.

The next day, Sarah, Trevor, and Noah decided to spend some time at the beach. The pool had been a big success, and they thought giving the ocean another try might help Noah get over his fear of the waves.

Once again she put his arm floats on and took Noah's hand. This time Trevor joined them. Noah seemed less afraid of the water and every time a wave came, the three of them jumped over it. Being in the pool seemed to make Noah less afraid, and they made plans to go to visit his grandparents again on the weekends.

As they walked back to the blanket, Trevor surprised Sarah. "So, I was thinking about adding on to the house."

"How come?"

"Well, there will be four of us soon, and the kids each will need their own room. I love living on the beach, and I wouldn't move for anything, but more room is definitely needed. I own a little more than two acres, so we've got the room."

"Two acres? Why didn't you tell me?"

"You never asked."

Sarah laughed. "I guess that's true."

Her cell phone rang, and Sarah could see it was Meredith Carpenter.

"Hello?"

"Hi, Sarah, it's Meredith Carpenter. Sorry to bother you on the weekend, but I thought you'd want to know that the Gallos' need to take a break from fostering any more children. Her mother is ill and needs to move in with them. I'd rather not move Sophia to another foster home, only to then move her again when you and Trevor adopt her. How do you feel about taking her now, as her foster mother?"

Sarah jumped up from the blanket. "Are you kidding me? Yes. I mean, absolutely I want her. How soon can I come get her?"

Sarah could hear Meredith laugh, "I thought you'd ask that. How does Tuesday sound—ten o'clock?"

"I'll be there, and Meredith, thank you so much."

Sarah's eyes started to water. She looked down at Trevor and Noah and her heart beat fast in her chest.

"I can foster Sophia starting Tuesday. The family can't take any more children right now because the woman's mother is sick and moving in with them. Do you realize what this means? I'm going to be a mother."

Trevor pulled Sarah down onto the blanket and hugged her.

"This is the best news. We'll have to get shopping. She's going to need a lot of stuff."

Sarah sat looking out at the tide coming in. She suddenly realized what she wanted to do with Sharon's ashes.

"Sophia won't be the only one coming to live with us."

Trevor was confused. "What do you mean?"

Looking around the beach, Sarah smiled and answered him. "This is our home—Sophia's home. When we're married and we've added to the house, I want to spread Sharon's ashes on our property. It seems only right that Sharon lives here too. After all, she gave Sophia to me. It's the least I can do for her."

THE END

Thank you so much for reading. I hope you enjoyed this story.
Stay tuned for many more books in this series.

Read on for a sneak peek at Book 3
CAPTIVA MEMORIES

CAPTIVA MEMORIES

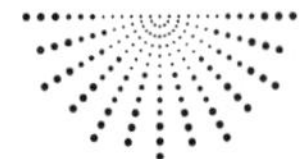

Christopher Wheeler watched his mother lift his seabag and place it in the corner of the room. Maggie leaned the crutches against the nightstand so that he could easily reach for them from the bed. He admired the cozy atmosphere of the place, but this room, in particular with a chair near the window, appealed to him. *A perfect place to hide out.*

His mother had taken great care to help him settle into his new home. The Key Lime Garden Inn, although a traveler's destination, would serve his desire to enjoy his surroundings while staying invisible. Any interest in him would fade as soon as the guests went about their vacation. A corner chair provided a perfect spot for him to look out the window and watch the butterflies swoop in and out of the bush, and he could hear the ocean waves crashing against the sand.

The awkwardness that hung over them started the minute his mother met him at the airport. Christopher wondered how long before he would wear out his welcome. Perhaps he should have had a Plan B if this arrangement failed.

He could tell that his mother didn't know how to talk to him, and that suited him fine because he didn't want to talk, anyway.

She and her new husband, Paolo Moretti, had built a ramp for wheelchair access when they took over the inn. Such things were required for establishments these days. He imagined that his mother had no idea at the time that one day her youngest son would have need of it.

"Would you like to take a tour of the place? I know you must be tired, but I'd love to show you around."

"Not right now, Mom. I am tired. I'd like to take a nap if that's all right with you."

"Of course."

Maggie turned down the bed and then the shades. "We get lots of sun here. You'll need to keep the shades down if you want to sleep in the middle of the day."

Christopher smiled and nodded. "That's fine."

She stood in the doorway and seemed unsure of what to do or say next.

"Do you need help getting into the bed?"

"No."

The second he answered her, he regretted it. He sounded angry, and he was, but none of this was her fault.

"I'm sorry, Mom. I can manage on my own."

His mother looked lost. He could see her wanting something more to do for him. The look on her face convinced him he needed to reassure her.

"Mom, you're going to have to get used to this. We all are. I'm going to be in this chair for the rest of my life. It's probably a good idea for me to get on with it. I've got to learn how to live with this. I'm sure I'll probably fall now and then. You can't always be there to pick me up. Do you think you can stop hovering?"

"I'm sorry, Christopher. I didn't mean to hover. I understand what you're saying. This is all so new and I'm not sure when to help and when to leave you be. I'm used to taking care of you."

"I know. It's going to take some time."

He could tell that she heard his words but was a long way from accepting his situation.

"I've got to run over to Chelsea's for a bit. If you need anything at all, send me a text."

Christopher held up his cell phone and wiggled it. "If it makes you feel any better, I'll put my cell phone right next to the bed."

His mother closed the door behind her as she left, and he immediately wheeled his chair to the window instead of getting into the bed. The garden looked beautiful and abundant with flowers and vegetables. He could see his stepfather, Paolo, cutting the grass.

He looked down at his legs and cringed. They had amputated his right leg just above the knee; his pants folded under what remained. No matter how many times he played the day of the bombing over in his mind, he couldn't make the leap from laying on the ground to sitting in a wheelchair. Piecing together what he remembered with what he was told proved almost impossible. Too many days and nights passed before he found himself under his mother's care once again.

He wheeled himself back near the nightstand and pulled one crutch close. Standing on his left leg, he leaned his right side onto the crutch. Moving the wheelchair down a bit he turned to sit on the bed.

What seemed like a small maneuver drained him quickly. These were the moments that frustrated him. He ran marathons and jumped out of airplanes, for heaven's sake.

Realization set in fast—that was before. Before he lost his closest friend in the world. The day that ended everything for him and began a new life that would expect much of him. It would demand that he believe in a future filled with joy and happiness and would insist he get on board with living.

Except he didn't know how and felt no desire to find a reason to go on. The days following post-op were a blur. Surgeons, nurses, occupational therapists, physical therapists, and social workers, each involved with his care and rehabilitation annoyed him and he did little to assist in his own recovery.

His lack of interest in a prosthetic device fitting, kept him firmly in his wheelchair most days, and although he'd met with a psychiatrist a few times, he hated those sessions and dismissed the man after four appointments.

With very little interest in healing, Christopher struggled to get out of bed every morning. His family's love and support meant the world to him, but he couldn't forgive himself for being alive when so many of his friends were dead. That pain tortured him every minute of every day. Now, living on Captiva Island, he planned to lay low and keep his suffering confined to his room as much as possible.

He placed the crutch up against the other and lay back on the bed. He longed to be back in Iraq. He wanted to fight those who killed his brothers and sisters. The military had become his home, but now all he had left of that life were memories.

He lay staring at the ceiling, feeling untethered and alone. It would take a miracle to bring him out of this darkness. If he could only sleep. Maybe when he next opened his eyes, that miracle would come. The only problem was that he didn't believe in miracles. He didn't believe in anything anymore.

He reached inside his shirt and pulled out the dog tags that hung around his neck. Everyone had a set—one to stay with the body for identification, and one to be sent back to the family in the event of his or her death. Christopher wiped the tears that fell with the sleeve of his shirt. He never knew what happened to Nick, only that he'd been killed in the blast.

For now, finding out what happened to his friend was the one thing that gave him purpose. As soon as he was able, he made a promise to himself that he would visit Nick's family and tell them what a brave son they had. How, more than once, their son saved his life. He'd explain it all, and then whatever happens after that, he didn't care.

ALSO BY ANNIE CABOT

THE CAPTIVA ISLAND SERIES

Book One: KEY LIME GARDEN INN
Book Three: CAPTIVA MEMORIES
Book Four: CAPTIVA CHRISTMAS
Book Five: CAPTIVA NIGHTS
Book Six: CAPTIVA HEARTS
Book Seven: CAPTIVA EVER AFTER

THE PERIWINKLE SHORES SERIES
Book One: CHRISTMAS ON THE CAPE
Book Two: THE SEA GLASS GIRLS

For a **FREE** copy of the Prequel to the Captiva Island Series, **CAPTIVA SUNSET** - Join my newsletter HERE.

Reviews are tremendously important to an author. I hope you will leave a review of this book on Amazon. I read every review because I want to hear from my readers. You can go directly to the review page by clicking on this link.
https://amzn.to/3u3oIUV

ACKNOWLEDGMENTS

As I continue my writing journey, I've added a few wonderful people to my team, and I honestly couldn't do what I do without them.

A huge thank you to Lisa Lee of Lisa Lee Proofreading and Editing. I'm so blessed to have you in my life. You are fast becoming a dear friend as well as an amazing editor.

To Michele Connolly and Anne Marie Page Cooke, thank you for agreeing to read and reread my books. Chapter by chapter, you have brought your vision and insight into my creative space, and I'm forever grateful.

To Marianne Nowicki of Premade Ebook Cover Shop. I'm not sure if you are aware how much your book covers inspire me to develop the perfect setting for my stories. Thank you so much for being such a beautiful, and creative soul.

To Otis who sits by my side every moment of every day. I know you'd like more credit than I give you, but what you don't realize is how much comfort you give me on those days when I think I can't write. You've been my buddy for seventeen years, and I wish we could have seventeen more.

And, as always, to my sweet husband, John. Your encouragement means the world to me. It's no small endeavor to write a book, but having a cheerleader who daily motivates me to keep going, means the world to me. These books would never get written without you. I love you.

To my readers:

You made my first book, Key Lime Garden Inn a huge success. I've received emails from several people telling me how much they love this series. Imagine that? With only one book, people are excited in anticipation for what's to come. I thank you so much for your support. Because of it, I'm able to do the thing I love most in the world, and that's to write.

If you keep reading, I'll keep writing.

May you get to wiggle your toes in the sand,

Annie

ABOUT THE AUTHOR

Annie Cabot is the author of contemporary women's fiction and family sagas. Annie writes about friendships and family relationships, that bring inspiration and hope to others.

Annie Cabot is the pen name for the writer Patricia Pauletti (Patti) who, for the last seven years, has been the co-author of several paranormal mystery books under the pen name Juliette Harper. A lover of all things happily ever after, it was only a matter of time before she began to write what was in her heart, and so, the pen name Annie Cabot was born.

When she's not writing, Annie and her husband like to travel. Winters always involve time away on Captiva Island, Florida where she continues to get inspiration for her novels.

Annie lives in Massachusetts with her husband and adorable new puppy, Willa.

For more information visit anniecabot.com

Made in the USA
Monee, IL
01 June 2025